In Valerian

By

Sophia Worden

Sophia Worden x

Little Red Hen Books, Cornwall, UK

Cover Lettering by Emma de Cruz

Copyright © Sophia Worden, 2023

ISBN: 978-1-4467-03830

Published by Little Red Hen Books, Cornwall, UK.

Thank you to everyone who has taken an interest in the *Valerian Trilogy*. Your kindness and support are the lifeblood of these books.

In Valerian

1. Violetta the Vampyre, *Part I*
2. Snow White and Rose Red
3. Forests For All Forever
4. The Lady In The Tower
5. Morgana of the Fruitful Isles
6. Un Beau Reve Rose
7. Violetta *or* The Titrations, *Part II*
8. Lions Are Better-Looking

Violetta The Vampyre

Part I

For a split second, Aurélie De Lys wondered if she had seen a dwarf, a real dwarf out of a fairy-tale, wearing a motley cap with bells on it, and Turkish slippers with curled toes, walking down the train platform at East Grinstead. Then she sighed and shook her head. Surely not. She had been up late the night before finishing a painting of a dragonfly and a hummingbird for her end-of-year show, and now she thought she must be imagining things.

Aurélie was from Ile-Grande, an island to the west of Avalon. She had been in Valerian for nine months, since September 1983, to take up a scholarship at the Valerian College of Arts, but she had no real idea what she wanted to do after that.

'Hey, I might join the circus,' she joked with her best-friend, Harmony, on a sunny afternoon when they were both wearing rainbow-coloured dresses and big floppy ribbons in their hair.

But today, Aurélie had travelled down to the Bluebell Railway in East Grinstead to look at an installation her fellow students from the college had set up in an old Victorian railway carriage. Now, however, she found she was rather more interested in taking a centenary ride on the train. It was annoying then, that her classmates were holding things up. It meant hanging around the quaint, pretty station for an extra half hour.

Of course, it did give her a chance to look at some nice Art Deco posters one of the students had put up in the platform waiting room. There were six of them, framed, in shades of golden and blue. Seaside scenes. *Maman et papa et pique-niques, les bateaux, les familles.* But beneath the posters, the artist's bio revealed he was from Ile-Morville. A surprise. Maybe you had to be a visitor to Valerian to appreciate it properly.

Finally, finally, they let the few stragglers hanging around on the platform, or in the waiting-room, onto the train.

Aurélie sank against her carriage's cool leather seat and glanced round its interior. Opposite her, there was a white parasol, an ornately bound leather journal and a fine quill pen. All part of her classmates' installation, she thought to herself crossly, and not worth holding the train up for. Still, curiosity got the better of her, and she found herself unhooking the journal's amethyst clasp and peeking inside.

On the inner cover, someone had pasted an old black-and-white photograph of, she assumed, the owner of the journal. It made an attractive frontispiece. The woman's slightly curly dark hair was bound back severely, which served to emphasise her fine, dark, luminous eyes and the pale strength of her features. The serene, pensive expression in those eyes made Aurélie hope that the lady's immortal soul was not yet in peril.

She wore a white cameo at her throat, strung on some ebony beads, and her dress was made of some dark stuff with paler stripes. She had slung a dark velvet shrug with delicate tassels over her shoulders, and her sleeves were black and lacy. Beneath the photograph, someone had written, in an elegant, cursive script: *My birthday portrait, 8th November 1888*. Then, beneath that, in Times New Valerian capitals was printed:

C, R, & O. HAWKINS, 32, 33 & 38 PRESTON STREET, BRIGHTON SCHOOL OF PHOTOGRAPHY. NEGATIVES KEPT. COPIES OF ENLARGEMENTS CAN BE HAD AT ANY TIME.

Aurélie turned over the front-leaf of the journal and on the next page, beneath a smudged, inky date, someone, the lady of the frontispiece?, had begun to set down her memoirs. They were written in a language that Aurélie could not read, but as she turned over the pages, she found a section pasted in that seemed to be a translation. She scanned the first few paragraphs of this translation, only to realise that she was becoming engrossed in the confessions of this lady.

The purpose of my costume is disguise, *(the journal's author had written,)* though I would not wish for anyone to see me dressed so humbly anyway: red headscarf, black dress, long, grey coat trimmed with dark, sable fur, matching grey gloves, and stout, fur-lined boots. These clothes are *almost* enough to keep me warm. However, my legs are so tired that they don't seem like my legs anymore. Yet though I have been walking for miles and miles, still I have no desire to stand still. It is too cold. My breath turns to frost flowers if I unwrap my scarf, and the tips of my fingers are numb despite my gloves.

As I walk across this land, it is so vast that I am dwarfed by it. It stretches for thousands of miles to the north and the south, to the east and the west: on one side, it's all forests, and on the other, a region of treeless wastes. Then too, there's the Black Land, with its fertile prairies, and elsewhere, the barren steppes, fit only for wandering herds and the tents of nomads and shepherds.

And if I see, in the contrasts of this landscape that is my Motherland, a metaphor and microcosm of myself, let it be known that I, Violetta Valhallah of the House of Vladimir of the Sabre, am *nosferatu*, and plagued with the paradoxical curse of complete self-obsession and self-awareness.

So then, for me, the drama of this landscape is both a projection and an externalisation of my own inner being. I can almost convince myself that the flow of the myriads of meandering streams out into the rivers, and then into the mighty seas, is because I will it; that the storm winds howl, and the winter sun beats down, all at my whim. For it is not true that all nosferatu cannot bear the rays of the sun. As long as I wear my headscarf, I am protected from both snowflakes and sunlight!

I will not pause for respite before I climb the hill. It is still too cold, and besides, at its summit, I can look out at the broad, low-lying meadow filled with morning mist, that dense, white shroud under which everything lies hidden until the sun begins to rise. There, I see it now, vague forms dimly appearing, magnified and monstrous in their outlines, the shapes and shadows of a buried wonderland. Then, as the white curtain begins to lift, living and moving objects appear below, strange outlines and unnatural dimensions, a vast phantasmagoria which is impossible to comprehend in its entirety.

Would then that I had Merlin's wand, that I might make these mists vanish, that I might glimpse once more these dear, familiar lands, these trees and houses, men and herds, all bright and glittering beneath the wintry, solar rays.

It is over these broad plains that the fierce horsemen of the East found an easy pathway to the rich and doomed cities of the West, where I am bound. Though I will be sad to bid farewell to this my Motherland, this, the land of my forefathers, where great fagots of grain and ancient iron swords were sacrificed to the god of war, as well as cattle, horses and prisoners taken in battle. One out of every hundred prisoners died to honour the god, their blood being caught in vessels and poured onto iron swords.

As I walk across the land, I seem to remember it all. And yet, was I really there, in those ancient times, stepping forth from the mists for my share of blood and victory?

Perhaps, even in my own journal, I should not reveal all my secrets.

Yet it is true, in those ancient times, at our high feasts, we drank the blood of our first enemies, killed in battle. We used drinking cups made from the skulls of our foes. For I was like an Amazon then, and my childhood companion was from the Neuri tribe and changed once a year into a wolf. Alas, he was not immortal, nor had he any wish to be. A spear through the heart brought an abrupt end to our friendship.

My own immortality came about in the following way. At the age of fifteen, I was forced to leave the house and protection of my father, Vladimir of the Sabre, because I refused to marry a neighbouring landowner of more than sixty years of age. My father declared that he would have nothing more to do with me, and so I packed my bags and left. But my fortunes fell so far that I was forced to begin working as a servant, rather than something worse, until the master of our household, Zhdan, died. As was the custom, all the male and female servants were asked who would like to be buried with the master. One might assume that our answer would be a resounding *no-one*, but we were told that at least two of us must volunteer.

My lover in those days, Daedalus, nominated us both – I think, to spare our fellow-servants. At that time, I did not know that he was nosferatu, vampire, though his energy and virility had surprised me.

They took Daedalus away to another part of the house, whilst the other servants displayed the depth of their grief by getting drunk on koumiss over the corpse. I followed after and watched as he was placed in chains, whereupon he shouted out to me, 'Fear nothing, for we will soon be reunited.' Then I too was taken away, bathed, adorned, and attired like a princess. They set jewels upon my brow, and then I had nothing to do but drink hydromel and koumiss, and sing loudly, all the while the obsequies lasted.

On the day fixed for the end of the ceremonies, my master, Zhdan, was laid in a boat with his weapons and his clothes. Next, his favourite horse was slain and laid beside him, and with it the body of his manservant, my lover. Then I was led up to the boat, a young and exceedingly beautiful sacrifice. I took off my jewels and sang a farewell song whilst they placed a glass of kvass in my hand.

All at once, the old woman who was with me, and whom they called the Angel of Death, bade me drink up quickly for I must enter the cabin where the bodies of the dead lay. When I protested, the old woman seized me by the hair and dragged me onto the boat. The men began to beat their shields with clubs to prevent my friends from hearing my cries. But my lover on the boat heard me. He was not dead, not slain, after all. He was nosferatu – immortal!

He jumped up from the semblance of death which he had assumed. He rushed over, wrestled me free from the old woman and bit my neck. But it was not fierce love-play. His fangs sank into my neck and his vampire blood mingled with my own. I was being reborn into a new kind of life. Even when the boat was set on fire, to serve as a funeral pyre, we two did not perish. We stood there on the prow of the boat and gloried in the flames. Neither fire nor sunlight could harm us. When the fire had consumed the boat, we clambered forth from its charred wreckage, then swam to shore, ready to begin our new lives.

When we reached the shore, we ran towards the forest, a smooth road of ice beneath us. The path seemed easy to follow though the wind blew us round, the snow fell upon us, and we were swaying this way and that. But new-born as I was, I felt little sense of labour, nor of chill. With vampire blood in my veins, I was faster now than I had ever been before, and stronger too.

By and by, the snowflakes feel smaller, and the wind ceased howling in the woods. Only the darkness was drifting above us, and the trees were spinning round us. Then I saw the lane of paleness where the moon had fled before us. That was when, my lover said, I became enamoured of the moon. The forest was whispering all around, and for all I knew, my master's household were in pursuit, and yet there I stood, stock still, gazing at the moon. It was as if I had never seen it before, nor ever noticed its brightness and beauty.

'I should have told you,' said Daedalus, 'that in your new state, your senses are heightened. And that we vampires are drawn to worship the moon goddess, Selene.'

Right dizzy I felt, gazing up at the moon, and down I fell. Daedalus gathered me up and carried me to the bank. There, all around us, hissed the larchwood. He carried me into the trees and cut down branches to shelter us there. Then he laid me against him, like a nut within a shell.

'Sleep,' he said, and I did.

The next day, it had stopped snowing. The light that the morning brought us showed a castle on a hill-top, with square crenelations and wondrous turrets pointing to the sky. My father's mansion had been grand enough, but it was nothing compared to this castle.

'I believe,' Daedalus said then, 'that we have passed into Kief, where Oleg is overlord. For over there is the mountain, the Zamikova Hora, and beneath it is his castle, where we might be able to get work.'

'Do such as we are still have to work?' I asked, sleepily, taking in a blurred impression of turrets and towers, and above them the grim shadows and peaks of mountain rock.

'It is good to have shelter,' said Daedalus. 'Besides, there will be roast meats and cold meats in the kitchen, and we will be close to the forests too, for days when we wish to hunt live prey and drink fresh blood.' Then he prepared a trap, and presently, showed me how to slaughter a hare and drain it of blood. And this was breakfast. Shortly afterwards, we stopped at a stream and broke its ice to wash away the sticky remnants of blood from our hands and faces, and all the ash from the day before.

'We look no better than we ought to be,' I said ruefully, looking at our scattered reflections. I was also much paler than I used to be, ivory-skinned, and we both had dark, unruly hair, and shadowed, bloodshot eyes.

'We'll do,' he said. 'For now.'

Then we clambered through the snowy drifts that had settled on the great mountainous hill until we reached the courtyard of Oleg's castle. Daedalus stomped round the side of the main keep, to a window through which we could peer inside. And there it was, a splendid place, with woven rush-mats on the stone floors, and oak chairs and tables. The ceiling was white, bordered with gold, and at its centre, a shower of glass drops, shimmering with tapers of light. For a moment, it was as if we were contemplating Paradise.

I felt a sudden, searing pain in my ankle and cried out.

Daedalus glanced down, swore, then yelled, 'They have set the mastiff hound on us.' And he began to make the most bloodcurdling noises to scare off the dog, and when that did not work, he got a stick and tried to thrust it between the dog's jaws.

Out came the servant with a flaming torch, shouting, 'Hold them fast.' He seemed to change his tune, however, when he saw who the dog was holding between his jaws. The hound was throttled off, his huge, purple tongue hanging out of his mouth, and his pendulous lips streaming with bloody saliva.

The servant picked me up, for I was sick, not from fear, but from pain. He carried me into the castle keep and Daedalus followed, grumbling curses and swearing vengeance.

'What's all the noise? Who do we have here?' asked a thick-set man with long red hair who was standing in the entrance.

'The dog has caught a girl, sir,' replied the servant, 'and there's a lad here too,' he added, making a clutch for Daedalus, which he could not well do, since he was still holding me.

'We were only looking through the window,' I said, at which the red-haired man smiled.

The servant placed me down on the settle, whilst Daedalus continued to curse. Then the man with the red hair ordered the servant to take Daedalus off. I heard him refuse to go without me, but there was some sort of scuffle, and it seemed that my lover was dragged back out into the snowy courtyard.

Since I could not walk, and was half-swooning in pain on the settle, there was little I could do. By-and-by, the servant brought some warm water and washed and bound my foot, and the red-haired man brought me a flagon of koumiss.

This then was my first meeting with Oleg the Vangarian, the owner and overlord of the castle.

The wound that the hound had inflicted proved severe, and it was some six weeks before I could walk again. To this day, and despite my vampire blood, my ankle is weaker than it used to be. At that time, it was hard for me to think clearly through the pain that reverberated throughout my frame, or the sudden great longings for sleep which their herbal potions of valerian induced. But when I could think, there was sufficient time for my mind to dwell on Daedalus. After he had become a servant in the household of my master, Zhdan, he had told me all about himself.

Born and raised in Greece as a goatherd, Daedalus had always longed to have his fortune told by the Oracle of Delphi. When he was fifteen, he climbed on board a ship and sailed to the western edge of Greece, near Astakos. He then travelled east until he reached the city of Delphi. Delphi was home to a great temple of Apollo, the sun god. It was also home to the Pythia, or Oracles. The Pythia would sit in a chamber within the temple and speak to those that came to seek the Oracle's wisdom, and prophecies inspired by Apollo.

When Daedalus finally arrived at the temple, he went to speak to the Pythia. The Pythia, whose words were often cryptic, said to him: *'The curse. The moon. The blood will run.'* Daedalus did not know what this curse meant but he did not like what they had told him. He decided to travel as far away as he could to escape his fearful destiny.

Once again, he went east by ship. Eventually he arrived on our shores and came to work in the house of a different master, Drozd. This is where he first met me, when my master Zhdan came to visit, bringing with him a retinue of his own servants to display his wealth and status, as was the custom. Daedalus later told me that dressed in my grey furs and white robes, I reminded him of the maidens of the Pythia.

Unfortunately for Daedalus, his master Drozd fell in love with him. Already at that time, he was a striking youth with olive skin and eyes like the seas when the storms have fled. When Daedalus refused his master's advances, Drozd decided to turn him into a vampire to exert greater control over him. Drozd bit his servant's neck and then drank his blood, claiming that this would ensure Daedalus remained in perpetual thrall to him. However, it also conferred immortality upon him, and made him a great hunter, with the speed and strength of a god, and fangs with which to drain the blood of his prey.

Daedalus did not relish this destiny. As the Pythia had taught him to do, he killed a swan and with its sacrificial blood, wrote to them about what had happened, asking for their advice. The Oracle's reply was again cryptic: '*Silver. Moon. Crown his dreams.*' However, Daedalus's new vampiric blood had sharpened his intuitive abilities, so this time, he understood what they meant. He took the silver coins he had earned from his master and had them melted down and beaten into a coronet. Then he then placed this coronet under the full moon at midnight so that the vampire goddess, Selene, might bless his endeavours. Whilst his master was asleep, Daedalus pressed the silver coronet onto his head. He told me afterwards that Drozd woke up, cried out, then shrieked and snarled as the life drained away from him.

When Drozd had ceased writhing and lay still, Daedalus removed the coronet, covered him over with a fur, and went to tell the rest of the household that the master was dead. Shortly afterwards, he decided to obtain work in Zhdan's household, and in such close, daily proximity, became ever more deeply enamoured of me.

My time resting on the settle in Oleg's castle was not entirely taken up with recollections of Daedalus. Oleg the Vangarian also made considerable demands upon my time and attention. He had initially said that once my ankle was better, I would be set to work assisting the cook. However, the assiduous attentions I showed him, such as inquiring daily after the health of his hounds (even the one that had bitten me) or ordering that another log be placed upon the fire when he returned to the castle, storm-beaten and weary, convinced him that the kitchen was not the right place for me – and this, without tasting a morsel of my cooking!

The day on which I persuaded Oleg to turn the back of his chair towards the hearth fire to dry his cloak upon it was the day he asked me to marry him. It was just three weeks since the servant had first carried me into the castle and placed me upon the settle. It would be another three weeks before I had any word from Daedalus.

On that day, I had just made my first tentative steps around the castle courtyard, gazing up at its lofty heights and turrets and rejoicing in the fact that I was soon to be its mistress, when a servant approached me with a letter. I examined it carefully: my name, *Violetta,* on the front, looked as if it had been written in blood. That was how I knew, even before I unfolded it, that it was from Daedalus. I paused for a moment and remembered the delicious crunch of the fragile bones of hares.

Daedalus wrote that he had been sheltering in a cave on the outskirts of the forest, some way up the mountain. He had been feeding on hunted animals and sacrificing swans to the moon goddess, Selene. He also wrote that it was dark and cold in the cave, and on the nights when there was no moon, there were no stars either. No stars. He asked me to join him because it would be better to live together as outlaws in the forest than to live like this, apart.

I spent the rest of the day thinking about what my answer would be. I am a vampire. I am selfish. I will always put my own needs first. And it seemed to me that there was a measure of comfort, and perhaps even happiness, to be found here in the castle of Oleg the Vangarian. And yet…

I did not know whether, in becoming a vampire, I had sacrificed my immortal soul, but surely there were parts of my soul which touched the soul of Daedalus. How then could I forsake him?

That evening, I still hadn't decided what my answer would be when Oleg brought me news that Daedalus was dead. At first, I did not know what he meant. He described a feral creature living in a cave who had been poaching game from the forest. He and his servants had discovered him as he slept, smeared with the blood of his kills.

'Poaching is a crime punishable by death in Kief,' said Oleg, but he would not look me in the eye.

'You killed him as he slept?' I asked.

'He looked half-savage,' Oleg protested, 'and the evidence of his crimes was all around him. I shot him through the heart with my silver bow and arrow.'

'Silver?' I repeated, stupidly. Then I remembered how Daedalus had killed his vampire master with a silver crown. 'Did the poacher in the cave look like the boy who came here with me, a few weeks ago?'

'How could I tell?' Oleg said. 'I only saw your friend for a moment. And this creature was filthy, unkempt, sleeping in the shadows. All I could see clearly was a swan's wing.'

I knew then that Oleg had killed Daedalus. And the part of me that was supremely selfish thought, now I will never experience perfect and unalloyed happiness. For no matter what I do, or where I go, throughout all of my long, long life, I will always wonder what it would have been like if Daedalus had not died. But it was easier for me to convince myself that Oleg did not fully know what he had done, that he would not have killed Daedalus if he had known who he was or what he meant to me. Certainly, it was never referred to by either of us ever again. And if part of my heart died that night, what did it matter? I was a vampire now, after all.

Just, sometimes, it was awful to wake in the night with the moon shining full through the window, feeling bereft, as if the best and worst part of me was gone. Who would join me now in the hunt?

In fact, during my time at the castle, I was forced to conceal many of my nocturnal activities. When I went out into the forest to hunt, I would crouch down on all fours until I caught the scent of my prey. Then I would pursue the creatures of the forest with fleet, four-footed speed. When I had fed, I crept back to the castle with blood smeared all over my cheeks. Then I poured water from the pitcher in my bedroom into the bowl. I washed my face fastidiously in the water.

'Just like a cat,' said Oleg from the doorway, making me jump. Despite my heightened senses, I had not realised he was there. But I nodded and smiled, and all was well. When he wasn't looking, I poured the bloody water out of the window, onto the rosebush growing there. Now the roses would always bloom in brilliant, baleful splendour.

After our betrothal, Oleg insisted on showing me the castle portrait gallery. The men and women were most of them handsome, and all of them were very grand. I thought I saw a family resemblance, particularly among the men, who were tall, strong, brown or red-haired, hazel eyed, and a bit grim about the mouth. Then too, they all had the same proud tilt of the eyebrows, chin and shoulders.

'My ancestors,' said Oleg, and he promised me that after we were married, my portrait should join them.

He kept his word. Shortly after we were wed, he commissioned an artist, Fra Pandolf, to paint me. Unless they have removed it, my portrait should be there still in the castle corridor, at the end of a row of gold-framed paintings. It was a fine one: my dark hair was pulled back into a severe chignon, and I wore a blue velvet dress, my favourite at the time, with an eight-sided pentacle embroidered onto the bodice. Then, too, I liked the contrast of my raven-black hair and ivory skin, and the way I appeared both soulful and expressive.

Of course, in the throes of creation, Fra Pandolf had muttered something about paint not being able to reproduce the dainty half-flush which died upon my throat. It was an unfortunate comment since it annoyed Oleg, who had particularly drawn attention to that same roseate flush during the moment of sweetest surrender in our lovemaking. However, I smiled, first at my husband, and then at the artist, graciously accepting such courtesy as Fra Pandolf's wont and my due. Only, after Oleg had paid Fra Pandolf his full fee in rubles, the artist was never seen or heard of again.

I made inquiries, but it seemed that Fra Pandolf never returned to his native Ferrara. But then, ours is a savage country. Perhaps he had been murdered for his rubles upon leaving the protection of our castle? It is a great shame, for he was a fine artist, and a charming one, besides.

After the painting of the portrait, I settled into married life, whether happily or no, to Oleg, the master of the castle, the overlord of Kief. He was regent of the realm for Igor, who was only four years old when his father, Rurik, lord of Novgorod, had died. Oleg, barbarian, soldier, brave, crafty and adventurous, was loyal to those he loved but treacherous to those he did not. I found I could love him in fits and starts, and yet, at other times, my heart was quite cold, though that was not his fault, nor mine either.

Since the death of Daedalus, it seemed hard to love – and harder even to love as humans do.

A few years went by, and Oleg grew older, but I did not. There were days when I was tempted to rub flour into my hair and upon my face to make it seem that I aged. For Oleg was a superstitious man, and the knowledge that he had married a vampire might well have proved his undoing. As it was, I played my part well enough: I even sat beside him in the family pew in the chapel every Sunday, with my eyes raised towards the angel pointing heavenwards. I knew something of the Christian faith by then, and I was not opposed to its ceremonies.

Alas for Oleg, it might have been better if he had looked to his priests rather than his fortune-tellers for advice. For his death came about in a strange way through their prophecies, though I swear it was none of my doing. Throughout our marriage, I had remained modest and restrained - and grieved fully as much as anyone upon his death, until I was made regent.

It so happened that Oleg had a favourite horse which he rode alike in the hunt and in battle. Eventually, a prediction came from the fortune-tellers and soothsayers that this cherished horse would be the means of his death. He was indeed a superstitious man, and so he sent the horse far away into the country, and for several years he avoided even speaking of it. Nearly a decade had passed since we were wed, and to me, he seemed quite an old man - whilst, as for me, it became more and more difficult to conceal my continuing youth and beauty. Eventually however, like Eve in that ridiculous story of the expulsion from Paradise, curiosity got the better of Oleg and he could not help but ask what had become of his horse.

'It died many years ago,' was the reply, 'and only its bones remain.'

'So much for the soothsayers then,' he said, with a curious mixture of relief and contempt. 'That is all their prediction is worth! But where are the bones of my good old horse? I would like to see what is left of him.'

He was taken to the charnel house where lay the skeleton of his old warhorse and I was later told he gazed with some show of feeling at its bleaching bones. Then, setting his foot on its skull, he cried, 'So this is the creature that was destined to be my death.'

At that very moment, a deadly serpent that lay coiled up within the horse's skull darted out and fixed its poisonous fangs in the conqueror's foot. In this way, Oleg, who had slain men by the thousands, and who had conquered an empire, met his death. And yet, shortly afterwards, another soothsayer told me that my husband's enemies, the Drevlians, knew of the prophecy and of Oleg's curiosity to learn his horse's fate. According to this soothsayer, it was the Drevlians who had placed the serpent among the horse's bones.

I have to say, there then rose within me a terrible desire for vengeance. Whilst I was waiting for my husband's ward, Igor, to return to the castle and rule the land, I continued to reign as its regent. I had absolute power, and I was determined to avenge the death of Oleg. Besides, in addition to killing my husband, the Drevlians had decided that they would not accept the authority of Igor, and that they would marry me instead to their own prince, Male, who would rule instead.

I cursed my fatal beauty that made me so desirable I could not even mourn in peace. For I had no wish to marry this haughty barbarian. So I only pretended to listen with modesty and obsequiousness when the Drevlian ambassadors said that they would now find me a better husband. I told them that I would consider their proposal deeply, and that they must return tomorrow for my answer. But after they had left my court, I had a deep, wide pit dug in front of the castle. The next day, there I stood, waiting for them with smiling lips but a ruthless heart. And when they came towards me, I ordered my servants to throw the Drevlians into the pits.

'How do you like your accommodation in my realm?' I asked them as they tumbled down.

'Oh!' they cried out in terror, 'pity us!'

But they begged in vain, for I commanded that the pits should be filled up so that those particular Drevlians were buried alive. Before the news of their deaths could reach their countrymen, I sent a message to their greatest remaining ambassadors, demanding that they come and court me as befitted my great status. My message had the desired effect, for the chief men of the country were now sent before me. They entered Kief riding over the graves of their murdered countrymen, not knowing where their horses trod. They were expecting to be hospitably entertained. I had baths made ready for them and sent word that they should refresh themselves after the fatigue of the journey.

The baths were soon heated and the Drevlian ambassadors entered the bath houses. But, to their dismay, and my delight, smoke began to circle round them, and flames flashed before their frightened eyes. My servants had fixed it so that they could not open the bath house doors, and thus they perished in the flames. Once again, news of their deaths did not reach their countrymen, and so I made ready for another act of vengeance.

I sent the Drevlians another deceitful message. 'I am about to set off on my journey to you, and so I ask you to prepare a large quantity of hydromel in the place where my husband died. Then may I weep over his tomb and honour him with the *trizna*.'

The foolish Drevlians were full of joy at this message. They gathered honey in large quantities and brewed it into hydromel. Then I sought out the burial place of my husband, followed by a small guard who were only lightly armed. For some time, I wept over the tomb of Oleg, who had been buried there with his horse. I ordered a great mound of honour to be heaped over it. When this was done, I commanded the funeral banquet to be set out.

The Drevlians drank freely until they were stupid with drink.

'Where are all the friends we sent out to you?' they asked.

'You will be joining them soon,' I replied, and then I bade my guards to draw their weapons and slay my foes, which were the great enemies and murderers of their overlord, Oleg. And in this way, the Great Slaughter began. When it was over, five thousand Drevlians lay dead at my feet.

When I think about what happened to me at that time, a kind of mist descends over my thoughts and much of my motivation is lost to my own understanding. All I know is that the rage of vengeance inspired me, and that the more I fed my thirst for blood, the more it refused to be sated. This would eventually be a source of great sorrow and shame to me, but at that time, in the land of the Drevlians, I had no hesitation in laying waste to the country and destroying its towns.

At last, I came to their capital, Korosten, which was a town made of wood, and my soldiers laid siege to it. But to my surprise, Prince Male and its inhabitants defended themselves obstinately, and for a long time. Finding then that force would not serve, I resorted once more to strategy.

'Why do you hold out so foolishly?' I cried. 'You know that all your other towns are in my power, and your fellow countrymen are peacefully tilling their fields whilst you are dying of hunger. You would be wise to yield, for then you need have no more fear of me.'

To conciliate me, Prince Male, the haughty aristocrat, offered me a tribute of furs and honey. I well recalled long nights of lying on bearskin rugs whilst honey was dripped onto my naked flesh, yet still, I refused this tribute. For, though of late, all the soothsayers had abandoned my realm, nevertheless, a queenly, red-haired woman dressed in long robes, like a priestess, had begun appearing in my dreams. In my dreams, she guided me to ask instead for a tribute of three sparrows and a pigeon.

So then, not knowing what the visionary queen had advised me, Prince Male and the Drevlians gathered together these birds and sent them out to my armies. That evening, I let the birds loose with lighted sticks tied to their tails. Back to their nests in their native towns they flew, and soon Korosten was in flames in a thousand places. And then, its inhabitants fled in horror through the gates, but my soldiers awaited them outside, swords in hand, and cut them down, without mercy. In this way, Prince Male and all his remaining ministers perished, and only the lowliest of his people survived.

Thus it was that I took full revenge upon the murderers of my fallen lord. And the rumour came about that I had unleashed a mighty dragon upon my husband's enemies, though in truth it was no more than three sparrows and a pigeon.

That night, after this final, greatest slaughter, I expected to sleep well. Instead, I was troubled again with strange restlessness and stranger dreams. In my dream, I saw once more that woman of great beauty, with her pale skin and red hair, at the helm of a barge which she was rowing through the mists. And on that barge were two other queens also, and six priestesses wearing black hoods and cloaks, as like to me as my own sisters, whom I had not seen now for many years. Lying huddled in a great cloak at the back of the barge was a man, sleeping or dying, with a look of Oleg about him, and yet not like Oleg either, though he wore a king's crown upon his head. And in my dream, it seemed to me that the queens and the priestesses were taking him away to be healed, though perhaps they could not reach the island that they sought. But then, it is like that sometimes in dreams.

Still, when I awoke, I thought the dream meant perhaps I hadn't done as well as I ought in killing so very many of my husband's enemies. And that perhaps the time had come for me to repent of some of my misdeeds. I therefore decided that I must likewise sail across the waters to be healed.

Within a few months of this dream, Igor returned to take over the rulership of Kief and so I departed from the castle, freely renouncing my title of Regent. And that is why I am now walking across the land towards the harbour. Sometimes I hitch a ride on a cart, but I have very little money, or indeed anything at all, for everything now belongs to Igor, not Oleg. But I would not rob my husband's ward, and pride prevents me from asking for his succour.

In any case, Oleg's cousin, Prince Nikolai of Novogorod, wrote to us from the court of King Leopold in Valerian some months ago. By his account, this court is a pleasant and hospitable place. So, I have arranged for my passage on a ship called *The Phoenix*, sailing West for Valerian. I will see there what fate my talents and instincts can win for me. And in order to embrace fully this spirit of enterprise and adventure, and to feel more at home with a different language, I resolve from now on to write all my future journal entries in High Valerian.

Meanwhile, blood-pickings have been scanty enough on my journey across the land, and it is a long time since I last fed. Selene knows I am weary enough - I expect I shall sleep soundly on-board ship tonight. But perhaps a long and restful sleep will restore a measure of my composure. For I have no real desire to cause trouble: I am, at heart, a peaceable creature.

There followed a couple of blank pages in the journal where the pasted, translated section had come to an end. Aurélie found herself turning over the pages more and more quickly until a single paragraph, now written in Victorian High Valerian, arrested her attention:

Lord Darvell is travelling to Russia, to the land of my forefathers. He has left Crowcroft Grange and gone to find someone who can tell him the truth about the past life of

23

Violetta, Regent of Kief. I have counselled him to reveal nothing of my vampiric origins, for they might tear him to shreds for daring to love a vampire woman. But beyond that, I do not know how to resolve the many troubles that have arisen between us. If only I had learned more of the Dark Arts, I could take psychic possession of a female mortal, perhaps even one who reads this journal and, in that way, become human for him. Or, if it can never be that I join him in human life, perhaps he could join me in vampiric immortality. And who is to say which way is sweeter? But I do not possess sufficient knowledge of the Dark Arts, and I have vowed to make no more of my kind. There is too much cruelty in the vampiric form of immortality which I do not wish to bestow on those I love.

How to reconcile this paragraph with everything that had gone before it, wondered Aurélie, for it seemed to have been written at a much later date. Though the mention of psychic possession gave her a momentary jolt, she decided to ignore it, for Violetta had claimed not to possess such knowledge. Besides, thought Aurélie, she was surely not the first woman to read this journal – which might, in any case, merely be an art student's hoax.

Nevertheless, reading the journal was, for her, a strange act of beguilement, and to learn what came next, she must keep turning over its gold-edged pages.

But a moment later, some fairy tales, and then a letter written by an entirely different person, *Arabella*, fell out of it. The handwriting was a child's loops and curves. Aurélie picked up the pages from her lap. First, she felt a curious sense of disappointment that she must relinquish the society of Violetta so soon, but then, with growing interest, she turned her eyes to the tales and letter set down by this new narrator, and in the slow-burning act of reading, they began to yield up their treasure:

By night, she comes to me, and she comforts me with fairy tales. For since my mother died, and I have come to this oh-so-strange Crowcroft Grange, I find I cannot sleep. And so, at night, Morgan-Le-Fay of Avalon tells me stories. One is about a girl with hair as black as ink, and hair as white as paper, one, about a girl with the heart of a rose, and one, about a girl trapped inside a mirror-tower – though there are other tales, besides.

She does not flatter herself, for she is rarely the heroine of these stories, but she is always there, as part of them, and even when her character is behaving most wickedly, *très méchant,* as she says with a glint in her ghost-eyes, it is perhaps her storyteller's way of trying to kindle some answering spark of animation in me. For sometimes she says the word, *'wicked'* so many times, and in such a droll voice, that it makes me rock with laughter. And the next morning, I always write her stories down, because I find them beautiful, and sometimes sad, and they help me to remember… someone loves me…

Snow White and Rose Red

One of the most popular tales in Avalon, that its fairy-children learned even before they attended their rune-reading and cat-nurturing classes, when their Queen, Morgana, was still dreaming of a School For Magical Miscreants, was one that began upon a dark winter's night, in the kingdom of Valerian…

On a dark winter's night in the kingdom of Valerian, Eva, a childless queen, was sighing over her needlework, wishing she had a little girl to benefit from her fine stitching. She could almost see the child's fair features forming in the fine flurry of snowflakes that tumbled past her ebony window-frame. But the mournful caw of a raven startled her, and she pricked her finger.

A single drop of blood soaked into the muslin cloth before her. As she sucked on her wounded finger and gazed at the glistening drop of blood, she said to herself, 'Oh, how I wish I had a daughter with skin as white as snow, lips as red as blood, and hair as black as ebony.'

The gods and stars heard her, for some months later, she gave birth to a baby girl, with skin as white as snow, lips as red as blood, and hair as black as ebony. They named the little princess Snow White, but then, not long after, the loving queen, her mother, died.

Soon after, King Leopold married another queen from a distant land, a widow, Morgana of the Fruitful Isles, which is to say, Avalon. Ah, but she was fair and proud and ever-so, ever-so wicked, with the blood of generations of witches running through her veins. She brought with her, her own child, another beautiful girl with wistful green eyes and a pointed chin, and long, nut-brown hair, that, in certain lights, shimmered honey blonde. However, her complexion was rosier than Snow White's and her name was Morfydd. But after they left the land of her father's passing, the little girl announced, to anyone that would listen, 'Henceforth, you will all address me as Rose Red.'

'Snow White, Rose Red. Rose-Red, Snow White,' said the new stepmother, introducing the two little girls as perfunctorily as she could, for she was determined to start as she meant to go on. This attitude meant that she would not feign an affection she did not feel, nor waste energy she could not spare, on a child not of her blood. For a child of her blood, however, she would be tender and fierce, passionate and strong. For the people truly of her heart, she would risk everything.

If Snow White had been older, she might have appreciated her stepmother's lack of hypocrisy; as it was, she was only a little girl who had recently lost her own mother, and above all, she craved love.

Alas, Queen Morgana's heart was like her pincushion, and so pricked and stabbed was it with her own concerns that she paid scant attention to her new stepdaughter. Instead, she stretched and yawned, so that her teeth glinted in the firelight. Then she turned her face towards her husband, the king, so that all her smiles were for him.

After a few moments of shyness following this brief introduction, Rose Red took Snow White's hand and they wandered out into the palace gardens, one, a dazzle of scarlet in her crimson cape, the other, as white as an angel's feather in her pure muslin gown.

'But your hand is so cold,' Rose Red said to Snow White, then.

'I'm always cold since mother died,' said Snow White.

Rose Red squeezed the slender fingers that grasped her own. 'It was cold in Caer-Ligualid, where my father ruled,' she said. 'But after my father died, my mother took my twin brother, Ywain, and I to her realm of Avalon, where the fairy-folk live, and where it always seemed like summer.'

'Do you miss your father?' asked Snow White.

'I miss my brother Ywain more,' said Rose Red. 'There was a plague and mother said some spell-words and I recovered. But my brother - she nursed him, yet still, he died.'

A raven flew above their heads then, uttering its mournful cry. Rose Red gripped hold of Snow White's hand, tighter.

'Don't be afraid,' said Snow White. 'All the birds and animals here love me, and now you are my sister, they will love you too.'

'I'm not afraid,' said Rose Red stoutly, though her poor little heart was knocking against her ribs. 'My mother is a witch, and she can put a spell on anyone or anything in the kingdom.'

'But witchcraft was outlawed here some time ago,' said Snow White, shocked. 'It's dreadfully wicked.'

Rose Red pursed her lips and put her dainty head to one side as if considering her mother's true nature for the first time.

'But there are many witches in Avalon,' she said then. 'And my mother is queen of them all. Besides, she is like a biscuit with weevils in it. There are good and bad parts to her. As long as the magic mirror tells her she is the fairest in the land, she is happy.'

'What do you mean?' asked Snow White.

'Come, I will show you,' announced Rose Red, grandly. A moment later and they stood shivering outside the queen's arched window, holding hands for warmth and solace, as they gazed inside.

The new queen, Morgana, was stood inside her chamber, arching her back slightly as she looked into her full-length cheval mirror. Her long, red-brown hair glinted in the firelight, rustling and flaming against the dark, green velvet of her dress.

'Mirror, mirror on the wall,' she intoned softly, 'who is the fairest of them all?'

Then her fair self was covered over with a dark mist in the glass, from which a wizened mouth began to speak: 'Thou, O Queen, are the fairest of them all.'

'But the mirror might just be saying that to please her,' protested Snow White.

'Oh no,' Rose Red replied, 'the mirror always speaks the truth.'

'Well, your mother *is* beautiful,' said Snow White softly, and perhaps she wished that she too could arch her back with the same feline grace as her stepmother, or that her own raven-black hair glinted red-gold.

'Everyone is beautiful in their own way,' Rose Red whispered. 'Let's creep back inside the castle and see if the cook will feed us some porridge.'

As the weeks passed, the two girls developed a close friendship that was akin to sisterhood. Rose Red discovered that Snow White was more at home in a library than a ballgown, that she could write and tell wonderful stories, but that often she could not contrive a happy ending. Sometimes, she grew pale with sorrow, and then Rose Red would timidly remind her stepsister to take a little refreshment, a bite of an apple, a morsel of porridge, or even to put some thick winter stockings on to guard against the palace chill.

Of Rose Red herself, Snow White learned that she had a love of flowers that was at times so intense, it was as if she had imbibed the very quality of the flower into her soul. When she was still quite young, she would nibble on honeysuckle and imagine she was a little bee drawing the honey from it. When she grew to be a maiden, she would hold roses up to her mouth, as if the deep red colour might pour into her throat and infuse the veins in her neck.

Both girls grew in wisdom and beauty, and both at times felt a little fearful of the fair shapes their mirrors revealed. This fear was not due to maidenly modesty but because they both realised that the queen could broach no rivals. Then, alas, one day, the inevitable occurred. The oh-so wicked queen stood in front of her magic mirror and ran her fingers through hair that was still auburn, a flaming mass against the severe cut of her dark, velvet gown.

'Mirror, mirror on the wall,' she husked, in a voice that had grown thick with too many Valerian cigars, 'who is the fairest one of all?' Was it her imagination, or did the enchanter whom she had imprisoned in the glass, and whose name was Merlin, give a little smirk before he replied,

'You used to be the fairest in the land,
But now, my queen, Snow White has the upper hand.'

However, the Magician might have wished he had held his tongue, for his words brought about a terrible change to Snow White's existence. Her stepmother ordered that she was to be taken from her pretty room, with its wallpaper of white butterflies, and be sent to work in the palace kitchens. Her fine gowns and her silver-backed hairbrush and comb were to be given to Rose Red, and from now on, Snow White was to be dressed in rags. Snow White's father tried to protest, but his queen admonished him,

'It is a terrible thing for a child to attempt to outshine her mother. She is a spoilt, unruly girl, and she needs to learn some discipline.'

Perhaps the king wondered whether, under these strictures, the queen's own daughter, Rose Red, would soon be joining her stepsister in the kitchens. However, he said nothing, for he was a weak man at heart, still besotted with his queen's beauty - and fearful of her sharp tongue.

And so, Snow White went weeping to the palace kitchens where her thick, dark hair was tucked beneath a scullery maid's cap, and she was given a servant's frock to wear. It had once been serviceable brown holland but now it was reduced to sooty rags. She worked long hours too, from six in the morning until past midnight, with nothing but a little bone broth and an old potato to eat each day.

But sometimes, when she could, her stepsister would creep down the staircase at night and rub a little rose ointment into Snow White's blisters, and brush out her long, dark hair with the silver-backed brush and comb. Sometimes, the two girls wept together, and clung to each other, and read fairy tales. In this way, they found a little solace.

However, it seemed that whatever privations she endured, Snow White's beauty did not diminish. She grew thin, even angular, but her skin still shone with an unearthly radiance. But one day, when her gown was covered in cinders from scrubbing out the hearth, and she had a terrible cold to boot, her stepmother felt confident enough to peel back the cloth from the magic mirror. Thrusting her proud face into the glass, she intoned, *'Mirror, mirror on the wall, who is the fairest one of all?'*

'Fate has dealt you a cruel hand,' replied the Magician in the mirror, *'for Snow White is the fairest in the land.'*

When she heard his words, the queen gave a scream so shrill it threatened to pierce the magic glass, and she stamped her feet so hard on the stone floor that sparks flew out from the soles of her pointed slippers. Then she covered the mirror over with its cloth, embroidered with sacred symbols, and summoned her huntsman to her.

He came and stood before his queen, a gruff, bearish man with a flowing, dark beard, and wondered what on earth she could want. He found out soon enough.

The queen said, 'Snow White has not been outside the Palace for months, and yet she grows fairer by the day. You must take her out riding in the forest on the pretence of granting her some fresh air. But then, when she's in a state of rapture over some stray leaf or forest fern, you know what these girls are like, you must dispose of her.'

In his heart of hearts, Hunter John was a good man, but he knew better than to protest at the queen's wicked words. He went to the stables and asked them to prepare Snow White's horse and a riding habit for her. The next day, he thought she had never looked so beautiful as she rode beside him on her snowy steed, with her pale, ermine cloak fluttering out behind her. Hunter John had a tender spot for her in his old, wounded heart, so he took her to a little cottage that had once belonged to his mother, which lay on the farthest edge of the forest.

'You may live here safe from hate and persecution, dear Snow White. And you can cook and keep house for me, for I shall return to you each evening when the sun has set.'

Privately, Snow White wondered whether she had not merely exchanged one form of servitude for another. For the moment, however, she voiced another, more pressing concern.

'But what of my wicked stepmother,' she said, 'who out of envy of my great beauty, wants me dead?'

'I will kill one of the wild boars that roam in the forest, and I will soak your horse's reins and bridle with its blood. And then I will cut out the boar's heart and take it to your stepmother,' cried Hunter John. 'And in this way, I will convince her that the dearest, sweetest maiden who ever lived has died at my hands.'

'Well,' said Snow White, 'if you think you can. But remember how dreadfully cold-hearted and cunning she is. Now, I'm going to sweep out the house and make this place fit for us to live in.' So that is what she did, glad of an activity that kept her cheerful and busy. For there was something satisfying about ridding the place of dust and cobwebs, and turning chaos into order, though she would still rather have studied magick, from great spell-books the size of doorstops, like her stepmother did.

Snow White decided that she was going to sleep in the attic. She liked the skylights there, and the glimpses of clouds bearding the blue. Sometimes, at night, she gazed up at the glistening stars from her narrow bed. But she could hear Hunter John's snores travel up the rickety staircase from the bedroom beneath. Then too, she missed her little stepsister, Rose Red, terribly. She began to train the birds that perched upon her skylight to send messages back to her. Snow White was careful not to reveal her location, nor who she was living with, but whatever the messages were, love was always what she meant.

Snow White and the Hunter continued their strange existence together. For all that he was a royal huntsman for the queen, he also poached pheasant and deer in the forest. He taught Snow White how to turn his killings into great, hearty stews which he ate with gusto, whilst she nibbled on some roast chestnuts. She washed his shirts and darned his socks, and sometimes, when his clothes were pegged on the washing-line, or draped over bushes and shrubs, she caught herself thinking of the man who wore them with a sudden, tender pang.

One time, Snow White laid down upon his bed and looked across at the imprint in the pillow that his head had made. But at other times, she was bitterly angry with him, and felt that she had merely exchanged one prison for another, and that he was her gaoler. Was this all the life that she would ever know, she who was the fairest and most nobly born in all the land?

One night, Hunter John brought Snow White a basket of rosy, ripe apples from the palace orchards, which had been seeded from the queen's apple-grove in Avalon, but the girl found that she was afraid to eat them. So, much to the Hunter's consternation, they withered in the stone fruit bowl on the cottage table.

Another time he bought her an exceedingly strange gift, purchased from a passing pedlar. It was a small glass coffin, about the size of her little finger, most ingeniously contrived with a real gold handle and hinges. Printed on the bottom in gold letters were the mysterious words, *'Tirra Lirra.'* When Snow White opened up the coffin, she gave a scream, then thrust it away from her, because a perfectly formed, minute ivory skeleton fell out.

Hunter John sighed at his love-gift's lack of success and his heart grew heavy. An awkward silence sprang up between them.

Presently however, Snow White retrieved the tiny coffin from under the table because she was intrigued by the strange inscription printed beneath it. To her, it seemed like a spell or a charm.

Another afternoon, when Snow White was watering the poppies that were shooting up resplendent in the cottage garden, a little dwarf appeared on her doorstep. He had a smoking pipe, a white wisp of beard, and his eyes were shrewd and blue.

'Could you please help me, dearie? My companions and I have been set a task which is impossible to do.'

'What is it?' asked Snow White.

'The wicked Queen Morgana is jealous of the gold and jewels that we find in the hills. She's sent great piles of wheat, millet, poppy seeds, peas, lentils and beans to our dwelling-place to be sorted into separate piles by tomorrow night. If we can't complete the task, she'll take everything we've mined in forfeit, just like she did last year.'

'Oh, isn't she a wicked one,' cried Snow White, 'but how can I help you?'

'The little birds of the forest have told us how fond they are of you. If you call on them for help, they'll do your bidding.'

Snow White nodded her ebony head and having locked the Hunter's cottage up carefully, she followed the dwarf, whose name, she soon found out, was Guinan Guineafowl, back towards his abode. As they travelled through the woods, this green, unfallen world, two notes of birdsong rose up into the air as if, Snow White reflected, all her girlish loneliness had been made into the sound.

Upon their arrival at the dwarves' cottage, Guinan ushered her through the house so quickly, she had no time to gain much impression of it beyond a dark, cramped interior, in need of a good spit-and-polish. Once they were out in the backyard, he marched over to the cider-pump by the dovecote and pumped himself a pint of cider. Then he pumped another one for Cooey, a quiet, younger dwarf who was sitting on the back-step, staring dolefully at the heaps of seeds and lentils piled up in the backyard. Eventually, Guinan inquired of Snow White,

'Would you care now for a spot of liquid refreshment?'

'Not when there's work to be done,' said Snow White.

'You may be right about that, after all,' said Guinan, as sagely as if he had thought of it himself. 'Our Dagonet likes to tell a tall tale or two, but in doing so, he developed a terrible thirst for the cider. He couldn't pump it out fast enough to meet the wild dryness that he had, so he started reaching down inside the barrel with his cup. But though the cider level went down, it's not as if his arm grew any the longer. Eventually he fetched himself a rickety crate and stepped upon it so that he could drain the barrel of its very dregs. But somehow, Valeria knows how, he toppled right down inside the barrel and there we found him, singing about the Queen's diamonds when he should have been mining them. We left him there until he had sobered up a bit, and then we hauled him out.'

Snow White shook her head, as if she was banishing the temptation of the dwarves' cider, and then she called out some words that she and Rose Red knew from a glimpse into one of Queen Morgana's spell-books:

'Birds of sea and skies,
Birds of finest feather,
Relinquish the celestial skies,
Let's work on this task together.'

There came a great flurry and clamour of wings as all the birds came pouring out of the sky, ravens, crows, doves, robins, even the pigeons were roused and came whirring round the seeds. They began to nod their heads; there was a soft, chirruping jostle, and then *pick, pick, pick* until all the grains and seeds were sorted into separate bowls.

Within the hour, the task was complete, and Snow White was accepting the dwarves' congratulations. Emboldened by their praise, she said, 'I couldn't help but notice the state of your home. What you little men need now is someone to come and help you with your housework.'

'Would you be volunteering, Snow White?' asked Guinan.

'Er- no,' she said. Then she thought about it, and added, cautiously, 'well, maybe, if you all follow my instructions, and help me properly, and if, when the work is done, we can sit in the kitchen and talk and laugh and play cards. For what I crave most in the world is some company.'

'You see, Cooey,' Guinan said, nodding at the younger dwarf still sitting on the back step, 'loneliness isn't just a dwarfish curse. Even the great five-footers feel it too.' Then he added smoothly, to Snow White, 'certainly my dear, you would be most welcome.'

As Guinan led her back through the forest, Snow White's heart felt a little lighter that she had made some new friends. For it was still sometimes gloomy living with Hunter John. He continued to pass his days with the oh-so wicked queen and his evenings with Snow White, of whom, by now, he was most passionately fond. But in the dangerous, secret way they lived, he did not feel that he could tell her of his love. All he knew was that he wanted her to stay with him, always. He thought that he was being kind to her and protecting her from harm. He did not understand how much selfishness lay at the heart of his love.

The forest outside the Hunter's cottage was overgrown with thickets of fern, plump and filmy from recent rainfall, and radiant in green and emerald. One evening, the soft rustling of a simple dress among the feathery fronds could be heard. Not long after, Snow White appeared between the branches of the trees, panting from her hasty scramble through the forest on her way back from the dwarves' cottage. Her cheeks were ruddy as the heavy bunches of red berries clustered around her, and her eyes shone with the unaccustomed exercise.

Soon however, she was forced to stop. A stranger stood in the centre of the forest clearing, brandishing his sword.

Snow White watched as he struck out at his imaginary foe. The sun's low rays were reflected in beams of light from the revolving blade. His scarlet arm circled, and the sword hissed silver through the air as he pursed his full lips in sustained effort. But despite his focus on the sword, the stranger's keen blue eyes seemed intent to hold her gaze. Eventually, however, the sword slowed, and then its revolutions ceased entirely.

'I heard you before I saw you, pretty maid,' he said.

'Then all of that was for my benefit,' she gasped.

'Most certainly,' said the stranger, with a bow. 'What do they call you?' he asked.

'Snow White,' she said. 'And you?' she added, suddenly emboldened by the sense of exhilaration coursing through her veins.

'Your Royal Highness, mainly,' he replied.

'You're a prince,' she said, scanning the taut, muscular shape of him, the bristling black hair, the piecing blue eyes. 'And yet,' she added, 'how could you be anything else?'

'In the company of royalty,' he said then, 'you should wear your hair a little neater.'

'I'm sorry,' she said, self-consciously, reaching up to smooth back her raven locks. 'It was so windy, and the tree branches did tear it so…'

'Wait,' he said, 'I'll do it for you.'

An arc of silver shone on her right side: the sword had descended. A lock of her dark hair slithered to the ground.

'Oh, oh, oh,' she cried.

'Why, I haven't hurt you a bit,' he said.

'No, but I wasn't expecting it,' she said.

'You're not expecting this either,' said the prince, and he stepped closer, dipped his head, and kissed her full on the mouth. But then he stepped back, and the hot, quivering sensation between them was over. He stooped down and picked up the winding lock he had cut from her tresses. He twisted it round his fingers, unfastened the brocade buttons of his frockcoat's left pocket, and, half-reverentially, half-carelessly, placed the lock of hair inside.

'There,' he said, as much to himself as to Snow White, 'a souvenir of my last bachelor days.'

'A souvenir?' said Snow White, standing square in front of him so that he was forced to look at her. 'I don't understand.'

'I am Prince Nikolai of Novgorod, and I am travelling to meet my betrothed for the first time,' said the prince.

'Your betrothed?' said Snow White, stupidly.

'My betrothed,' said the prince with a half-smile that showed the gleam of his white teeth. 'The young, and, by all accounts, very lovely, Princess Rose Red.'

'Rose Red?' said Snow White, and now she could feel her heart pounding full and hard in her chest.

'Yes, pretty maid,' he said, sauntering over to the dark horse he had tied to a tree. 'And so, my dear, this really is goodbye.' And with that, Prince Nikolai of Novgorod climbed onto his horse and raised his hand in farewell, before riding off into the last glimmers of sunlight between the ancient oaks.

As Snow White stared after him, dumbfounded, she reached up to touch her hair, her cheek and then her lips. She thought to herself that for all he had stolen a lock of her hair, and then a kiss, he had not once called her by her name.

Snow White never forgot her encounter with Prince Nikolai, but, in time, as she roasted the Hunter's pheasant, and scrubbed his pots and pans, she began to think of the prince as a kind of meteor that had once blazed across her sky, never to return. However, one evening, as the sun was setting, Hunter John returned to the cottage with astonishing news from the palace.

As he sat on an old wooden chest, pulling off his muddy boots, he said gravely, 'Your stepsister has run away from the Palace, and her betrothed, Prince Nikolai of Novgorod, has been murdered.'

'Oh, my sweet little stepsister,' said Snow White. 'And oh, poor Prince Nikolai. But surely no-one suspects her of having anything to do with his murder?'

'All I can say,' said Hunter John, 'is that we are living in very strange times. Leaving the palace in the way that she did is bound to cause suspicion.'

'Well,' said Snow White, 'whenever anything terrible happens, rightly or wrongly, I tend to put the blame at my stepmother's door.'

'After everything she has done to you, you can't be blamed for that,' said the Hunter, but his brown eyes looked troubled. Handing Snow White his muddy boots, his voice dropped to a whisper. 'One afternoon,' he said, 'when I was waiting in an antechamber for an audience with her Majesty, I heard an uncanny voice call out:

*'Morgana, so fair, it's true,
But now your own daughter,
Your sweet Rose Red, outshines you.'*

'The Magician in her magic mirror,' said Snow White. 'The enchanter she imprisoned. Some say he is the great Merlin himself. Have you not heard tell of him?'

The Hunter slowly shook his great, shaggy head. 'No,' he replied. 'Though it was rumoured at court that the queen was beginning to spend just a little too much time with her daughter's betrothed.'

'But what has happened to Prince Nikolai?' asked Snow White, remembering a pair of keen blue eyes intent upon her.

'Some say he was poisoned,' said Hunter John. 'For there is not a mark upon him. But whether it was hemlock, or deadly nightshade, or wolf's bane, is not known. Still, they will take a vial of his blood and then his body will be dismembered for burial, as is the custom of his land.'

'It is a strange custom,' said Snow White. 'What is the purpose of it?'

'His are a superstitious people,' said Hunter John. 'The corpse is dismembered so that the dead cannot return as a vampire - or a ghoul. Two dwarf undertakers have already been assigned the task.'

'The dwarves?' said Snow White. And then she recalled how two of Guinan's companions, Kilkenny and Fieldung, had told her of the dead things they buried. 'And the birds – the little birds –?' she asked.

'What do you mean?' said Hunter John.

Snow White shook her raven head and did not answer, for despite everything he had done for her, she still did not entirely trust the Hunter. So, she did not tell him of her plan, which was to ask the birds of the forest to find Rose Red, wherever she may be, and guide her to the safety of the dwarves' cottage. There, Snow White would be reunited with her - and they could ask the dwarves to make them cups of tea.

It took the mere blink of an eye and the repetition of a charm to summon the birds from the sky:

'Doves and larks and sweet black crows,
Follow the path where my stepsister goes –
Guide her, protect her, lead her to be –
In a safe place, to reunite with me.'

Soon the air was thick with the flurry and bell-beat of wings. Then, as Snow White craned her neck upwards, she watched as they soared over the canopy of trees to locate a young woman in a crimson cloak. And then, a week or so later, on her allocated cleaning day, she set off through the forest to the dwarves' cottage, only to be confronted by a chaotic sight.

Rose Red was sitting at the dwarves' kitchen table, dressed all in black, in a gown of a cut-and-colour that was too severe, only serving to emphasise her pallor. Where once the roses had bloomed in her cheeks, now they were white, gaunt, even, and dark circles had appeared like bruises beneath her weeping eyes. For she was sobbing loudly, whilst three of the younger dwarves, Pippin, Voldip and Cooey were scampering around in attempts to console her.

Pippin was fetching her tea; Voldip was winding up a small clockwork mouse and Cooey was reaching for a biscuit for her from the barrel, which greatly interested the pet rat peeping out of his pocket. But Snow White could have screamed at how inadequate these attempts were to comfort her stepsister.

'Rose Red,' she shouted, and she ran to the girl, and enfolded her in her arms, hugging her so hard it was as if she would never let go. 'My dear, my most precious one,' she said. 'It's been so long since I last saw you and yet I thought about you every single day. You were always, always in my heart. And now, my darling, what has been happening to you?'

'Oh Snow, oh Snow,' sobbed the younger girl. 'He's dead. Prince Nikolai has been poisoned.'

'Did you love him?' asked Snow White, though she felt a bittersweet pang when she asked the question.

'Love him?' said Rose Red. 'I barely knew him. We met at a formal banquet. His hair was like yours, as black as a raven's wing, but there was something sardonic, cruel, even, about the curl of his mouth – and a glitter in his eyes that I just didn't like. Mother, however, seemed very taken with him. She sat next to him and Sir Pinel le Savage at the banqueting table, but she ignored the knight to feed pomegranates to the prince. It made Sir Pinel and all the other knights very angry that she favoured the prince above all – for in truth, it seemed she had eyes for no-one but him. And for a while, Snow White, he acted like her little puppy-dog. Ah – I didn't like it at all,' she cried, with all the passion of a heartbroken child.

'But why do they think you poisoned him?' asked Snow White.

'So that I could escape an unhappy betrothal,' said Rose Red. 'All the court pitied me for how he and my mother behaved. Sir Pinel, so woebegone that he was no longer my mother's favourite, often tried to talk to me about my plight. But then,' said Rose Red, with a sudden flash of insight, 'I think it is less frightening for the court to believe that I am the guilty one and to condemn me, rather than my mother. Can you imagine all the curses she would drag up from Hell if they tried?'

'I think your mother is a wicked woman, my dear, and it is so much better that you are no longer at the Palace. For you are my own, my dearly-beloved Rose Red, and I will care for you – and together we will grow strong.' Snow White took hold of Rose Red's hand and squeezed it so hard that she left the red imprint of her fingers on the younger girl's flesh.

'Ah, it's too late for her,' said Rose Red. 'I don't think the splinter of ice in her heart can ever melt.'

'Then let her be,' said Snow White. 'Leave her to her black heart, her dark thoughts and her misery.'

'But the prince?' said Rose Red. 'The poor, poor prince. He is lying in pieces in a glass coffin in the dwarves' courtyard.'

Snow White released Rose Red's hand and went out into the courtyard. Beneath a canopy of red spreading leaves, there lay a gleaming glass coffin with hinges and handles of ornate gold. Snow White climbed the two steps of the dais and peered inside. The prince's dismembered body parts were covered in a black velvet cloth and his pale, dreamless head was resting on a purple cushion.

Snow White reached inside the coffin and clasped his head with her hands. When his face was level with her own, she could see how pale his flesh was, paler even than her own, and that his dark hair writhed, snake-like, round the severed veins in his neck. She pressed her crimson lips to his own and as she did so, his eyelids fluttered open. His eyes were blue and filled with starry light. But it was not enough. Her kiss was not enough to impart life to the dismembered prince. So, she wondered, most bitterly, what could be done.

Meanwhile, the Hunter had returned to his mother's cottage only to find that Snow White was no longer its chief pride and ornament. He saw that her portmanteau had gone, along with her walking-stick and boots, and her ermine cloak was no longer hanging on the peg by the door. Nor was there any fresh, herb-scented dinner waiting for him. He let drop the little bunch of wild crocuses he had brought back from the forest for her. Then he sank down beside them onto the floor and sobbed with all the strength and vigour of his broken, manly heart. But in the midst of his tears and lamentations, the glimmer of an idea took shape.

He rose from the floor, saddled his horse, and galloped through the rain-sodden forest, the branches of the trees tugging at his cloak and shirt. In this way, he soon reached the Palace. He hid in the shadows in the corridor outside Snow White's stepmother's chamber and waited for her to depart. Then he went and stood in front of the queen's looking glass and wept out the story of his lost love. And the magician trapped within the magic mirror, took pity on him because he could perceive an honest, loving heart when it was stood there in front of him. From the depths of the silver glass, he called out:

'Foolish boy,
Turn your sorrow into joy.
She does not know her love for you.
Show her that your heart is true.'

Then the Magician caused the mists within the mirror to part, to reveal Snow White and Rose Red, reunited, in the cottage of the dwarves.

However, the sudden, staccato clacking of the stepmother's glass slippers along the corridor's stone flags alerted Hunter John to her imminent reappearance. He quickly re-covered the mirror with its dark, velvet cloth and turned to face the vulpine stepmother. Before she had a chance to react, he stepped behind her, drew out his hunting knife, and held it to her throat.

'When I brought you the boar's heart all those months ago, and told you it belonged to Snow White, I lied,' he said. 'Snow White lives yet, you wicked woman, and I love her.'

'Then you disobeyed my commands,' choked Queen Morgana.

'And I would do it again,' said the Hunter.

'Do you mean to kill me?' asked the stepmother, with a sardonic twist to her lip, so that for all she was so cruel, Hunter John was compelled to admire her bravery.

'I would not waste even my second-best hunting knife upon you,' he replied. 'But if you promise not to harm any of us, I will let you go free.'

'What is to stop me sending my guards after you and killing you both?' asked the Queen.

'I know where Rose Red is too,' said Hunter John, 'and if you harm just one hair on Snow White's head, I will bring your daughter to you and cut her heart out in front of your very eyes.'

'My daughter?' said the queen, and now the thwarted mother-love crept back into her slanted green eyes. 'Very well then, I shall do what you say. But suffer my daughter to be returned to me.'

'Oh no,' said the Hunter, 'and let her face murder charges for a crime she did not commit?'

'But I would never have let it come to that,' gasped the queen.

'All the same,' said Hunter John, 'I believe she is happier where she is.' However, he relented slightly at the look of anguished love upon the mother's face. 'You may see your daughter at my wedding,' he announced, moving his knife away from her neck with a majestic flourish.

'Your wedding,' repeated the queen, and her hands stole around her neck and began to rub the cool place that the blade had left.

'Yes,' said Hunter John, feeling as if he could soar with his new-found sense of exhilaration and confidence. 'If Snow White'll have me.'

He strode through the corridors of the dark, wintry palace to the tavern where he had stabled his horse. An ale or two steadied his nerves and readied him for his journey. He mounted on his midnight-black steed and thundered through the forest to the dwarves' cottage. All the while, he was wondering if Snow White's stepmother would indeed come to their wedding, and whether she would hurl stars and roses, perhaps hoping that a jagged point or a sharp thorn might take out someone's eye. Finally, he resolved to pay her less attention in his thoughts, and to concentrate instead on the bright future opening out before him.

Presently, he reached the dwarves' cottage, where, to his great joy, Snow White was tending the plants in the courtyard. There she was, his raven-haired girl, pruning them, watering them, and trying to decide which ones needed to be brought inside to be protected from the winter frost.

Hunter John took the watering-can from her hand and placed it on the ground. Then he took her hand in his own.

'Snow White,' he said, 'when you left me, I felt as if my heart would break. But now I ask you to no longer be my housekeeper, but my bride.'

'Isn't that much the same thing?' asked Snow White tartly, for keeping house for seven little men had made her more or less wary of tending to others' needs.

'Oh no,' said the Hunter. 'For I will cherish you and I will cook for you, though I am not much good at cleaning. But I shall bring you bluebells from the forest every day, and when your stepsister comes to visit, you shall paint watercolours and embroider together like you used to do. And you shall feast upon honey and meringues and be my very own darling.'

Snow White nodded and then put her arms around the Hunter's great neck and kissed him on the mouth. Then he felt inside his breeches' pocket for a little gold ring that had once belonged to his mother. He slipped it on the ring finger of Snow White's left hand, and it fitted perfectly.

Though she felt a little flame of happiness rise up within her, all the time, she was aware of the poor, dead prince lying out there in the coffin, and of those poor, parched lips that she had once kissed. Nevertheless, she took her leave of Rose Red, and of the seven dwarves, and went willingly enough with Hunter John back to his cottage. But that night, in the attic room that would remain hers until she became a bride, she said a prayer for the prince.

The following day, after Hunter John had left to poach in the forest, she scraped her hair back as tight as it would go, rubbed mud from the garden into her face, and took an old, plain, patched cloak from the wardrobe. This then was her disguise, and having mounted her recalcitrant steed, she rode off in the direction of the Palace. When she arrived there, she tied her horse to a tree and waited outside the arch-shaped window where she and Rose Red had once spied upon the oh-so wicked queen, so many years ago.

Once again, her stepmother was standing by the mirror, arching her supine back so that it pulled taut the blue velvet of her dress. Snow White could not help but admire the sinuous grace of the devilish thing. Only now, when the stepmother entreated the magic mirror for answers to her questions, the magician stayed mute. Snow White had the impression that her stepmother was beginning to lose her sway of power in Valerian, and that the enchantment was nearly at an end.

The stepmother glared once more at the mirror, then turned on her heels and departed from the chamber. Now it was Snow White's turn to assume ascendancy. She darted through the window and, shouting out the words, *'Tirra Lirra,'* she threw the ornamental coffin that the Hunter had once given her into the looking glass. The glass shattered and fell down, and inside the frame, there stood an elderly man, wan and wizened, with wispy tufts of white hair. He was smiling.

In his right hand, he held a red rose, and in his left, a white rose, which was of such a pearly, iridescent sheen that all the radiance within the room and all the quicksilver light from outside seemed to gather in its petals. This was the rose that he presented to Snow White.

'Thank you for freeing me, beloved child,' he said, and then he added, 'I wonder that no-one thought to do that before – I left the magic words wherever I could. I'm glad you broke the mirror - and the spell,' he continued, glancing at the shards of glass on the floor. 'Such a cruel enchantment.'

'But you can help me now,' said Snow White, eagerly. 'You can help me mend a broken man.'

'Child,' said the magician, 'perhaps you are too young to know this now, but all of us are broken, to a greater or lesser extent.'

'But Prince Nikolai?' asked Snow White.

'Him? Once the light shone through him, right enough. But first came one crack, and then another, and then another, until, inside, the prince was broken up entirely. It happened long before the dwarves wanted to chop him into pieces.'

'But you can help me mend him,' Snow White repeated, her voice rising.

'Well, maybe together with your love, we can,' said the Magician kindly, and he began to intone, over-and-over, *'under the stars, the lost things are found.'* And then Snow White caught the words of the spell, and clutching the rose to her, she also began to murmur, *'under the stars, the lost things are found.'*

The breeze picked up outside the palace-window and carried the words through into another chamber. There was Snow White's father, King Leopold, lying on his four-poster bed, watching his wife comb out her auburn hair at her dressing-table. As the words began to infiltrate his heart and soul, they slowly enkindled a light that had not shone there for many years, not since the death of his first wife, Eva. In remembering the tender grace of Snow White's mother, he gazed in horror at his second wife, the wicked creature that he had married.

'Begone from my sight and my kingdom, foul witch,' he cried, 'for there has been nothing but strife and misery since you arrived.'

Queen Morgana stood stock still and put her hand to her heart, as if, all of a sudden, there was a pang of feeling there, which, strange, misbegotten thing that it was, she did not know how to recognise or own. She gave a whimper that might almost have come from a new-born child, and then she retreated to her chamber, only to find that her mirror lay in shards upon the floor. The ancient curse was undone, and the magician had departed. The stepmother took hold of a piece of shattered mirror glass and held it contemplatively against the longest vein in her wrist.

Meanwhile, Snow White and the Magician were journeying through the forest, over and under the leaves, and all the while they intoned the magick words, *'under the stars, the lost things are found.'*

The words were weaving their magick. Rose Red, who was sitting by the prince's coffin in the dwarves' courtyard, gave a sudden cry, for now a golden light appeared around each disembodied part of the prince, and each severed limb began to knit itself to its brother. Then too, the air shone and there were stars suddenly at the prince's elbow and foot. And amidst this vast expanse of tranquil light, the prince sat up, rubbed his eyes, then smiled at Rose Red. Only now there seemed to be a new sweetness to his smile, and a kindness to those blue eyes which had not been there before.

Slowly, the prince sat up and began to shake the accumulated stardust from his limbs. Leaning on Rose Red's shoulder, he stepped out of the coffin. But though there was radiance all around him, he seemed not to see the sheer goodness of Rose Red. She seemed not to have the power to touch his heart.

Rose Red understood this and curtseyed to the prince and gave him a gentle half-smile. She knew full well that her destiny did not lie with him. And yet, she was compassionate enough, for she led him into the dwarves' kitchen, and gave him a hunk of bread and some goat's cheese, and a glass of elderberry wine. Then she stepped back out into the garden, only to be confronted with the sight of the magician on the other side of the gate. He bowed his head to her and offered her the red rose.

'You are much too good for him,' he said, 'but now, my dear, it is time to leave this forsaken place, and travel with me onto your new path. For you are to become a guardian of the forest, and there are many trees in need of healing.'

Rose Red gave a proud toss of her head, and a sudden gleam came into her eye. All her life, she had been at the beck-and-call of her mother's whims. Now, however, the Magician had granted her a glimpse of what her purpose in life might be. The red rose she pinned to her scarlet cloak shone bright, but not as bright as her own hopes and dreams for the future. The day that she put her hand to her first elm to heal its inner anguish was a proud one; the day that she made her first tincture of hornbeam as balm for a hurt mind was a day when she rejoiced in her calling.

With the oh-so wicked queen now banished from the kingdom, there was nothing to prevent Snow White's triumphant return to the Palace. Her father had written her a letter which began, *'My own, dearly beloved child.'* It consisted of a plea for forgiveness, his blessing on her engagement to the Hunter, and his promise to throw the most splendid ball in celebration of her impending nuptials. To convince her of his sincerity, he undertook to send a magnificent golden coach, decked out with crystals shot through with rainbows. Inside the coach, there was his gift: a long, champagne-coloured gown and an intricately wrought tiara replete with pearls and diamonds. The coach itself was drawn by a pair of white horses with scarlet plumes.

Snow White and Hunter John climbed inside the coach in great delight. They sank back against the satin upholstery, which had the sheen of a Faberge egg. Then Snow White smiled with such innocent radiance that the Hunter took her hand and raised it to his lips.

Soon the Kingdom of Valerian loomed into view, its golden towers and turrets gleaming in the light from the ostlers' lanterns. The carriage swept over the dark drawbridge and clattered into the courtyard, where Rose Red was eagerly anticipating her stepsister. She was wearing a crimson gown and there was a dash of red cochineal on her lips which, combined with the dark sweep of her hair and her tiara with its jewels like rosehip berries, gave her a look of unprecedented sophistication.

'You're here,' she called out, joyfully, 'both of you.' After they had alighted from the carriage, she began to pull Snow White towards the black-and-white tiled lobby that was lit by beacons of flames. Then she stepped behind her sister, and put her hands over Snow White's eyes, only removing her fingers once the great doors to the ballroom had been flung open.

The magnificent rococo chandelier at the centre of the high domed ceiling was carved in the shape of a rosebush, and each white rose was crowned with a candle that spilled pellucid light onto the polished wooden floor. The arched, stained-glass windows bore heraldic images of lions, gryphons, dragons and unicorns amidst forest leaves. They created further corridors of light through which ballgowns fluttered, iridescent as butterfly wings. On the ceiling were paintings of hosts of angels, some with harps, some with flutes, and all clad in white and golden gowns, with starry haloes at their heads.

Beneath the painted ceilings lay trestle tables which were covered in plates of dainties and cold meats, as well as glistening fruits: peeled grapes, quarters of tangerines and nectarines, and rosy apples.

Rose Red pulled Snow White to the centre of the ballroom, and the two girls began to dance beneath the shimmering light of the chandelier. The light spilled out into their hair, made the highlights of their cheeks and wrists and ankles gleam. How they laughed, and the peals of their laughter flowed out into the arched dip and swoop of the cascading violin-music. And so, they whirled into the music's ebb-and-flow, until the Hunter politely, but firmly, tapped Rose Red on the shoulder and claimed his betrothed for the next dance.

Snow White gazed at him with new appreciation. She had persuaded him to rinse his hair in lemon and thyme and now it shone. He was wearing a loose, white, flowing shirt with a diamond pin at the collar over a leather jerkin. He took her in his arms, and all the tenderness he was feeling rose up to his eyes and into his smile. Together they danced beneath the chandelier, and the radiance it released was not brighter than the love-light which emanated from each towards the other.

At that moment, the ballroom's mahogany double doors burst open, and Snow White's wicked stepmother stepped through them. She was dressed in a charcoal-grey gown trimmed with raven feathers, and she wore in her hair, a tiara that resembled a forest fire. Around her neck was a ruby choker, two inches wide, like a particularly precious slit throat; and her ears bore earrings that looked like sparks of orange flame. Across her eyes was a black and diamante mask, but it was the repellent, sinuous grace with which she moved that revealed her identity. She sidled up to her daughter, who began to back away, slowly, in alarm. The other couples came apart to allow Rose Red to disappear through the corridor their parting bodies made, and then to vanish into the night.

In the more than awkward silence that ensued, the lead violinist, perspiring heavily on his rostrum, struck up a lively Tarantella, in which he was soon joined by the other members of the orchestra. Now Queen Morgana began to move in time to the music, and then she began to twist like flame. As she span, it seemed that sparks emanated from her layers of charcoal-grey silk and feathers, and from the pointed toes of her glass slippers. Like the tongue of a darting match, her dance flickered in the ballroom. It seemed that her red hair was also ignited, and then, whirling faster-and-faster, her long arms uncoiled, and her dress fanned into passionate flames. Now she moved with complete and perfect confidence, and the slash of scarlet that was her lips became an exultant smile.

Suddenly, all at once, she was completely aflame - a sheer wall of lambent fire that hurt the eyes of its beholders. But, as the flames dispersed, the ballroom guests were astonished to discover that the wicked queen had completely disappeared into the dark, quiet night.

Snow White's father stepped forwards and ordered the orchestra to begin a different tune. Then, as King Leopold approached his daughter and her betrothed, the sweet slurs of the violin became a wistful, haunting refrain. When he put his arms around them both and recommended that Hunter John fetch a plate of fruit for Snow White, he did not know that someone who hated her had laced one of the apples with a tincture of wolfbane and belladonna.

And oh, the Hunter brought Snow White the poisoned apple, for how could he not? It was so much brighter and rosier than all the rest!

As Snow White took a bite of the apple, she began to experience the strangest sensation. Something was coming to her. What was it? Her heartbeat quickened. She did not know; it was too subtle and too elusive. And yet there it was, creeping through and through the candle-lit air. She took a few deep breaths to steady herself. Her bosom rose and fell, and her heart beat loud and fast – there *was* something approaching. She was fighting to beat it back with her will – and yet, her two, little, white, slender hands could not restrain it.

The double doors of the ballroom flew open, and there, standing in a stream of light, was Prince Nikolai. Flakes of snow had settled in his dark locks and dark cape – and in the fur that gathered at the tops of his ebon boots. His lined, handsome face was slightly flushed, as if he had been riding hard through the starry night, and his hand strayed to the silver pommel of his sword as if he were yet uncertain of his welcome. The blue-and-quicksilver of his eyes surveyed the gathered throng of guests until he found the one for whom he was searching. Once again, the crowds of guests parted as he strode slowly and purposefully towards Snow White.

She saw him pacing towards her through the rustles, scents and colours of the assembled throng. Her pulses beat faster, and her surging blood warmed and then relaxed every inch of her frame. Two bright spots of scarlet appeared upon her cheeks, which were otherwise as ghostly as the winter snow. Out of the corner of her eye, she saw the Hunter gazing at her in consternation as still the prince approached her with, she supposed, dark intent. Snow White muttered a few words of a broken prayer, of which only the word, *Mother,* was discernible. Now her pupils dilated, and her eyes glittered until, with a single, piercing cry, she dropped the apple from her grasp and sank to the ground.

Hunter John, his own heart beating wildly, stepped forwards to shield her from the curiosity of the other guests. He watched in alarm as the prince came and stood beside her prone form. Each man was now level with the other whilst Snow White's father summoned a doctor, all the while none of them knowing if she were alive – or dead.

Death did not claim her. But, in the ensuing days, as Snow White lapsed in-and-out of her mysterious malady, calling sometimes for her mother, Eva, sometimes for the Hunter, and sometimes, for someone strange in a language of her own invention, even the doctor could not say whether it was the effect of strong and contradictory emotions or the trace of belladonna he had found in her blood which was weakening her.

'Love - or - poison?' the doctor mused to himself from his patient's bedchamber.

Through the arch-shaped window, patches of blue sky fought their way amongst snow-clouds, whilst one black raven flew across the ancient Kingdom of Valerian on crooked wings.

Forests For All Forever

When she was telling me her stories, Queen Morgana recalled how, as a child in Avalon, Rose Red once dreamt that her ginger kitten had grown to human size and offered her a huge, golden wedding ring, large enough to slip over her head. It was a strange dream, but, said Queen Morgana, everything else about my daughter's subsequent history was also a little odd.

For a time, Morgana said, Rose Red lived with the Magician in the cottage of the dwarves, who were away on what they claimed was an Important Mining Expedition. That was their story, but they were fooling no-one, since Pippin told everyone they met that they were now the Travellers of Space and Time.

'Hush, hush, Pippin, son,' Guinan had said to him. 'It's tip-top secret business, not to be revealed at this time, remember?'

Pippin nodded. 'Strictly on a need-to-know basis,' he replied, nodding solemnly, for he remembered the words, if not their import.

Rose Red was not at all sure what to make of this, but she thought to herself, there are dwarves who live in cottages, and there are dwarves, and elves too, who live in the forest, little grey or fawn-coloured men, a different species of fae entirely. So, perhaps there are also dwarves who can slip in-and-out of time.

That was just one of the things that Rose Red learned. She learned too that the wise toad who natters with the kingfisher by the river in summer has a precious jewel in his head. She learned that at midsummer, valerian produces pink or white flowers, beloved of the bees, that can sometimes be mistaken for poison hemlock. She learned that its root clusters can be hung to dry for teas or tinctures for hurt hearts and minds. And she learned how to heal the inner anguish of a line of mighty oaks by placing her hands upon them. In all these things, she was guided by Merlin the Magician, her teacher in forest lore – but, my goodness, he worked her hard!

She caught herself scrutinising him one afternoon after she had lived with him for nearly a year. Physically, he had not altered very much in that time. His hair was still snowy-white on top, but tapering down into long strands of iron-grey, smooth in some parts, straggly in others. He still had grey tufts of beard on a surprisingly square jaw, and a jutting brow with those same tufts of grey, like sprigs of gorse on a cliff. Only something had shifted in his eyes, so that sometimes the lost expression in their watery depths was at variance with the overall impression he conveyed of strength and purpose.

Since the Magician did not wish to repeat the same mistakes he had made with her mother, Morgana, and with others besides, he did not teach Rose Red much spellcasting. Still, they both knew that she had a quiet power of her own.

One day, when he was leaving the cottage for a few days, he asked her what he should bring back. First of all, she wanted to ask for a singing bird. Then she thought about how long it had been since she was last at the Palace, and how bedraggled and faded she was now with all the many tasks she must do. So, she asked him if he would bring her back another rose, that its beauty and freshness might revive her own.

The Magician set off on his travels. Far ahead of him, he thought he saw a bruise-coloured dragon, scaly, black and purple, running ahead of him on a dark slope. But he was not sure, for the beast made no sound. Then too, it seemed that the stars above the hills were no stars his eyes had ever seen before – he, who prided himself on his knowledge of all things celestial!

Perhaps he followed the dying dragon too far – this dying dragon, who suddenly seemed the emblem of his own fading power. For in his heart of hearts, he knew that Morgana, once his lover, was now his implacable foe, and that whilst she lived, his magick was always in jeopardy.

Now he was alone on the dark hillside.

He turned slowly. Slowly, he set one foot and then the other to climb back up the hill. Step-by-step he went, and each step was harder than the last. The stars did not move. No wind blew over the steep ground. In all that vast kingdom of darkness, only he moved. He came to the top of the hill and then he looked out across the Kingdom of Valerian. He knew that he must gather all his power to cast the spell that lay ahead of him.

Right glad Rose Red was when the Magician had gone, and she was at liberty to walk once more into the forest that was ever her comfort and her consolation. She walked towards the forest spring, which flowed into a mossy pool where river shingle gleamed. As Rose Red glanced down at a quick-darting minnow, she caught a glimpse of herself instead. Her silky brown hair was piled high on her head, luxuriant as a queen's, although a few strands escaped and blew around her face. Her face itself was sweet but pained, the pucker of her brow and the shadows beneath her blue eyes belying the blooming roses of her lips and cheeks.

She blinked, smiled, then shook her hand in the water to break up the reflection. Was it then that she heard the trickle and murmur of the forest spring? For, over-and-over, it seemed to say, *'Marry me, marry me, marry me,'* and even, *'oh marry me at last, or else my heart will break.'*

The voice reminded her of Nimue's, an aunt of hers, the Lady of the Lake, who always dressed in white. Rose Red recalled a time when she was very small, when Nimue had left her home beneath the sea to visit them in the Kingdom of Avalon. She still shivered when she thought of Nimue's cool, webbed, touch, and the beseeching look in her eyes, eyes that seemed to take their colour from whichever part of the lake where she swam, sometimes turquoise, sometimes sapphire, sometimes violet – although, at this time, when she was far from her watery home, they were grey as the mists which circled round Avalon, with a black sun for each pupil..

She also remembered her mother Morgana saying to Nimue, 'If there is no human man, there are no babies.' Then, what an unearthly, determined look had appeared on Nimue's pale face and since that time, strange stories about her had circled in Avalon.

In the forest, Rose Red soon reached a place of beheaded statues. These were fixed above the graves of suicides or thieves, or poachers, who could not be buried on holy ground. It was even said that some of these statues were not statues at all, but rather men and women who had been taken in adultery and then turned to stone. Afterwards, their jealous spouses or lovers had crept into the forest in the middle of the night and overcome by rage, had lopped the statues' heads clean from their shoulders.

Rose Red knew that she had a great gift for healing, but she did not know what she was meant to do with these beheaded statues – or even, if she was meant to do anything at all. Just, she was fascinated by them, and she could not stop thinking about them.

However, that night, when she lay beneath the stars in the very heart of the forest, she had the feeling that she was being transported beyond them into a strange, starry realm. Yet she was still there in the forest too, for she could feel the grass beneath her and the great sway of forest fronds all around her. Then she felt that she had the healing of the earth and trees and skies and stars all within her power.

The next morning, she returned to the cottage and thought on the great mysteries of the forest.

But that evening, when the Magician came back in a fierce rage, Rose Red knew that something was terribly wrong. The shadows that roamed around him now seemed much darker, the spiders scuttled about him, and high above in the cottage eaves, an owl began to hoot.

'It's your mother,' said the Magician. 'Something must be done about her. She stole the Spell of Immortality from me, and you remember how she bound me in a mirror. And today, I heard on my travels that she rules again from the Fruitful Isles, where she continues to work her evil magick.'

'But what can be done?' asked Rose Red, faintly. She looked all around but it seemed that the Magician had forgotten his promise to bring her a rose.

'I need a lock of your hair,' said the Magician quickly, 'and then you must join me in cursing her. For you are of her blood, and that will make the curse more potent.'

Rose Red did not want to act against her mother, and she began to pray for strength to resist the Magician's imprecations. But just now, she did not know whether to pray to the Goddess Valeria, who was waiting to reincarnate in human form, or to the Holy Virgin, or even to the source of the power that daily she felt growing within herself. And whilst she thus hesitated, the Magician thundered,

'You shall live on, Morgana, for many years, as beautiful and as wise as you are now. And you will come to feel that you are blessed and healed. But just when you are in the moment of your greatest triumph, everything will turn to ashes.' Then he took a knife, and from the top of Rose Red's head, he cut a lock of her nut-brown hair.

At this point in the story, Morgana told me she had felt something dreadful was occurring. She tried to cast a spell of protection, but only the vestiges of it clung to her, wraith-like. So she began to magick a counter-curse. But, alas, she was no longer in her heyday. The Magician and the reluctant daughter were draining the magick from her. So, in her state of diminished power, she cast a spell that within a hundred years, Merlin must return to the prison of the mirror unless he could find someone else to take his place.

Now the malevolence of the Magician was terrible to behold, and he continued to curse, comprehensively, every part of Morgana, from the crown of her head down to the arch of her slender feet.

And for Morgana, deeper and darker even than the Magician's curse was the knowledge that her own child had joined forces against her. The pain of this betrayal was more than she could bear. She whimpered and her black cat slinked between her legs, and then neither she nor the cat could find comfort. Outside, a storm sprang up on the Fruitful Isles, and how it raged and howled, and inside her palace, the dark blood ran chill in her veins.

Rose Red was right: the Magician had forgotten to bring her the rose. He muttered a few gruff words of apology, but she could not help recalling those older, kinder days, when he had won her friendship with warm words and the gift of a flower. But now, how vastly changed she felt things to be, both between them, and in their lives together. She suffered from the creeping taint of the Magician's presence around her, and yet, she also wanted that feeling of happy companionship to return.

So, the Magician promised that the next time he was away, he would return with this gift for her. And in a few weeks, the Magician set off once more on *a sacred quest*, not for the rose, but in order to learn secrets from the dryads of the trees.

As soon as he was gone, Rose Red felt again that glorious sense of freedom that came in his absence.

She pulled on her fox-pelt slippers, and ran out into the snow-laden forest, where she span round-and-round, her arms outstretched, shouting, 'What's going to happen?'

Then she heard once more a sad female voice murmuring in the water of the spring, '*O marry me, marry me at last.*'

She did not know that at that very moment, the Magician was galloping into the forest clearing where lay the beheaded statues and their severed, upturned limbs. And there, in the centre of that clearing, the Magician saw, blooming on a bush full of dead flowers, a last, single, red rose.

It glistened, crimson as blood.

The Magician bent down low on the neck of his dark horse and reached out to pluck the flower. His fingers had barely touched the stalk, when he heard the strangest sound in the world, a great roaring, as of a beast of prey.

Suddenly, there appeared in front of the Magician a being who seemed vaster than the mighty sway of the forest, solid, massive, yet swift. And how the sunlight glittered on his great, leonine head, and on his eyes, blue as celestine, and on the golden hairs of the great paws that now grasped his shoulders so that their claws pierced the thick wool of his magician's cloak.

The lion shook hm like a child shakes a snowstorm.
'Thief!' he roared.

All the little moons and stars on the Magician's cloak scattered and he fell, sprawling, to his knees. 'Forgive me,' he wheedled. He began to try and draw up a spell of protection, but he quickly realised that it would have no power against the lion, who was already a creature under a powerful enchantment. And just as the Magician feared the lion, so too did he fear this magick, which he knew was more ancient, and possibly more powerful, than his own.

But a cunning look crept into the magician's eyes and he said, 'The rose was for my daughter, a maiden, young and fair.'

'Take her then the rose,' said the Lion, 'and bring your daughter to me as my bride in yonder castle,' and he inclined his head towards the northernmost part of the forest, where purple turrets loomed above fir trees.

What was to be done? The following day, the Magician led Rose Red to the castle, which now appeared in the forest like an enchantment coming undone. It rose up before them like sunrise, towers and battlements reaching hundreds of feet into the sky. For, behind wrought-iron gates, a path led to a massive square building of pale grey stone, block set upon block, half-hiding behind its own pillars and turrets, and how the stone glittered in the pale morning light. To Rose Red, it seemed as vast as a city, not just one building, but many, tied together by corridors and a courtyard with a sweeping cypress tree.

Despite this, it was a lonely castle indeed, save for the one light that flickered from an upstairs window in the most eastern tower, that Rose Red would later learn was the library, the domain of the Lion Baron's former tutor, Friar Long. This light was so dream-like and evanescent, it might have been the flicker of a star.

She and the Magician parted company then, for he had traded her life for his own, and what more was there to say? There was only the sadness of a parting that should have occurred much earlier.

Rose Red crossed the courtyard, entered the castle gates, and stepped into a white and mahogany hall. Here, the morning sunlight slanted through tall, narrow windows. Their coloured glass held pictures of golden heraldic lions with long, waving manes, and bright, dark eyes, or silver unicorns that shimmered with a mysterious moon-glow.

From the ceiling, there hung a chandelier suspended on a golden chain, with crystals that tinkled with the draft from the open door. Its candles threw light across the hunting stags and heraldic shields set at intervals across the white walls. Yet there was no living person in the hall.

But inside the hall, there was a table with a dinner service upon it, covered in red flowers. Beside one plate was a silver bell, with a little note beside it which said, *'Ring Me.'* And so, of course, Rose Red did.

Then the goblet in front of her, which was shaped like a unicorn, with its horn the stem of the bowl, filled with a sweet, piquant liquid, like lemon and grapes cooled with sherbet. When Rose Red tasted it, she realised it was most exactly the drink she wanted.

After she had eaten, the Lion Baron came to join her in the hall. When she first saw him, she could not help but shudder, for though lions are infinitely better-looking than men, yet theirs is a different order of beauty. Nevertheless, there was a kind of sadness in his celestine eyes which moved her.

He drew back his head and gazed at her with those eyes, in which she saw her own face, repeated twice, like a glimmer within a pearl.

'I am Lowenhardt, the Baron of Astalot,' he said. 'I am the owner, and guardian of this castle.' To Rose Red, it seemed his voice issued from a cave full of echoes. He grudgingly admitted what she had already guessed that he disliked the presence of servants because constant human company reminded him too bitterly of his own otherness.

Rose Red found his difference from herself strange; his presence, heavy and choking, in a way which reminded her of her time with the Magician. And with this sense of his mystery came a feeling of pressure, as if the castle itself was about to be submerged beneath water.

That evening, she watched the firelight play on the gold strands of his mane. For a moment, it seemed as if he were haloed.

Still, his strangeness made her shiver. When he helplessly fell before her to kiss her hand, she would retreat into her flesh, flinching at his touch. It was difficult to forget completely her fear of someone as large as a bear, maned like a lion, and silent as the sun.

But presently, when she found herself yawning, she bid him a polite good-night and walked down the corridor to a door carved with twisting roses. Her bedroom. A glance between the window's heavy velvet curtains revealed an ivory landscape of fresh, fallen snow. Shivering slightly, she clambered into her comfortable four-poster bed with its brocade curtains and silken canopy.

After she had blown out the candle, a man came and laid beside her. It was the Lion Baron, who had cast off his lion pelt this night. It was so dark in the room that she could not see him, but she could discern his massive bulk. He slipped a ring onto her finger, and while she was twisting it round in wonder, she fell asleep. When she woke in the morning, the ring was still there, on the third finger of her left hand, but Lowenhardt was gone. Suddenly, she remembered her childhood dream about the ginger cat, and she smiled.

She found Lowenhardt soon enough, in the library in the easternmost tower, poring over a dark-bound leather volume with a gilt clasp and a lion, a unicorn, and a girl holding a mirror to its face stamped in gold on the front.

'It is the book of my ancestors,' said Lowenhardt. 'I was looking to see where I should record our betrothal.'

'Our betrothal?' asked Rose Red.

'Didn't your father make it clear to you the conditions upon which you were to stay with me?' asked Lowenhardt, gravely.

'No,' said Rose Red, and, with a sudden flash of anger, she added, 'and he isn't my father.'

At that, the Lion Baron's massive brow furrowed. 'Then we have both been deceived,' he said. He added, more earnestly, 'Rose Red, I will not keep you here against your will. But do you think you could stay here with me for a while? If you grow to like me enough, perhaps you may consent to be my bride.'

'I will stay with you for a year and a day,' said Rose Red, 'and after that time, I will tell you my answer.' She slid the betrothal ring from her finger and tried to give it back to him.

But he waved it away with his great paw.

'Keep it,' he said, 'you may find that you want to wear it again.'

When he left the reading-room, she saw, with a touch of shock that seemed to pierce through her languid enchantment, that he moved on all fours.

After that, he came no more to her room at night, but was ever courteous and attentive to her by day. He chose the finest books from his library for her entertainment, and he walked beside her in the castle gardens, gathering flowers for bright nosegays.

As the months passed, she came to realise how passionately he cared for her. The realisation moved her almost to tears. And when, at the end of each evening by the fireside, he put aside the great volume of poetry from which he had been reading aloud, it was often in her heart to drop a kiss upon his mane. But though, every evening, she reached out her hand towards him, still, she could not bring herself to touch him of her own free will.

The days went by, and she marked them off with a stub of pencil in her notebook. When she had made three hundred and sixty-six pencil strokes, she knew she must give him her answer.

She paced down the corridor that connected her chamber to his own. A tentative rap on the door. No answer. But then a gust of wind sweeping down that corridor blew the door wide open, and Rose Red stepped inside.

His grey hunting sable, his sword and sash were laid out on the leather chair; one fine burgundy gauntlet was placed on each arm. Candle flames on the brink of extinguishment, about to drown in pools of wax, flickered on the solid stone hearth.

She saw them reflected in the ominous caverns of his eyes.

Then too, he was pacing backwards and forwards, forwards and backwards, so that the tip of his tail kept brushing against her dress.

Surely if I accept him, he will devour me, she thought.

She stretched out her hand to him and he became as still as the statues in the forest. Perhaps he was more frightened of her than she was of him. This thought made her angry, for reasons which she could not quite explain.

'Yes, Lowenhardt,' she said into the silence, continuing a conversation that had started over a year ago, 'I will marry you.' She took the bright gold ring from her reticule and placed it back on her finger.

Then the room began to shake with the tremendous thunder of his full-throated purr. This purr was enough to rock the walls; the candleholders on the great stone hearth started to dance. The sound ricocheted round the room: its reverberations forced open the shutters so that scatters of starlight shone through.

Then the Lion Baron stood up from all fours and dragged himself closer and closer to Rose Red. He put his great paws on her narrow shoulders so that she could feel their pads through her dress. What if his claws should rip the thin silk of her sleeves?

'Very well,' he said.

She found that she could not read his expression.

After her consent to his proposal, Rose Red was struck with strange misgivings. She wished, more than anything, that there was someone in whom she could confide. She sent messages to her dear stepsister, Snow White, but Snow White was in confinement, expecting the birth of her first child, and considering the Great Matter of the Abdication, besides.

Finally, Rose Red thought she could do no better than to reconcile with her mother Morgana and discuss everything with her in Avalon.

So, she told Lowenhardt that she was lonely and had a great desire to visit her kinsfolk again.

'It is not for me to prevent you,' said Lowenhardt, 'but you must promise not to talk to your mother alone, but only when there are others around. You must not allow it, otherwise you will bring great misfortune on us both.'

Rose Red gave her word. So, he told her to take the silver bell from the dinner-table and ring it and wish herself home. Then she would find herself back in Avalon. She retrieved the bell, did as he said, and there she was, walking through a great field upon the Isle of Avalon's distant shores.

It was her first visit home in many years. She remembered the island as fruitful, green and mysterious, with willow trees overhanging vast swathes of water, and apple trees growing in groves on the outskirts of the forests. But now, to her sad eyes, the willows floundered wild, and the partly uprooted trees were obscene.

Was it true then, that the island took its power from its great queen, and that as Morgana waned, so too did Avalon? But surely, Avalon was the heart and seat of her power.

Some cleared space had been enclosed with a rough wall, and peering over it, Rose Red saw old ivy that had struck root anew and was growing green on the quiet mounds of ruin. Still, that single patch of bright green drab was a welcome sight to Rose Red.

A gate was standing ajar; Rose Red pushed it open and went into the garden.

Here, a cool mist wreathed the trees. She began to pick her way along the garden-path when she suddenly beheld her mother's summer hall, with its glass walls and black-and-white carved mosaic floor. Inside were people that she remembered from long ago, the faery butler Henri, and the footman, Josef. They recognised her too and were overjoyed to see her.

Henri was thin and sharp-featured, with a bright beak of a nose and little gold-rimmed spectacles perched on the end of it. Josef was more heavy-set, with a rugged face, and a shock of dark hair, glossy as blackbird feathers. Maybe they had both been too long at fairy court, thought Rose Red, for they had an odd, constrained way of walking, more like bird steps than purposeful strides.

'I am to be married,' she said to their inquiries. And she told them it was very good to live where she did, and to have all that she wished. She didn't tell them the whole story, nor did she have the chance, for in that moment, her mother swept into the room.

To Rose Red, her mother seemed somehow smaller, though her belly was swollen. Morgana's hair was lightly peppered with grey and held back from her face with a clasp of hawthorns and dewdrops. Her large, amber-green eyes fastened on Rose Red, so that the daughter felt the coldness of her mother's still gaze.

'Daughter, we must talk,' said Morgana, and she dismissed Henri and Josef with an imperious wave of her hand.

Rose Red watched as they gave bird-like hops out of the hall. What could she do? After all, this was her mother's kingdom. Despite the ravages wrought by Merlin's curse, still, Morgana's will was sufficiently powerful that Rose Red felt some of her own sense of purpose draining from her.

She had promised Lowenhardt - something - what was it? She couldn't remember. She couldn't even remember what she had eaten for breakfast that day. So, she allowed her mother to lead her away as if she were a little child. They walked into an antechamber which contained a fine blue glass vase, on which a marble mermaid swam with her arms around the neck of a dolphin.

'A sculpture of your Aunt Nimue,' said Morgana.

'How is she?' asked Rose Red.

'Middling,' said Morgana. 'She is sad that her water babies must one day go to court. She wanted me to cast a spell so that they never grew up. I had to tell her that they were only borrowed children, and that in time they must go and live their lives in Valerian.'

'What did she say to that?' asked Rose Red.

'All I could get her to promise was that one day she would send Lancelot off to court in Camelot, clad in armour white as snow.'

By this and other family reminiscences, Morgana won back her daughter's trust. Rose Red began to tell her mother about Lowenhardt, how he wore a lion body by day, but that the first night he had cast it off and lain beside her as a man. And she had not seen his face because the candles were extinguished, and then he was up and gone in the morning. She wondered if this was to be the pattern of their marriage, which made her so sad, because she wanted to see his face.

'But my darling,' said her mother, 'it may be that you sleep with a troll.'

'Surely not?' said Rose Red, aghast.

'It is just as well you came to me,' said Morgana. 'For I will give you a candle stub which you must carry in your bosom on the day you are married. On your wedding night, light it once he is asleep, and then you may see his face. But be careful not to spill any tallow on him.'

Rose Red took the candle and hid it in her pocket. Then she took out the bell, and rang it, and a moment later, there she was, back in her room in the castle at Astalot, rubbing her eyes and wondering if it had all been a dream.

Yet when she glanced back down at the bell, she found she had rung it so hard that it had cracked through and through – so that now it could give no more peals or wishes. She wondered how she might go back to Avalon again - and if it mattered, for soon she was to be married and to take her place among the finest ladies in Valerian.

The outer walls of the wedding chapel were covered in a green and shining shawl of ivy, with turtledoves perching in the tracery of its arched window. Angel wings carved upwards gave this window its shape. It depicted a Pieta of Madonna and child, whilst its colours, blue like flood, red like fire, darted across the congregation's faces and hands in benison.

On the day of the ceremony, Rose Red sighed at herself in the looking glass. There were red roses twisted in her hair, and she wore a long-sleeved, white gown covered in gold thread. Around her throat was a choker of pearls. But though her mother's hair was red as beech leaves, all she had bequeathed to her daughter were clusters of nut-brown with a faint shimmer of gold. It was only later, as she walked down an aisle resplendent with candles, that Rose Red felt beautiful again.

Lowenhardt was there, waiting at the altar, beneath the window's vivid and shifting hues. He wore a simple, dark tunic with a fine gold chain round his neck which accentuated the majesty of his leonine features.

Standing in front of them, Friar Long, who looked both sharp and pleased, pronounced them man and wife.

As a boy, Lowenhardt had believed that Friar Long, his tutor, knew everything, and it had been a great disappointment when he realised that the older man could not find the words to reverse his enchantment. For the curse had come from Avalon, from Morgana herself, who deemed that Lowenhardt had treated her disdainfully.

Friar Long well remembered his pupil's crime: the spoilt and haughty youth had refused to offer hospitality to the fairy lady. For this, he had been condemned to a lion's body. So then, Friar Long had to contend with his pupil's passionate sense of injustice accentuated by the lion's rage. Over the years, Friar Long had done his best to curb the excesses of his student, but at times it had been very difficult, almost impossible. Now, however, the friar's face was wreathed in smiles, as the bride and bridegroom kissed.

But this was not the moment for Lowenhardt's curse to come to an end.

That night, Rose Red entered Lowenhardt's chamber, now their chamber. Here, an enormous four-poster bed stood on a dais, canopied in gold, with a white counterpane worked in citrine silks. She readied herself for bed, blew out the candles, and then lay in complete darkness. Soon after, Lowenhardt entered the room and took off his lion pelt. Then he lay down beside her and his touch was like honey and steel dipped in velvet. He took her to himself, knowing that she was his.

After their lovemaking, he fell asleep, and she noticed then that he snored, not lightly, but with a deep, full-chested rumble. Just as she was beginning to wonder whether she would ever get used to the noise, she felt the tallow-candle against her arm, that had fallen out of her bosom and into the bed. So, she clambered down from the great, four-postered canopy, retrieved the candle, lit it, and held it up so that the light shone upon him.

Ah, he was handsome indeed, but not handsome as men are in storybooks and fairy tales, but as they are in the wicked world, when they must walk its paths and by-ways and endure its pains and woes. For a moment, she felt in awe of him, and his strange, intangible maleness, and yet he *was* just a man after all, with a shock of brown hair tinged auburn, and a broad, wide, flat nose.

She felt then that she loved him truly, and so she leaned down and kissed him. But, as she kissed him, she let three drops of hot tallow drip onto his shoulder, and he woke up.

'What have you done?' he cried, but his words sounded distant, as if they were echoing down a cold corridor of decades. 'Now you have given us both sad destinies. Had you but waited one year more, I should have been free. For now, I must tell you, your mother has bewitched me so that I am a lion by day and a man by night. Due to your fatal curiosity, the curse remains, and you must leave me to learn how to undo it.'

Rose Red cried at that and drew out great shuddering sobs in answer from Lowenhardt, but still, there was no hope for it, she must go. But where, and how? For the bell was broken. Nevertheless, she returned to her old room and readied herself for the journey.

Whilst she was packing her few dresses, and shaking out the folds in her cloak, she heard the distant sound of birdsong and cattle lowing. Then, the strangest thing occurred. As she turned towards the sounds, a great gale of wind rushed through the room. The sounds grew louder and became a shrieking and fluttering from all corners.

The room twisted on its axis, and then it snapped in two, with a loud crack, like an egg breaking. Rose Red found herself hatched once more in a familiar place, the summer room of her mother's palace in Avalon, restored to some of its former glory. Here, there were misty mirrors with sepia stains perched on ornately carved tables, reflecting fine-blown green glass vases.

Queen Morgana turned towards her daughter.

To her astonishment, Rose Red saw that the front of her mother's tunic was unbuttoned and that she was suckling an infant boy with a shock of dark hair sticking up like the quills of a porcupine.

'Your brother, Mordred,' said Morgana, and Rose Red could hear her own dismissal in the words. For she felt something had shifted within her mother. Always before, she had known that Morgana loved her, that no matter how possessive or craven she became, her behaviour was the dark shadow of her love. Now, however, Rose Red was left feeling unloved and unnerved.

'Or rather, your half-brother,' Morgana said, 'for you are not a Pendragon.' There was a sharpness to her voice, the edge of a blade of ice, or cold, moon-bright metal.

After everything she had endured, this was too much for Rose Red, and she burst into tears.

'Why are you weeping, child?' asked Morgana as she handed the infant over to the handmaiden who had just entered the room. For a moment, it seemed the chilliness of her demeanour might thaw, deceptive and treacherous though that hope was, because Rose Red was now all too aware of how quicky her mother could turn to ice again.

'Surely a new bride should look happier?' Morgana continued.

Such was Rose Red's consternation that she did not know whether to speak, or to remain silent.

'Mother,' she said, finally, 'I have lost him. Or perhaps -,' she added sadly, 'he was never truly mine in the first place.' Was it her imagination, or was there now a gleam of pleasure in Morgana's eyes?

'Then there's work to do to get him back,' her mother replied.

'Work?' asked Rose Red, 'what work?'

'Three tasks for you to complete,' said Morgana. 'The youth was insolent,' she muttered to herself, 'and doubted my power. How ironic that he should be dependent on my daughter for the curse to be lifted.'

'But if I complete your tasks,' said Rose Red, 'will you keep your word and remove the curse?'

'And will you, daughter, complete the tasks?' asked Morgana, so that Rose Red felt a pang of self-doubt.

'Love isn't for the faint of heart,' Morgana cried into the ensuing silence. The pallor of her face increased; her still, sculptural quality turned to strange dismay. Then it seemed as if all the light in the room gathered up brighter, and more malevolent, in her eyes, amber in dark hollows.

'There are three tasks which you must complete, each more difficult than the last,' she said. 'But the first is quite simple. I want you to place a thousand flowers in this casket which was a gift from your Aunt Nimue.'

Rose Red took the delicately carved, ivory box from her mother and opened it. The entire box was only large enough for the girl to place her hand inside. She tried to imagine it full of blossoms, or tiny, bright-coloured flowers, but, somehow, she went wrong in her imaginings, for the visionary petals parted, and instead, she saw the castle courtyard at Astalot, with its great cypress tree and a bench beneath it.

Two boys and a girl with a long, flaxen plait down her back were sitting on the bench. For a moment, Rose Red fancied they could see her, for they looked startled, but then courtyard, bench, children, all, faded away.

Rose Red remembered then that both her mother and her aunt had the Gift of Sight and she thought that perhaps here in Avalon, she possessed it too – or, at least, a latent aspect of it. But the vision had gone – even the imaginary flowers had gone – so that Rose Red found she was staring at nothing more exciting than the purple velvet lining of the ivory box.

'How will all the flowers fit inside?' she asked her mother, bewildered.

'That is the nature of the task, for you to find out,' said Morgana. 'Your second task is to restore all the beheaded statues in the forest clearing to life.'

This time, Rose Red knew better than to protest. Instead, she began to think, slowly and carefully. She remembered all the rumours she had heard that some of the statues were actually lovers caught in adultery, and she wondered whose magick had turned them to stone. Perhaps her mother was giving her a hint when she mentioned Nimue, who was indeed gifted with her own peculiar abilities.

For, like Morgana, Nimue had once been a pupil of Merlin's. Unlike Morgana however, Nimue had not become his lover, for she believed her power derived from her purity. She had learned some of Merlin's secrets, but she had not sacrificed herself. She was strengthened in this resolve when she saw how her sister, Morgana, had suffered at the hands of men.

Was it then, Rose Red wondered, that the springs of water in Avalon, and even in Valerian, began to murmur, *'Marry me, marry me,'* to ears attuned to fairy music? And not long after, strange stories were heard across the land, of baby princes snatched from their cradles, Lionel, Bors, and even the infant Lancelot. Hadn't Morgana claimed that she had sent messages to her sister beneath the sea, demanding that the stolen babies be returned to Valerian?

Perhaps, thought Rose Red, Nimue still longed for human love, and yet she continued to believe that her power derived from her purity. Was it Nimue, who, in one of her fits of bewildered rage, turned all the lovers to stone? But how to reverse this magick? For many of Rose Red's formative years had been spent in Valerian, not Avalon, and she did not believe she possessed the power of her fairy kin.

'And so, to the third task,' said Morgana, who had been watching her closely. 'I have a mind to build a wall of birds.'

This seemed very cruel to Rose Red. Did her mother wish to drown out the little voice that was the last vestiges of her conscience with birdsong? For Rose Red knew that her mother could not beguile herself with music. Why, over there, propped up against the hearth was the broken frame of Morgana's violin – and whenever her mother put her hand to any musical instrument, it likewise snapped in two.

'What do you want me to find for you?' asked Rose Red.

'You must send me the nightingale of love, to be the chief prize and ornament of my collection,' said Morgana.

'That doesn't sound so difficult,' said Rose Red.

'Oh, but it will be,' said Morgana, 'for the nightingale will bewitch you with such sweet songs that you won't know what to believe. Besides, you must capture the nightingale in a special cage woven from osier twigs and emeralds, which I shall teach you to make, and which you must carry with you, always.'

Despite her promise, Morgana was Queen of Avalon and could not spare much time for her daughter. And so, Rose Red often found herself wandering in the palace gardens, alone. Here the trees were heavy-laden with fruit, but the different apples, pears, damsons and figs did not confine themselves to their own trees but mingled in riotous confusion. There were lemons and oranges too, growing together on the same miniature trees, and olives and pineapples, and other fruits and spices, that were new to Avalon since Rose Red's time, and which filled the air with their fragrance.

Yet Avalon was chiefly famous for its apples, and Rose Red gathered up a basket to take back with her to Valerian, for none there were so ruddy, red and gold, so perfect and magical.

Sometimes, when Rose Red was walking up-and-down the twisting garden paths, she noticed that the stunted, wizened shoots were beginning to bloom again, and that green stalks were showing red-and-purple buds. It was something, Rose Red thought, to feel the sunshine of home once more upon her face. To her fancy, it seemed that her bright presence was pushing back the encroaching decay, so that Avalon began to be more as she remembered it from her childhood.

For there were times, too, when it was lovely to be on the Isle of Avalon – the sand, the sea, the sky, which was the colour of gull's eggs. Here, she could do whatever she wanted, lie on the warm rocks for long hours with the sun on her face, shining colours through her eyelids. Everything was peaceful: the soft lap-lapping of water on the shore and the gulls crying high overhead. Sometimes, she waded so far out to sea that she was swimming.

Occasionally, she encountered old servants from the Palace taking their exercise on cliff pathways. The butler and the footman now seemed less fae and puckish, and rather more sober and substantial, as if great state matters weighed upon them. Rose Red noticed too that the curious bird-like quality of their movements and the glossy, feathery sheen to their hair had gone. Perhaps it was dangerous now for anyone to attempt even a partial bird transformation at Queen Morgana's court. For Morgana kept her word, and taught her daughter, and those priestesses and handmaidens who had a mind to learn, how to weave osier twigs and emeralds, or hawthorn twigs and rubies, into bird cages.

At night however, Rose Red often dreamt of the Lion Baron and the castle in Astalot. In her dreams, she was walking quickly down its corridors, seeking for something, yet troubled in heart and mind that she could not find it. But she did not hesitate as she turned corners, went upstairs and downstairs, opening doors to search through fine rooms with their tapestried wall-hangings, the frescoed ceilings of cupids and angels, the carved furniture, the portraits on the walls. Her sleeping-self was both dazzled and bewildered, but her dream-self proceeded on, ever yet more anxious.

On Rose Red's last morning in Avalon, she woke abruptly as the sun was rising. The first thing she saw when she stepped out onto her balcony were two porpoises at play in the azure depths of the water, and beyond them, paddling lazily in the shallows, young children from Valerian. She wondered whether Nimue had stolen them from their cradles and left changelings in their place, or whether they had been sent here to learn such wisdom as Avalon could teach.

Later, she bid an awkward farewell to her mother, and readied herself for her journey.

The silver bell was broken, but one of the few non-magical ways to leave the Fruitful Isles was by boat. And so Rose Red embarked on her voyage, sailing through the mists of Avalon. When she had reached the island's furthest shore by water, she clambered out of her boat, then journeyed on through a great tract of woodland. Here, the branches were like hair among the starlight, and the boughs of the trees creaked above her. This woodland, she wondered, was it Avalon or Valerian, or a hinterland, for she could not tell where one ended and the other began. Then too, what strange eyes gleamed out at her between the branches, what spirits hovered above her in the draughts of air? Almost, she could feel them there now, whirling and blowing about her.

Morgana's tasks were arranged in order of difficulty, and the first was to fill a purple casket with a thousand flowers. Rose Red could not think of a way to do this, and she fell to haunting many a walled and many a wild garden, staring at the beautiful array of flowers, searching for the answer. And then, one day, she fell into the company of a travelling pedlar, a shrewd woman with iron-grey hair, wearing a patched, russet-coloured dress.

The pedlar, Maisie Heckles, looked at Rose Red quizzically as the girl told her tale, then, when she had finished, offered her a vial of perfume.

Rose Red took the dainty, diamond-panelled glass bottle from Maisie, removed its stopper and sniffed the contents. And oh, but the scent was glorious! She could smell French orange flower, jasmine, osmanthus, tuberose, labdanum, patchouli, violet, ombrette, white magnolia, hyacinth, bergamot, pink pepper, briar rose, iris, and many, many other flowers, more than she could name.

'It takes a thousand different flowers to fill each bottle,' said Maisie, smiling at the look of wonderment on Rose Red's face.

Rose Red paid the pedlar a golden sovereign and placed the little vial of perfume inside the purple casket her mother had given her. Then she simply said, 'To Morgana,' and the casket disappeared, to be opened by her mother in Avalon.

The next task that Morgana had assigned to her daughter was to mend all the broken statues in the forest clearing. As Rose Red approached this clearing, she wondered if she should gather all the mutilated limbs of the statues together and hold them close to her heart, intoning the words, '*Under the stars, the lost things are found.*' For her stepsister Snow White and the Magician had once used this magick on Prince Nikolai, so that each of his severed limbs had knit to its brother – and Snow had placed stars too, where each break had been.

But Rose Red knew that spells, like the people of our hearts, are not interchangeable. If it was Nimue who had turned the lovers to stone, it was an aspect of Nimue's magick that must return them to life. So, Rose Red ran to a forest spring and filled gourd upon gourd with water. For a moment, she wondered if the splash of it inside the bottles was indeed the voice of a lonely water goddess.

Then Rose Red made her way to the forest clearing and stared all around. Against the dark, gnarled barks, the white limbs of the mutilated statues gleamed. She began to dance around them, scarce knowing what she was doing, but scattering spring water all over them. And then something began to move. A shadow? No, not a shadow. A statue of a nobleman unfurled his limbs, planted a foot upon the grass, then, beneath the dazzling sunlight that slanted through the trees, gave a sudden, joyous shake.

Now. Now was the time.

A headless statue of a woman was entirely covered in cracks. But a spray of water struck her, and the cracks began to dissolve. Then everything was still. Not a breath. Not a whisper. Then Rose Red realised that the cracks covering the woman had entirely disappeared. All those pieces of stone, covered in cracks and lichen and moss, were now arms and hands. The hands picked up every lost and broken limb and restored them to their rightful places. The spring water was a blessing singing over their bones.

Finally, there were no statues left at all, but only lords and ladies laughing, returned to the first freshness of their youth, free to roam the forests, to return to court, or to travel further yet, to kingdoms beyond the sea. After they had fled the forest, Rose Red walked round the clearing where the statues had once stood. 'I did that,' she thought, proudly, 'me.' But then came desolate reflections. 'Where is my happy life?' she murmured. 'Where is the kingdom meant for me?' She sat down in the centre of the clearing and let her basket spill where it would, whilst she took one, single, desultory bite from an apple.

Avalon's fruit gave her fresh heart of grace, as indeed it should, and she began to look around her with more curiosity. Now the statues were gone, it was easier to discern a magnificent rosebush, right at the heart of the forest-clearing, the very one from which the Magician had plucked the fatal rose which had condemned her to the Castle of the Lion Baron. Here bloomed again a rose as red as the dawning of an eastern sky. Crimson was the halo of its petals, and ruby was its sacred heart. Its aroma was overpowering.

Even more beautiful than the flowers was the sound of the nightingale. Its notes and peals swooped and soared in synaesthetic shades of red. Rose Red could hear varying tones of scarlet, crimson and carmine, ruby and russet, coral and cerise.

From the sound of its song, Rose Red knew that her search was at an end. The nightingale of love was here among the roses.

How easy would it be to entice the golden bird into the cage?

Rose Red recalled a spell that she and Snow White had once read in one of Morgana's books. She began to repeat the words over now:

'Bird of star and sky,
Bird of finest feather,
Relinquish the celestial sky,
Let us work on this task, together.'

And, in response to her gentle entreaty, the nightingale flew down from the rosebush and alighted on the crook of Rose Red's wrist, where it perched with great trust. Such a brave, pretty thing it was, with a crimson flush upon its throat. Then too, it had the strangest eyes of any bird she had ever seen, an unfathomable blue, more human than fowl.

Quickly, and ignoring her misgivings, Rose Red took the cage from beneath her cloak and thrust the nightingale inside it. As she did so, she felt a sickening lurch in her belly and suddenly she was covered all over in sweat. And where before there were images of roses in her mind, now she could only picture blood.

'Mother mine, mother mine,' the nightingale sang out, 'O, do not give me up to Morgana.'

'But that is the third of her tasks,' said Rose Red, 'so that I may be reunited with Lowenhardt.'

'Mother mine, mother mine,' sang the nightingale, 'Morgana is twisted up with envy and lies. Why listen to her?'

Rose Red knew that the nightingale sang the truth, and she felt sicker, sadder and stranger than ever. But she did not know what to do, for she desperately wanted to see her husband again, and Morgana had told her that this was the only way.

'Mother mine, mother mine,' sang the nightingale, one final time, 'set me free at last.'

Now there was something so plaintive and heart-touching in the nightingale's voice that Rose Red drew back the door of the cage and set the bird free. The nightingale stepped out of the cage into the light of the forest, inclining her head graciously towards the sun. Perhaps it was a trick of the light, but now she seemed less like a little, golden bird, and more like a young girl, pale in the sunshine.

'I am the one they call Elaine,' she said, 'and you will see me again, by-and-by. But hurry you now to the castle to find the fulfilment of your heart's quest.' And with that, the bird who was the maiden flew into the sky, right glad to feel once more sunlight upon her wings.

Rose Red gathered up her fallen apples, then made her way through the woods, that were filling again with shadows. As she readied herself to cross over soft, green hills of pasture and arable land, she heard the sound of a distant roar, like a lion in pain. She knew then that she had tarried too long.

Now she trudged beyond the ruins of an ancient abbey. These ruins lay in a still, rich, meadow at the foot of the last fall of woodland, through whose oaks shone bluebells. But the abbey had been torched in the recent rebellions, forcing Snow White to call on Uther Pendragon and his warlords for their assistance.

When she reached the castle, Rose Red hesitated for a moment, though she could see quite clearly through the bars of the gate that led to the courtyard. But the gatekeeper's lodge appeared uninhabited – there was no welcoming rushlight in the window, nor plume of smoke rising from the chimney. Plucking up her courage, she pushed her way through the gate. In the courtyard, dark, uncontrollable bindweed threatened to strangle the green shoots of tender young plants. The branches of the cypress tree intermingled in a strange embrace which reminded her of the wedding ceremonies she had witnessed in the Fruitful Isles.

Then too, there were other trees that seemed to have taken root in the courtyard, displacing the neat mosaic of its tiles. Their gnarled roots looked like the unfurled limbs and wings of dragons, complete with talons. Squat oaks, ancient chestnut trees, a tortured elm or two, alongside monstrous shrubs and plants. Rose Red could not remember them from before. She wondered if Morgana was trying to establish a sacred, profane grove here in the castle's courtyard in Astalot.

The path towards the castle was buried beneath the undergrowth, beneath fallen trees and wintry ditches. Nettles had sprung up everywhere, too many for tea or possets. The sight of it all, so lost and strange, brought tears to her eyes. What she did not realise yet was that, over the weeks, where she walked, the flowers would bloom again. For her time in Avalon had brought her healing powers to their zenith.

Now she looked out towards the placid, silver sea. But whilst her eyes were turned away, the castle seemed to come to life. Light suddenly shone from its windows; the curtains blew out in the breeze. Then, too, in the reading-room of the easternmost tower, the faintest radiance appeared on the diamond-shaped windowpanes. The castle's great oak doors creaked open, followed by the sound of footsteps, and a tentative voice.

'Rose Red?'

She turned her head in the direction of that voice, and there he was, her leonine husband, standing beneath the cypress tree, some little way from her.

Now her tears were tears of joy, and she ran towards him and enfolded him in a tight embrace. His breath was hot upon her cheeks. She closed her eyes and laid her head on his great, billowing mane. She let her tears fall where they would. When she opened her eyes again, she saw that they had wrought a gentle transformation. For now, his bones were beginning to show through his pelt, and his flesh, human flesh, beneath the wide, tawny forehead. Where he had always kept his fists clenched, to shield his claws, now, slowly, painfully, he began to stretch out his fingers. His hands, she noticed, were broad and shapely, the hands of a hunter - and a scholar.

Then it was no longer a lion in her arms, but the man she had glimpsed in her bed, a sturdy man with an unkempt mane of hair, and a broad, wide nose.

'Rose Red?' he said again, as if by naming her he was reassuring himself that she would not disappear. 'You came back.'

In that dear, remembered voice, there was the sound of rose gardens in summer, tea beneath the spreading branches of the cypress tree, and the reverberations of the river that wound its way round Astalot.

The Lion Baron continued, 'You have released me from my enchantment.'

'I don't understand,' she replied. 'I failed to complete my tasks. I set the nightingale free.'

'Yes,' said Lowenhardt, 'but if you had given the nightingale up to Morgana, you would have condemned me to a lion's body forever. She tricked you to see what you would do. It is because you showed such a compassionate understanding of freedom that she allowed me to return to my human form.'

He kissed her and she found that his mouth was as loving as she recalled from their time as husband and wife.

He took her hand, and they walked around the castle gardens. A few flowers had indeed begun to bloom again, bright and proud, golden and red. They stepped back into the courtyard, and she whispered to Lowenhardt that some valerian might do well in the shade of the great cypress tree, and that they should place a bench there, beneath it. Then, hand-in-hand, they pushed open the great oak door and entered the castle that was to be their home once more.

If this ending seems happier than might be expected, remember that this is the story which Morgana told me, Arabella, about her daughter, Rose Red. All those that love Rose Red might choose to grant her in fiction the happy ending, which, alas, was not to be her ultimate fate in the castle of Lowenhardt, the Lion Baron of Astalot.

The Lady In The Tower

Once upon a time, so my ghostly companion told me, there was a magician who fell in love with a beautiful woman with red-gold hair, that glistened like blood and honey beneath the cruel sun. Her name was Morgana, and she was the Queen of the Fruitful Isles. Merlin the Magician so loved Morgana, and so wanted her to love him, that he told her all his secrets and some of his most powerful spells. And eventually, sweet, parasitic thing that they called her, she grew strong with his magick.

However, before she left the Fruitful Isles to marry King Leopold of Valerian, she decided to imprison the magician. She believed he was responsible for the death of her first husband, Urien – and besides, whilst he was at liberty, some of her own, wilder impulses could not have full sway.

Firstly, Morgana tried to imprison Merlin in a wall, but the plaster crumbled apart. Then she tried to capture him in a door, but the door's beams sprouted leaves and he laughed amongst them. So, finally, she wrapped him in her hair as he slept, and drew the magick water-words, *Tirra-Lirra,* from his mouth. This, she knew to be a powerful charm, so she said it three times, and then, alas, the poor, foolish magician awoke to find himself imprisoned in her looking glass.

There he was, daily forced to praise the wicked queen's great beauty. The vainer she grew, the sicker he became of her, so that right glad he was when Snow White threw a miniature coffin at the mirror, shouting, *'Tirra Lirra,'* which shattered his glass prison.

However, since the wicked queen had said the magick words three times over, the curse upon him was not fully lifted. To be truly free, the magician must place the curse upon someone else. His poor, hapless victim must be persuaded to venture into the looking-glass and remain there, so that the Magician would not have to return to the silvery realm. So, he gazed into the seeds of time to discover who this victim would be.

Decades passed. King Leopold was long since dead, and his daughter Snow White and her consort, Hunter John, had abdicated, and the line of succession had passed to Uther Pendragon, and then, finally, to his son, Arthur and Arthur's queen, Guinevere. In their time, a beautiful baby girl was born into the kingdom. Her parents, Sir Lowenhardt the Lion Baron, and his lady, Rose Red, named her Elaine le Blanc, the Lily Maid, for she was good and pure and fair.

However, Elaine's purity of soul and the fact that she was the granddaughter of Queen Morgana irked the Magician greatly. For these reasons, he wanted to entice her into the mirror realm, so that she should suffer as he once had. And so, one chilly spring day, he rode out with King Arthur to that part of the kingdom where Elaine lived, the castle of Astalot.

Here in Astalot, there was a river which wound through the castle parkland. It had its own vitality – it kept moving, despite the snow and ice, the jagged icicles that hung from overhanging branches. Beside the river, there was a path that curved, snake-like, towards a tower. A round tower it was, that rose up like a sharp tooth from its hilltop and overlooked a patch of frozen flowers: waterlilies and green-sheathed daffodils that dared not blaze their trumpets. Far to the north-west, small, white peaks stood sharp against the blue, and to the south, there was the shining sea.

The Magician decreed that this was the tower where the Lily Maid must be placed. He said the magick words, *'Tirra-Lirra'* once and then, there she was, imprisoned within its walls.

No-one could gainsay the Magician, not even the king, for his power had increased sevenfold in the time that he had been freed from the mirror. And Merlin had begun to feel that the mirror was now his friend, capable of deceiving and confusing his enemies with false and ghostly worlds. For, he argued, the mirror was both less than a complete copy of the world they called reality, and yet more so, giving rise to the wildest dreams and fables.

The years went by, and willows whitened and shivered, and yet every year, the cool sun made the tower cast a long and crooked shadow. Here, inside it, lived Elaine Le Blanc, the Princess of Inconsolable Insomnia. She was famous for her song and her invisibility. No-one knew her and yet she was known throughout the land. For sometimes she sang, and sometimes she scratched her fingernails along the bars of her window and sometimes she took out brightly coloured scarves and paraded around in them. Then too, she used to twist pearls through her thick, flaxen hair, and, upon occasion, rubies. She ran to the mirror to take a look, then fell back to sighing, for no-one could see her. At other times, she lay upon her bed and pulled up the silks and velvets and lolled against the pillows, fully dressed, incomparably sad.

Unlike the mining dwarves she knew from her childhood, who were seemingly content to accept the flickering shadows of torch-lamps on rock as their reality, she desired something more. For she could hear the river outside her window, and the bustle and noise of the city all around her. When she gazed into her looking glass, she could see the reflections of the city-dwellers clad in their bright scarves and hats, their shining cloaks, all their hopes ruddy on their cheeks. There were young women too, with all the dreams of their lives before them, or a girl and boy, in their best clothes, walking hand-in-hand to the church to be wed.

Sometimes, Elaine whiled away the tedium of her solitary existence by weaving with bright colours the enchanted realms she glimpsed within the looking glass. One day, half-dozing, half-dreaming, she wove on her loom the finest chalice she could fashion in threads of silver and gold. Then she took some cloth of red damson, and wove that into her design, so that now the chalice would contain the blood of Christ, the most sacred blood of all.

But there she was, in her tower, the Princess of Inconsolable Insomnia. She could not sleep. She could not sleep. Not in her cold room, while the snowflakes fell outside and the stars wheeled through the skies, trembling with love.

With love and with hope. She could not sleep because the enchanter had placed his curse upon her and what was to be done?

One night, however, she lapsed into an exhausted slumber and then, that night, she dreamed. She dreamed she was polishing a knight's shield. She was leaning over it, with her flaxen hair spilling against its silver, and she was breathing on it, creating a mist, then clearing it with her hands in a slow, circular motion. She woke the next morning and wondered what the dream could mean.

Was that when she caught her first glimpse of him in the looking glass, the Knight of Misbegotten Means? Did she polish *his* shield in her dreams?

He was riding into Astalot on a black horse. As he passed through her looking glass, he carried his secret with him, rusty beneath his suit of armour and blazing feather plumes. This was the secret of his true name, which no-one must know: Sir Lancelot Dulac.

He rode alone, singing a lullaby from his childhood. '*Tirra Lirra,*' he sang, and at the sound of his song, Elaine felt a sense of renewed, returning life. She thought then that she could leave her tower, where she had been a prisoner for so long, and take her rightful place in her father's household, with all its colour and bustle and life.

This Unknown Knight rode to the Castle of Astalot, where lived Sir Lowenhardt the Lion Baron, and his sons, Sir Torre and Sir Lavaine, as well as his daughter, Elaine. They were receiving knights who were attending the King's diamond tournaments. At this time, Elaine won great admiration from them, since she was passing fair indeed: her hair was twisted round a bouquet of lilies, and her pale flesh was whiter than the foam of a wave, though her cheeks shone red as foxgloves. Then, too, her palms and fingers were wonderfully whitened with weaving; they were whiter than buds of sweet clover in a field of daisies.

The Unknown Knight also won admiring glances, but later, when he sought to borrow a shield from his host to take part in the King's tournaments, they judged him by his noble bearing and ill-equipped state and called him the Knight of Misbegotten Means. In fact, the real reason he wished to borrow a shield was to hide his own true identity. The kindly Baron decided to lend him the shield of his eldest son, Sir Torre, who had been hurt the same day he was made knight and so would not ride in the tournaments.

Elaine's other brother, Sir Lavaine, wanted to win the diamond at the tournaments to give to his sister for safe keeping. One of her strange dreams had been that she had it in her hand and then down it had slipped, into the water. Sir Lavaine wanted to prove the dream a lie. But, jokingly, he added that such a diamond was for a fair queen and not for a simple maid. At which his sister flushed, and the Knight of Misbegotten Means, noting her discomfort, declared,

'Like should go to like, and this fair maid should then wear the fairest jewel on earth.'

Marred as he was by the competing loves he bore his queen and his lord, the Knight of Misbegotten Means yet seemed the goodliest man Elaine had ever seen. She raised her eyes upon him, bruised, bronzed, with an ancient scar upon his cheek, somewhat battle-worn, weary, and more than twice her age, and yet in that moment she knew that she loved him with the love that was to be her doom – or else, her salvation.

That night, the men spoke of the many, many battles they had fought, and Lancelot declared of his king that he had never seen his like; that, in his heyday, there had been no greater leader. Then the Lily Maid spoke thus, 'Save for your own self, oh lord,' for she loved to see the smile light across his face and chase away the melancholy clouds; the sudden, beaming tenderness that rendered him so dark-splendid.

Later, at night, in her room in the tower, his face lived before her as if she were a painter who had absorbed his very likeness into her soul. This was the face that came betwixt her and sleep; this was the face that caused her unquiet slumbers, that travelled into her dreams and haunted her there.

Up she rose the next morning to bid farewell to her young brother, Lavaine. She crept down from her eastern tower step-by-step. And there, in the courtyard, was the Knight of Misbegotten Means calling for his borrowed shield, and his hand strayed about his glossy black horse so that almost she envied the beast and crept ever closer.

He saw her then, the maiden standing in all that dewy light. Somehow, he had not realised before that she was so very beautiful. He had not seen this starry maiden; he had not realised her eyes were like lustrous violets beside a mossy brook. There came upon him a kind of sacred fear, for she was gazing at him as if he were a god.

And in this exchange of glances, perhaps there was something that might not have been there at other times, call it hope, or promise, or potential. And this thing, whatever it was, so emboldened her that for one brief moment, she braved her tumultuous heart and said, 'Fair unknown knight, (though noble I believe your name to be), will you wear my favour at the tournament?'

With heavy heart, he refused her thus: 'No fair maid, for I have never worn a lady's favour – and those who know me well know this of me. If I granted you that, I would do more for you than I ever did for any lady or damozel.'

This comment made the blood spring to her face as if a rose were crimsoning, but when it departed, it left her all the paler.

'All the better then, my lord, to maintain your disguise,' said Elaine.

The knight thought to himself that her words were wise, that if he wore a favour of hers, none of his own blood would know him. So, he continued, 'Fair Maid, I will grant you to wear a token of yours upon my helmet, and therefore show it to me.'

'Sir,' she replied, 'it is a red sleeve of mine, scarlet as the blood you must not relinquish.'

When she brought him the scarlet sleeve, made from the same piece of red damson with which she had woven the blood at the heart of the chalice, he saw that it was embroidered all over with great pearls, like tears. As he took it from her, he said, 'In honour of the trust you have placed in me, I ask you now to take my own shield into your keeping. Then I know that I will not be harmed, and that I shall return to you to collect it.'

'So, am I your squire, then?' she said, and suddenly the dimples in her cheeks coloured. Such reassurances granted them both good cheer.

Later, when her brother gave her a farewell kiss, and that rosy-kindled her face once more, she found herself wishing that it was not Lavaine, but the Knight of Misbegotten Means who had bade her such a farewell.

She enfolded her arms around the knight's shield as she watched them ride away. They paused briefly at the gates to her father's estate, as the sun shone down onto their armour, so that it sparkled like the river running beside them, sending up eddying gleams. Then she took the shield to her chamber, and there she kept it, and there lived in fantasy, whilst in the meadows all around the tower, tremulous aspen-trees and poplars quivered and their leaves fell.

High in her bedchamber, Elaine guarded the sacred shield of Sir Lancelot. Ever she placed it where the morning's earliest rays might strike upon it – and then she felt that she would know no more nightmares or fiendish enchanter's curse, but only the gleam from his shield.

Then, too, she fashioned a case of silk for it, replete with heraldic device and fantastical borders of branches and flowers, and yellow-throated birds so finely stitched that you would swear that they could sing.

Ever anon throughout the day, she would leave her household cares and her father, the goodly Baron Lowenhardt, and climb the stairs to the eastern tower, where she would strip the silken case from the shield, and gaze upon it. From this shield, she could have told you everything about the Unknown Knight: every battle in which he had fought, every strike upon him from every sword and lance, then every bruise and every scar, yet she could not have told you his name.

This beloved knight, who had left her now to tilt for the great diamond in the jousts.

These were King Arthur's fabled diamonds, from a time before he was king. For, once, Arthur was roving the realm of Lyonnesse when, there in a grey glen, beside a boulder, he trod upon a crowned skeleton. It was a skeleton from decades ago, when King Leopold's father had fought his brother, and each had slain his sibling. There they lay, with their bleached bones turning parchment yellow among the crags of rocks. When Arthur's foot crunched over that skeleton, the skull broke from the neck and then that crown rolled into the light, spinning like a glittering rivulet across the scattered shingle.

Arthur plunged after it, caught it in his hand and set it upon his head, and though it was the crown of a long-dead king, he actually murmured, 'Lo, I too shall be king.'

But when, years later, he became king, he had the crown's nine diamonds plucked from their setting. He felt that they were a gift from Heaven and belonged to the kingdom and not to himself. He therefore decreed that there should be a joust every year for each of these diamonds, so that they might learn who was the greatest knight among them.

Thus, it was that for the past eight years and the past eight jousts, Lancelot had won the diamond of the year, intending to present them to the Queen when all nine were in his hand. He had never said a word to her of his intention, meaning to win her favour at precisely the right time and not a moment before.

It was for the last and largest diamond that King Arthur was now holding the diamond jousts. Yet this year, Sir Lancelot had stayed behind at court, thinking to please the queen whilst she tarried there, heart-sick with recent sorrows.

Recently the queen had held a great feast in which she had assembled all manner of dignitaries and dainties. To this feast, she had invited as many of the knights of the Round Table as would come, to show that she had no especial favourites, but rather, great joy in all her knights. So, to the feast came Sir Gawaine, and his brethren, that is to say, Sir Agravaine, Sir Gaheris and Sir Gareth. Other knights were present there too, Sir La Cote Male Taile, Sir Persant, Sir Ironside, Sir Lanval, Sir Kay le Seneschal, Sir Pinel le Savage, Sir Patrise and so on, to the tune and number of twenty-four.

At the feast, the men grew boisterous and rowdy, and began to mutter dark imprecations, for if ever they felt sorrowful or unappreciated, they must have someone to blame. But now they were all befuddled in their cups and could not rightly decide who was the cause of all their misfortunes. Until at last, Sir Pinel thought on the queen of the olden times, the second wife of King Leopold, the Lady Morgana, lately exiled to the Fruitful Isles. Once she had smiled upon him, but then, he judged, she had proved fickle, and turned her favours to Prince Nikolai. Then, too, Sir Pinel was a kinsman of Snow White's consort, Hunter John, and a distant cousin of Lowenhardt the Lion Baron of Astalot, and well he knew the suffering that she had caused his kin.

One other legitimate grievance that Sir Pinel seemed to have against Morgana was that she had turned his latest mistress, his lady-love, Suzanna, into a wild boar, and ever since that day, Sir Pinel had known no love at all. In the years that followed Morgana's crimes, his sense of bitterness and resentment grew so that he began to harbour a hatred of all womankind, which had spread even to Queen Guinevere.

The more he drank, the more Sir Pinel hated Morgana, and in a moment of proud, drunken folly, he said he would ask Merlin the Magician, who hated her also, to help him destroy the wicked queen.

'Would it not be a grand idea,' he said to his companions at the feast, 'to scotch the viper in her nest before she has a chance to destroy the lives and happiness of others?'

'What do you mean?' asked another knight, Sir Patrise, from deep within his cups.

'I mean,' said Sir Pinel, 'that I will ask the wizard to send me back to the time when Morgana was passing young and fair, and kill her then, by poison, by sword or by whatever means I can contrive.'

'Think carefully on that,' said Sir Patrise. 'For I have heard it said that our king intends to make her son, Sir Mordred, his heir.'

'I have heard it said that Mordred is not his nephew, but his own son,' said Sir Pinel. 'Besides, our king would do better to choose another heir than to have the spawn of that she-demon upon the throne.'

This, then, was the charming dinner conversation which Lady Guinevere had to endure about her husband and his sister. But when Merlin was summoned to the banqueting hall, he vowed that he would not, after all, help Sir Pinel. This was because he had his own score to settle with Morgana which even now was playing out through the line of her descendants. He did not wish his careful spellcasting to be spoiled.

So then, what must Sir Pinel do but persuade Guinan, the leader of a band of dwarves and a close friend of the previous queen, Snow White, to steal one of Merlin's own magick books. For, after all, there was something of the riddler or conjurer about this dwarf, and he could figure his way through a spell-book well enough. And so, with a book of spells in one hand, and a blue celestine stone in the other, Sir Pinel and his seven dwarves, the Travellers of Space and Time, disappeared from court one day. Then the blame for this theft and disappearance was laid at the door of Queen Guinevere, for it was maintained that a truly virtuous woman could have dissuaded Sir Pinel from his task and turned the conversation to more wholesome matters, if only she had tried.

But then, so are women blamed for all manner of matters which are not their fault – or so, at least, it seemed to Guinevere, who felt it bitterly and sorrowed over it. Eventually, she began to wonder whether the disappearance of Sir Pinel and the disapprobation surrounding it were merely a cover to allow people to disapprove of her for the one sin of which she was truly guilty: the deep, grievous love that she bore Sir Lancelot.

In her distress, Guinevere grew sick and sad. But when Sir Lancelot volunteered to stay away from the diamond jousts to cheer her, she urged him on to Astalot. For the passing of the years had granted her a wisdom that she had not possessed in the first flush of youth. She therefore said that he must not joust under his own name, for the other knights were so greatly in awe of him that they bowed down before his spears at a touch.

'There is no true glory in that,' said the queen, with a mirthless laugh, 'but win you then under another name and only reveal your identity at the end of the tournament, and how the king will delight in you. It will put an end to all the rumours that circle about us, a fog that currently we cannot dispel.'

'But you, my queen,' said Lancelot then, 'will you delight in me?'

At that she could not answer, for there was something cold and pettish in her heart, born of long years of sadness and thwarted love. She let him kiss her hand in farewell, but she would not let him kiss her cheek. She turned her head away from him so that he could not see the tears forming in her eyes - and thus, he mistook her actions as a greater rejection than she had intended.

For all that, Lancelot was faithful to her, and true, and to heal the imagined rift between them, he resolved to follow her instructions to the letter – and then to lay before her the nine diamonds from the jousts. He spent some happy moments picturing her with his diamonds on her wrist or at her breast, diamonds like tears, but of joy.

For as he and Sir Lavaine rode out to the jousts, his head was filled with images of Guinevere as once she had been, when he had first known her, escorting her to King Arthur for their wedding, and then later, much later, in a forest far from

Camelot, alone with him. At that time, it had seemed not sin but love, pure and perfect, and that the blue skies of heaven were smiling down on their joy - a joy that seemed fit to fill the earth as the birds sang all around them and a sparrowhawk circled above.

As Sir Lancelot and Queen Guinevere had ridden through the forest glade, the river ran along beside them. To Sir Lancelot, she seemed part of the Spring itself, riding on her snow-white horse in her kirtle of green grass silk. She fled before him, laughing, and the happy breeze blew free her ringlets from her braid, haloing her sweet face. In that one perfect, crystalline moment, she won him body and soul, so that he gave up everything good that he was, and everything good that he might become, for the honour of bestowing his entire heart in a single kiss upon her perfect lips.

This then was the Guinevere of his youth, and he hoped that the bright lustre of the diamonds could return the sparkle to her eyes and the lightness of spirits, the loving, laughing grace that they betokened.

At the diamond jousts, Sir Lancelot and Sir Lavaine glanced all around the peopled gallery, which lay shaped and coloured like a rainbow, but amidst all the fine furs and silks, they could not see the Queen, who had remained behind, languishing in Camelot. But there was the clear-faced, brown-haired King, who sat robed in red samite, with a wrought-bronze dragon writhing down his back, and another clinging to his golden crown.

Later, Lavaine thought that if Sir Lancelot had not already confessed his identity to him on the ride to the diamond jousts, so he might have guessed it, by the magnificent way he fought, king, duke, baron, earl, count: whomsoever he smote, he overthrew. Yet it seemed right strange to Lavaine that none of Lancelot's own relatives could guess the identity of their prize knight from his grace and valour, simply because his visor was pulled down over his face, and on his helmet he wore a crimson sleeve all embroidered with pearls.

For it seemed, that, as intended, Elaine's favour misled them, as did their own foolish pride in the name of Lancelot. As they thundered down upon Lancelot in the name of Lancelot: a spear lamed his horse, and another spear pierced his side. There it snapped, and there it remained. And half miracle though it was, still he fought on in this seared and anguished state, driving back his kith and kin, and all the fabled Knights of the Round Table. Then the herald blew, proclaiming the prize, and the sun shone down on the scarlet sleeve with its bright pearls, and a greater jewel yet that they wished to bestow upon him.

Bleeding into the scarlet sleeve, he was brought before the king, with all the heralds blazing out, proclaiming as his, the diamond prize. But Lancelot gasped, 'Diamond me no diamonds, for God's love, a little air!' And a moment later, 'Prize me no prizes, for my prize is death!' And so, he departed, vanishing from the field and into the poplar grove beside it.

There, loyal Sir Lavaine awaited him. Sir Lancelot begged him to withdraw the lance-head, but Sir Lavaine protested, 'If I remove it, Sir Lancelot, then you will die.'

'But I die already,' said Lancelot.

So, Sir Lavaine withdrew the lance-head, and Sir Lancelot nigh-on swooned for pain as out gushed his blood in a crimson torrent. Then a hermit emerged from a little chapel in the poplar fields, and judging it dangerous to move him further, took Sir Lancelot to a nearby cave to tend his wounds.

The knight stayed there for many weeks amidst the rustle of the poplars and the trembling of the aspen trees.

Whilst he lay hidden from the rumours of the wide world, all the knights who had fought in the joust gathered around King Arthur and told him of the great marvels and the greater injury of the Unknown Knight.

'He has left behind his prize,' they cried, 'claiming that his prize was death.'

'He must not remain untended,' said the king, 'such a great knight as he has proved to be – why, twenty times I thought him Sir Lancelot.'

King Arthur then commanded his nephew, Sir Gawaine, to ride out and seek the knight, tend to his wounds, and award him his great prize. 'For since he comes not to us, unto him will we deliver the diamond.' Then King Arthur reached up into the carven flower above and plucked out the diamond at its heart, and handed it to Sir Gawaine the Courteous, a good enough knight after Lancelot, Tristram, Geraint and Lamorack. Yes, a good knight indeed, but from a crafty house, and one not always loyal to his word. And, in fact, Sir Gawaine was not well pleased at having to leave the banquet in quest of the Unknown Knight. Muttering darkly to himself, he mounted his steed.

King Arthur was also dark in mood, thinking that this Unknown Knight, this Knight of Misbegotten Means, might in fact be Lancelot. In the pursuit of glory, had Lancelot added wound to older wound, and then ridden away to die?

The King returned to the Queen and asked her if she was still sick.

'No,' she replied.

'Then, where is Lancelot?' asked the King.

'But wasn't he in your company?' she said, 'and didn't he win your prize?'

'No, said the King, 'only one featured like him.'

The Queen sighed, 'Well, and that was he.'

When the King asked her how she knew, she told him of a conversation they had after the King and his court had departed. She said that Lancelot had complained that because of his reputation, men went down at his spear at a touch, and there was no fair sport in that. And so, he had decided he would joust as an Unknown Knight. For this, he felt, would be a fair test of his skill, and would be in the name of purer glory, such as would please the King.

But the King was unhappy that such a secret had been kept – and even unhappier at its conclusion, the terrible wounds that Lancelot had received. Yet he tried to comfort himself with the thought that Lancelot was no more a lonesome soul, since he now wore upon his helmet, 'the gift of a gentle maiden, a sleeve of scarlet, embroidered with great pearls.'

'Yes, my lord,' answered Queen Guinevere, 'your hopes are mine.' But she turned her face away, then rushed to her chamber and flung herself down upon her bed. There she bit her lip until it bled and clenched her nails into her palms. 'Traitor,' she murmured into the silken hangings about the bed. But soon she dried her tears and took her rightful place in the Palace, moving about it, pale and proud.

Meanwhile, Sir Gawaine rode for miles and miles, growing ever yet more weary of the quest for the owner of the diamond. Finally, he rode into the groves of Astalot, to be greeted by a maiden as pale and precious as a pearl.

Elaine had espied him from a casement and her heart had leapt up like a salmon in a stream, for she thought it might be the Unknown Knight. But as Sir Gawaine rode towards her, she realised that it was not him, and down plunged her heart once more.

'What news from Camelot, my lord?' she asked, 'what of the knight with the red sleeve?'

'He won,' said Sir Gawaine, 'but he left the jousts wounded, hurt in the side.'

At that she caught her breath, as if she felt the sharp lance pierce her own side.

Sir Gawaine gazed at her, wondering at her great consternation. Then, from out of the castle came her father, the Lion Baron of Astalot. And Sir Gawaine explained to him that he was searching for the victor of his prize, 'a diamond that would not look out of place in a diadem for your fair daughter.'

The Baron took this for what it was, idle gallantry, but he told Sir Gawaine that he might bide with them a while, 'for my daughter guards the shield of this Unknown Knight and my son rode off with him, so sooner or later we must have news.'

Sir Gawaine acceded to the Baron's request with his wonted courtesy, and yet it was courtesy with a touch of traitor to it, for he found that he loved to gaze upon fair Elaine and hoped that he might gather up this wildflower for his very own. And so, often, over the coming days he met her among the garden yews and sought to win her with fine dalliance, and flashes of wit, and songs and sayings from the court.

But such court manners were not for the fair Elaine. Rebelling against what passed for courtesy, Elaine said to him, 'O noble Sir Gawaine, why don't you ask to see the shield of the one we named the Knight of Misbegotten Means – though that name seems now a jest.'

'To find this knight was the quest on which the King sent me,' said Gawaine, 'and yet I lose sight of it like we lose the lark as it soars towards the heavens when I encounter your blue eyes. But, by all means, bring me the shield.' Yet he knew he would rather have followed her to the shield's hiding-place, her chamber, and there, not to look at the shield.

But Elaine did as she was bid and went to her chamber and took the shield from the woven silken case that she had made. When Sir Gawaine saw its three azure lions, crowned with gold, rampant in the field, he laughed and said, 'So, the King was right! Our Lancelot was here.'

'And so, I was right,' said Elaine, 'when I thought my knight was the greatest knight of all.'

'But do you love this greatest knight?' asked Sir Gawaine.

'I don't know what love is,' said Elaine, 'my mother died when I was very young, and my only companions have been my brothers. I just know that if I don't love him, still, there is no other that I can love.'

'Then you do love him,' said Sir Gawaine, 'and yet perhaps you would not if you knew what everyone at court knows, and who it is that he loves.'

'So be it,' cried Elaine and she stepped away from him. For a moment, she experienced the strangest feeling, as if she were suddenly trapped in glass and silver gauze, and there was no way to escape. She had not known till now that her greatest love was likely to be her greatest curse - or that, even now, at that very moment, the Magician was poring over his spellbooks and muttering, '*Tirra lirra..*' She shivered and the strange feeling passed.

'Perhaps I am wrong,' said Sir Gawaine, 'but I have never known Lancelot to wear a lady's favour before – but then, after all, it is none of my business whom he loves.' He smiled beseechingly at Elaine so that she turned the cool light of her blue eyes back towards him.

'At any rate,' said Sir Gawaine, 'I'm sure that you and your family will soon know his whereabouts, so let me leave my quest and this diamond with you.'

'But why?' asked Elaine.

'If you love him,' said Gawaine, 'then it will be sweet to give him the diamond, and if he loves you, then it will be sweet for him to receive it from your hands. And if there is no love there at all, still, a diamond is a diamond.'

Elaine looked askance at these shrewd words, at which he laughed.

'If he loves,' said Sir Gawaine, meaning now to be kind, 'and his love holds true, then he will bring you to court, where you and I may meet, and know each other hereafter.'

He placed the diamond in the palm of her hand, enfolding her fingers round the stone, then lightly dropped a kiss upon the knuckles. He seemed not to know that the hand to which he paid such courtesy was now shaped like a fist.

Then Sir Gawaine, with laughing, careless grace, abandoned his quest and leapt lightly on his horse. Back to Camelot he rode, trilling a ballad of his own invention. And when Sir Gawaine reached the court, he told the King that he had left the diamond with the Maid of Astalot, 'for courtesy is our truest law.'

At which the King frowned and said, 'Your will go no more on quests of mine, for you have forgotten that obedience is the courtesy due to kings.'

And so, the king departed in ire, and the queen in sadness. But Sir Gawaine cared not – he had finished the ballad he was writing about the Lily Maid and her love, and soon the Knights of The Round Table were pledging Lancelot and Elaine rather than Lancelot and Guinevere.

Far away, in Astalot, Elaine kept the two-day-seen Sir Lancelot in her heart, polishing his shield and dreaming of him at night, until it made her feverish, tossing and turning. At one point in her dreams, she thought she heard him cry out, but she could not discern the words. Still, she prayed for his safe return – and for that of her brother, Sir Lavaine. Finally, she went to her father, Baron Lowenhardt, and told him some of what lay in her heart. She showed him the diamond with which she had been entrusted.

'I must find my brother and my knight,' she said, 'lest I be thought as faithless as Sir Gawaine, who abandoned his quest to me.' She told her father too of dreams she had where the Unknown Knight appeared in need of tender nursing. Since he had worn her favour, was not she, a gently born maiden, liable to render him this service?

'As to that child, I cannot say,' said Baron Lowenhardt, 'for I would keep you safe at my hearth, not roaming out on a knight's quest. At least take your brother Torre with you.'

'Will he ride out with me? For he has ever a mind to follow his own inclinations,' said Elaine.

'Oh yes,' replied her father. 'For he is recovered now and grows restless within these walls. And besides, the diamond is a great prize, which must be rendered to its rightful owner.' He added, 'Get you gone, child,' and gave her a farewell kiss on the forehead.

As she rode out on her own milk-white steed at the side of her brother on his black charger, content with her father's blessing, still she had that strange feeling of riding into the silver mirror-lair. Her head swam and her limbs grew as cold as if she were becoming glass. Yet she shook off that strange feeling as if it were a mosquito.

She and her brother rode on to Camelot, and there, just outside the city gates, she found her other brother, Sir Lavaine, making a roan horse caper and prance round a field of daisies. When he had heard his sister's tale, he said he would guide her across the poplar groves to where Sir Lancelot lay.

Seeing that his sister was safe with Sir Lavaine, Sir Torre declined to accompany her any farther and went his own way to explore the mysterious towers and turrets of Camelot. For sometimes he was prone to these strange, feline moods and then there was no point in trying to dissuade him.

Sir Lavaine and Elaine crossed the grove towards the caves and as she neared the entrance, there was her own scarlet sleeve, part torn and cut, with half the pearls ripped from it. It was tucked into his helmet and resting on a rocky ledge. Her heart was gladdened at the sight of it. He had not lost his keepsake and perhaps he meant to tourney in it once again.

But when she entered the cave, her joy turned to sorrow for Lancelot's arms and hands looked so forlorn on the wolfskin which covered them. There he was, so unsleek and so unshorn, as gaunt as if he were the skeleton of himself.

The unwonted sound of her footsteps woke the sick and sleeping knight, so that Elaine ran to his side. She held the diamond out beneath his fluttering-open eyelids. As his pupils enlarged to take in the glittering prize, she told him all the tale of the King and Sir Gawaine, and the quest assigned to her, the unworthy Lily Maid. Even as she said these final words, she thought to herself, 'am I not rightfully the daughter of Rose Red and the granddaughter of Queen Morgana Le Fay herself?'

She did not know then whether to stand tall and proud, or else kneel beside his bed. In the end, she knelt and placed the diamond in his open hand – and in this way, her face came level with his own.

Then it seemed quite natural for Sir Lancelot to kiss the dear child who had completed her allotted task.

But the touch of his lips was too much for her and she sighed aloud – though Sir Lancelot would have it that it was her ride which had so wearied her.

'You must have peace and rest,' he said.

'I have both beside you, my lord,' she said, and her face flushed the colour of a wild rose, and in all that roseate flame, her heart's sad secret burned.

But Sir Lancelot could not quite guess this secret, for he was weak in body and in mind, and just at that moment, he was indifferent to the love of all women, save one – and she, not perhaps as she was, but as she filled his feverish dreams, tender and full of concern, just out of reach and yet ever by his side. And it was to her that he wished to return in his sleep, and so he turned away from the rosy Lily Maid, sighed, and shut his eyes.

Elaine gathered herself up and glided out into the fields – and onto the city of Camelot, where dwelt both her distant kin and her brother Torre. Then, the following morning, she passed from the turrets of Camelot, back through the fields, and there to the cave where Sir Lancelot lay. And every day, she came there and tended him, and sometimes when he was most sick, she stayed far into the night.

For at times, the wound he bore made him brain-feverous, and then, though he was sometimes curt with her, how gentle and kind she was with him. Her great love gave her skill at nursing. The hermit that also tended Sir Lancelot with herbs, salves and ointments told him that it was Elaine's fine care which had saved his life.

In that time, Sir Lancelot came to cherish Elaine as his friend and dear sister, would listen out for her coming and then regret her passing step. He loved her dearly, but as if she were a good child. He would have given her anything, but not his life and not his heart, for these were dedicated ever to the queen who loved him in his dreams.

Just occasionally though, the thought crept into his mind that if he had met Elaine first, she might have made for him a better world, where the air was fresh and pure, a world in which he could breathe. But now the shackles of an old love held him fast; his honour was rooted in dishonour and held him falsely true. And as his strength began to revive, it was the face of this old love which swam before his eyes, and then he could not even see Elaine with all her gentle cares and graces.

All Elaine knew was that some ghost had risen up, unbidden, between them. She knew too that she could not live without his love. In those darkly sorrowful times, she felt as if a silver-grey shroud had fallen upon her.

'Must I die?' she said, and the thought of it was like ice and water and a tomb from which she could not escape. It seemed to her as if the Magician's curse had come upon her once more, and at last. Then tears dimmed her gaze and drove her out into the fields.

But with the blood of her kin, Morgana and Rose Red, surging through her veins, she knew she was braver than that. When Sir Lancelot's wound was healed, she rode out with him and her brothers to Astalot, there to feast and laugh awhile.

On that first evening back at the castle, she dressed in her finest robes, a kirtle of blue-grey silk shot through with silver thread. She looked so fair when she crossed the threshold of the banqueting hall that Sir Lancelot could not help but smile. That smile emboldened her so that she went and sat in the siege at his side.

'Sweet sister,' he began, 'how well you look tonight. It puts me in mind of what I have often said that you must ask of me some costly gift in thanks for your great care of me.'

'But I don't want a costly gift,' she said.

'Well, what do you want?' he asked, affectionate parent to a wayward child.

'Only, -' she said.

'Only what?'

'Only you yourself,' she replied, knowing now that she would not die for want of one bold word. And in truth, it was

Sir Lancelot and not herself who was dumbfounded, so that when she replayed this scene in her mind in the days that followed, she wondered whether, after all, it was he and not she who lacked courage – and whether it was the same pattern the whole world over when one loved and the other did not. But then, she had known so little of love that she could not tell.

'Sweet sister,' answered Sir Lancelot after a moment or two, 'what is this?'

She held out her arms to him in all innocence, and said, 'Let me love you. Let me be your wife.'

At these words, Sir Lancelot looked as grave as the statues in her father's courtyard. 'If I had wished to marry, dear Elaine, I should have wedded earlier. But now I know that I will never have a wife.'

'Then let me just be with you,' she said, 'let me go where you go, let me follow you throughout the world.'

'The world would not allow it,' said Sir Lancelot, 'nor your father or brothers either – and it would be poor recompense to them, and to you, for all your kindness to me.'

'But what about me?' asked Elaine, 'how shall I survive if I cannot see your face?'

'You will find someone else to love,' said Sir Lancelot, 'for you are but seventeen, still so very young, and in time, you will come to smile at the folly of your youth. And when you come to marry, I will endow you with land even to half my realm beyond the seas, if that will make you happy.'

'But I don't want your land,' she said.

'I can offer you nothing more,' he replied, as kindly as he could.

Still, she turned pale. The world seemed to shimmer all around her, and then turned silver-grey. She stood up, then walked away from him and climbed the staircase to her room. As she lay upon her bed, she felt so heart-stricken, she could not move. Then it seemed that she was trapped in a silvery cobweb with shards of glass all around her.

All her joy was sorrow. Everything ran backwards. Yesterday was tomorrow.

In a state of sorrow, she began to search through this moon of mirror land, this silver, splintered lair. She imagined herself diving down into the river, to search for lustrous pearls and diamonds on the riverbed. There was his face in the water, dreaming and asleep, for he had told her that he was the foster son of the Lady of the Lake. Perhaps he dreamt of being a knight in the land above.

But this was her curse, and this was the silvery realm to which she had been confined.

All around them the water was bitter and blue.

Though her limbs were slow and heavy, she swam to the surface of the river of her imagination and began to watch the patterns of light and leaf-shadow flicker across the ceiling of her turret room.

Towards evening, Sir Lancelot sent for his shield, so she roused herself from her bed and stripped off its case. She handed the naked shield over to the servant, feeling that she was handing over her heart's best treasure. The case, her own poor work, her empty labour, was left discarded on the floor.

That night was the worst she had ever known since the death of her mother. On that other night, they had taken her mother's corpse to the castle chapel to pray over it and then to bury it. By the time the priestesses of Avalon had arrived on their barge, to row the body away to the Fruitful Isles, it was too late.

The loss of her mother was terrible indeed, and for Elaine, this loss now approached the forsaken feeling, the desperate desolation, of that earlier time. For the ache of it, on-and-on through the darkness, was unendurable. Sometimes, to add to her woe, she tormented herself. Perhaps the Knight of Misbegotten Means was just waiting for the gathering stars. Or perhaps he was waiting for the arrival of the dawn. And then, would his songs finally have words? Would he then tell her everything she needed to hear, so that the Magician's curse might at last be lifted? Ah, let him come to her and part her hair and kiss her brow, and in this way, release her from her suffering.

But no. He would not.

When she rose in the morning and went to her casement, she saw Sir Lancelot below, throwing water over his face from the pump in the courtyard. Though he sparkled in the sunlit cascade of water, now her scarlet sleeve was gone from his helmet.

Elaine knew too that he could tell that she was looking at him, but he would not look up at her, nor even wave his hand. So now her sadness was complete. She felt as if she were being submerged in such dark, glassy starriness that she might never emerge. Then too, the calling of the birds outside seemed to wrap her in sorrow: *'Call and I follow, I follow, call and I follow – Oh let me die at last.'*

For there she was, trapped inside her looking glass, with her tower shuddering all around her, a tower built on despair, with nothing in it, and nothing to see. There came no answer when she sobbed aloud. Probably her father and brothers thought there was a ghost let loose on the stairs.

And yet, with the retreating gallop of his horse's hooves, she thought she heard the words of his song again, *'Tirra lirra.'*

Then it was as if the mirror, which had held her fast as a fly in amber, began to crack from side-to-side, so that in her bewilderment, she said, 'The curse is come upon me? – or – or is it lifting?' For now, she felt she could step free from the looking glass. She was returning to her own circular room in the tower once more and the strange, silvery realm seemed far behind her.

Down the winding steps she went, through rich rooms and halls, past high, stained-glass windows that looked north, south, east and west over the low green hills that endured houseless and treeless and changeless, clear to the summer skies.

She found her brothers and father in the banqueting hall.

'Do you remember?' Elaine said, running up to them, 'how when we were little, we used to visit our mother's friends, the dwarves, in their cottage in the woods? And the stories they used to tell us of great and faraway quests? And how then Lavaine would take me with him up the great river in the gatekeeper's boat? But we always reached the clump of willow-trees, and he would not pass beyond it, no matter how I cried – for far up that shining flood was the palace of the king. But now I will have my way and I will sail beyond the willow trees to that palace. And then, when I sail through its gates, no-one will dare to mock me, not Gawaine, who had a thousand farewells for me, nor Lancelot who had not one word, but only an old song of water magick. But the King himself will come down from his throne to greet me, and the Queen will pity me, and all the gentle court will welcome me – for then, after my long voyage, I shall rest beneath the turrets of Camelot.'

'Child,' said her father, 'perhaps you are light-headed, for why would you wish to go to Camelot and look at yon proud knight who has spurned you?'

At that, Sir Torre began to bluster. 'I was never like the rest of you,' he said. 'I loved him not a jot. And now he takes it upon himself to break my sister's heart, I swear that I will strike him down for the sorrow he has brought us.'

'Calm yourself, dear brother,' said Elaine, 'it is no more Sir Lancelot's fault not to love me than it is mine to love him.'

'But child, this man you love has faults enough,' said her father, wanting to break the knight's hold upon his daughter, 'for it is said he loves the Queen, and she returns his love in open shame.'

'Father,' said Elaine, 'the more noble a man, the more likely it is that he will be slandered. In my love, at least, he is peerless. But if you desire me to live, dear father, let me set sail as I have asked.'

Yet ten mornings passed before good Baron Lowenhardt would give his consent to part with his daughter. Only when morning had broken on the eleventh day, did he allow her to call for a priest and confess her few failings and petty sins, so that she should feel clean and light upon her voyage.

Then Elaine commanded the boat to be decked out like the Queen's barge, but with her own name emblazoned upon its prow, and she dressed herself in her finest gown of muslin-white enwoven with crystals, for she was going in state to court.

Next, she wrote a letter, for words she had enough since her mother had taught sons and daughter alike to read. She folded the letter over-and-over, and then, at last, she was ready.

Baron Lowenhardt placed his daughter on the barge of black samite and then the old man who lived above the gatehouse came down from his perch to row her to the very doors of the Palace.

Yet she had a sort of fancy that she was sailing not to the Palace, but to her death. For all among the gorgeous folds of black and purple cloth hung around her, that cursed feeling was returning, like a shadow streaking through a summer's day.

Was this barge to be her final dwelling-place?

Her brother kissed her farewell, and in truth, her cheeks were so cold that they did not know if they would ever see her again.

'I want to travel to a heavenly city in a boat shaped like a silver star,' she murmured. They did not know if she meant Arthur's Camelot, or Morgana's Avalon, or Paradise itself, and so they wept at this parting from her.

She clutched her precious letter in one hand; they set a lily in the other, and, in the cloth over her head, they hung the shield's silken case with its embroidered blazoning. And then their gatekeeper sat at the helm of the boat and steered his way upwards through the flood, while she glittered in white and gold, with her long flaxen hair spread out around her clear-featured face.

They were floating in smooth water now, across the overflooded fields. The gatekeeper rowed mechanically, whilst Elaine strained her eyes towards the sky. Its darkness began to be divided by the faintest light. Slowly, the overhanging gloom parted above the watery level below. How welcome then was the gradual uplifting of the clouds, and the gently defining blackness of objects above the grassy dark. There was the lines of black trees, then all the river lay open before her.

As they floated down the river towards many-towered Camelot, Sir Lancelot was already craving audience of Guinevere. The time had come to give her the gift of the nine diamonds, now strung on a bracelet. Yet he took less delight in the gift than he had hoped, for it seemed to him that for every sparkling diamond, he recalled every bruise and blow it had taken him to win it; every life it had cost him - and almost, at last, his own.

The Queen agreed to an audience, and they met in a summer oriel covered in vines.

'My lady,' he said then, 'take these hard-won diamonds from me to augment your beauty. I sin to speak of it yet grant you my worship.'

'These are not *my* diamonds,' she replied. 'They belong to your latest fancy – add them to her pearls so you can tell her she shines me down.'

'But they are *your* diamonds, my queen,' said Sir Lancelot, 'I fought only for you.'

'Then if they are mine or hers, or hers or mine – then – at any rate, she shall not have them,' said Guinevere, and she seized the diamonds from his hand and flung them down through the open casement.

In disgust, Sir Lancelot leaned out of the window to watch their fall. Down they fell, and flashed, and struck the surface of the river. And there they sank, among the pearls and eyes of sacred fishes. Sir Lancelot half remembered then the dream they had told him of in Astalot, of diamonds falling down into the water..

At that moment, beneath his very gaze, there passed Elaine on her barge, whereupon she lay, smiling faintly, half-dreaming, half-dozing, seeming dead.

At the doors to the palace at Camelot, Arthur bade gentle Sir Lanval, who had many misadventures ahead of him, and young Sir Galahad, who would later accompany his grandfather on a quest for the Holy Grail, to lift Elaine from the barge. Reverently, they bore her into the castle hall and placed her on a dais. There Sir Lanval gazed at her; Sir Gawaine wondered at her, and Sir Lancelot came and stood over her a while, until at last Arthur espied the letter in her hand. He stooped, broke the seal, and read it aloud; this was all:

'Most noble lord, Sir Lancelot of the Lake, I, sometimes call'd the Maid of Astalot, come hither, for you left me taking no farewell, and I would take my last farewell of you. I loved you and my love had no return.'

Thus, Arthur read the letter and all his assembled court of lords and ladies wept over the words and turned their gaze from the face of their monarch to that of the prostrate maiden. Sir Lanval was so touched by the sound of the king's voice and the sight of the fair maid that to him, it seemed her lips were moving.

Then Sir Lancelot needs must explain himself, to the King, the court, and most of all, to the Queen.

'Know you all,' he said, 'that this was a good maiden and true, but that she loved me with a love beyond love, which I could not return. Her own father counselled me to use some discourtesy against my nature to break her passion. It was for this reason that I left her and bade her no farewell. But had I known she would die from it, I would have found some other way to save her from herself.'

'You might at least have saved her from her death,' snapped the Queen, and her green eyes blazed at him, to be met by an answering blaze.

'Queen,' he said, 'she wanted to wed me, and this I could not allow.'

The queen's eyes dropped then, fast as flung diamonds.

'For all the virtues she possessed,' he continued, 'free love will not be bound.'

'Lancelot, forgive me,' the Queen said.

'Pass on, my Queen, forgiven,' said Sir Lancelot, but Sir Lanval looked askance at him, that the older knight had not valued the Lily Maid as she deserved.

The King and Queen, and all the court, save only for Sir Lanval and Sir Lancelot, passed from the hall in readiness to prepare a costly tomb for the Maid of Astalot. There they would lay the letter in one hand, the lily in the other, and the shield of Sir Lancelot with its three lions rampant at her feet.

Sir Lanval shot a parting glance at this sad tableau, then he too left the hall. Sir Lancelot mused a while. The diamonds might indeed have rained down upon Elaine, had the Queen's aim been better. Then too, perhaps it was more rightfully Elaine who should have worn them, for her love was pure and true, surpassing that of any woman he had ever known, whilst the Queen's fitful passions waxed and waned. 'Would that the good Lord would send me an angel to guide me now,' he thought, 'or else tumble me among the forgotten fragments of the hills or fling me headlong into the mere.'

He glanced a moment at the face of fair Elaine.

'Perhaps God did send me an angel,' he said, 'only how was it that I did not know her?' And so, he groaned in remorseful pain, not knowing that he should die a holy man.

'God in his mercy grant you grace,' he whispered to Elaine.

But then it seemed he heard another voice, rippling across the water outside, singing him an old lullaby. It was the voice of his foster mother, Nimue, the Lady of the Lake, who had stolen him from his cradle as a child. And so, '*Tirra-Lirra by the river,*' was the song that Sir Lancelot heard now, and repeated over to himself.

At the sound of this song, Elaine sat up on her dais, smiling, quite herself and fully recovered, for now the Magician's curse was entirely broken.

Morgana paused for a moment in the midst of her storytelling. I thought it was the grandmother's remembered joy at her granddaughter's recovery, *mais, Hélas,* it was no such thing. What she told me was altogether sadder. For though the

Magician no longer had any power over the fair Elaine, still, he had decreed that Morgana would die just when happiness was in her grasp.

Yet it was in the moment of Elaine's waking that Merlin vanished from his spell-casting room in Camelot's furthest turret. Strange stories were heard of him afterwards, but no-one seemed able to find him. Perhaps, Morgana said to me, with a strange glitter in her eyes, he remains trapped within another magic mirror, to this very day.

'I'm awfully hungry,' said Elaine plaintively now, so Sir Lancelot called for the servants, and they fed her with venison and pastries, washed down with strong cider. She ate and drank her fill, then walked around the Palace Gardens just long enough to turn down Sir Gawaine's proposal of marriage, and Sir Lanval's offer that they should feed the ducks on the pond.

Thereafter, following his rejection by the fair Elaine, the denizens of Valerian and Avalon gossiped about the marriage of Sir Gawaine to Dame Ragnelle, seemingly transformed from her previous incarnation as the Loathly Lady. Within three months of the wedding, the bride's desire for gold had grown so great that nothing could appease it. Sir Gawaine sent her then to the Compound of the Sisters of Valerian in the hopes that she might learn better ways. When it was found that she had a purse for a heart, she was exiled to Avalon.

Morgana gave her the choice of becoming once more the Loathly Lady or else, a wild boar in the forest. She chose the latter option, thereby dissolving all ties of matrimony between herself and Sir Gawaine. He, however, incorporated a wild boar into his coat-of-arms in memory of the one brief week in which he had been happy.

Meanwhile, the servants at Camelot's court gathered together sufficient provisions and better oars so that Elaine could row herself all around Valerian, and further beyond, if she wished, to Avalon, the Fruitful Isles. For she had a desire now to meet her grandmother, that everyone said was so very wicked, and learn what she was really like, and what it was to be Queen Morgana's granddaughter.

Presently, Elaine set sail. It was not until she had passed on nearly to Tintagel, ruled over by King Mark and Queen Iseult, that she could get the boat clear out of the current. Then, with one last yearning look towards Camelot, that lay much farther down the river now, she gripped both her oars and rowed with all her might across the watery fields.

Wide areas of watery desolation were spreading out in dreadful clearness all around her. Then whirls and eddies flowed across the stream while the boat sailed on. Swiftly now she went, with less effort, more and more clearly in the lessening distance. Onwards, Elaine paddled and rowed by turns to the dawning of the day and the energy of her own awakening hope. Her wet clothes clung around her, and her streaming hair was dashed about by the wind. Yet she was scarcely conscious of any bodily sensations. All she felt was strength and power, inspired by her own great determination.

Colour was beginning to awaken in the early morning sky. Now she could discern the tints of the trees, the old firs, far to the right, and the chestnuts of Astalot. Elaine looked for the stars that had led her thus far.

She knew now that never again would she be in thrall to any living man, no magician, no gatekeeper, no knights of dubious means. From now on, it was only the stars that would guide her path. And, in that moment, when her powers were at their height, she resolved to venture on a most sacred quest.

'*Zut alors*,' I cried out to Morgana then, loudly, in the still of the night, 'was it Elaine of Astalot and not this Sir Lanval, or this Sir Galahad, who would at last find the Holy Grail?'

'Patience, Arabella,' my ghostly lady said to me, 'and I will tell you what happened next.'

Morgana of the Fruitful Isles

So, Morgana told me that at the very moment when Elaine, the Lily Maid of Astalot, was setting sail for the Fruitful Isles, wondering whether her boat might pierce through its mists, Sir Pinel Le Savage and his companions, the self-styled Travellers of Space and Time, that is, the seven dwarves, were also contemplating a journey.

In the centre of Sir Pinel's tower-room in Camelot, where they were all assembled, was a huge, wooden chair behind a large, chestnut-brown desk. Sir Pinel was sitting in this throne-chair, which was carved with shameless, cavorting cherubs, and lined with pale blue brocade over straw-coloured satin. He was resting his slender hands on its wooden arms. Since it was the only chair in the circular room, and since it took up so much space, the dwarves had no choice but to stand, or sit cross-legged, or even, in the case of Cooey and Pippin, the youngest dwarves, to lie sprawled out on the tower's cool flagstones.

Sir Pinel was wearing a striking silver ring wrought with an intricate, circular design of an ebony gryphon and an emerald serpent. The gryphon was devouring the serpent's tail and was itself being devoured by the serpent's jaw. Nor was this ring the only striking thing about Sir Pinel, who, in his forties, would have been good-looking had he not been quite so sullen. Beneath a froth of dark hair and black, beetling brows, his pale-blue eyes were shadowed and sulky. His features were well-made, but the twist of his mouth and the jut of his ivory jaw made him look petulant. Some said that he grieved for the lost favours of Queen Morgana; others, that he missed his fairy mistress, the Lady Suzanna of Avalon.

Queen Morgana had exiled Lady Suzanna from the court of Avalon, for, like Dame Ragnelle, the lady's avaricious ways threatened to deplete the resources of the realm. This is because, every month, Lady Suzanna would travel back to Valerian by boat, dressed in her finest silver and gold. Here, she would present herself to unsuspecting artists as a patroness of the arts. By claiming she would richly reward them for their creations in her Palace of Art, she would entice them back with her to Avalon. However, upon arriving there, the artists would discover that the Palace of Art did not exist, and that it was their job to create it, for no reward, no promised, glittering prizes, and little food. For the Lady Suzanna fed them just enough to keep them alive in her service. Since she selected the youngest, most promising, and most naïve artists, their enchanted servitude was likely to last at least thirty years. As they became too famished and weak to rebel against her, many hoped that death would overtake them sooner.

However, one night, in a dream, Morgana was warned about Suzanna's antics, and how they were tarnishing the glory of Avalon. So, shortly after breakfast, and without much ado, Morgana turned Suzanna into a wild boar, to join Dame Ragnelle in grubbing for roots in the forests for their survival. The artists were then free to roam Avalon or return to Valerian, as they wished.

The artists vowed that they would never again be so foolish as to be taken in by a fanged fairy-lady.

The loss of this one person, Lady Suzanna, who had seemed to love him whole-heartedly, had done nothing to sweeten Sir Pinel's temperament, or to endear Queen Morgana to him. Now, he gazed at the scrolls of maps and timelines spread out before him on the wooden desk and across the stone floor and plotted his revenge. The dwarves were also scrutinising them intently, though not all of them could read.

They were trying to decide which period of Queen Morgana's history would be most auspicious to kill her.

Their problem was, they could not decide which year of her life would be best for her murder. For Queen Morgana had carried out many good as well as evil actions over the course of her reign, and whenever a dwarf jabbed a pin into her timeline, another dwarf with a different smattering of political knowledge would be sure to dispute it.

Sir Pinel watched them all in dismay, but since he needed the dwarf Guinan's ability to turn a spell, he let them argue as they would. Finally, Guinan, who was indeed the most forceful and experienced of the Time Travellers, banged his fist down hard on Sir Pinel's desk, making the maps of the two realms jump.

'You snivelling, cowardly, bloodthirsty lot,' he cried. 'If you're going to be like that, why not just go right back in time, and kill Morgana's mother, the Lady Igraine, and her father, the Duke of Gorlois, for good measure?' As he had hoped, his inflammatory words stunned them into silence. For, throughout Valerian, the Lady Igraine was still revered as a pattern of virtuous womanhood, besides being the mother of their current king, Arthur.

'There's no call now to be murdering the innocent,' said mild-eyed Cooey in response. 'And I don't think we wish to wipe out *all* the Pendragons, either.'

'Which would be treason,' added Sir Pinel, fearfully. 'But I do think the child Morgana, who has not yet learned the Magician's magick, would be much easier to kill.'

'Where's the challenge in that?' spat Guinan, with a look of disgust.

'Why do we want to kill her anyway?' asked Dagonet. 'Why can't we all just live in peace?'

'Dagonet,' said Guinan, 'have you been so long at the cider that you've forgotten all the terrible things she did when you were at court? And don't you remember how, after we settled here, she kept confiscating all the gemstones we found in the mines when we couldn't sort the seeds? If Snow White hadn't helped us that one winter, it would have been a lean time for us. We might have starved. And besides, the great six-footers have their own complaints against Queen Morgana. I'm sure Sir Pinel will remind you.'

But Sir Pinel clutched the dark fountain of his locks, curiously reticent. He merely muttered, 'It is known that she mistreated our beloved King Leopold, and made a servant of his daughter, Snow White. And that she imprisoned our court magician Merlin within a mirror after stealing all his magick.'

'I don't think she deserves to die because of that,' said Dagonet. 'Lots of people don't like Merlin.'

'And my own relatives, Hunter John, and Lowenhardt, the Lion Baron of Astalot, have bitter complaints against her,' added Sir Pinel.

'But isn't she the grandmother of the Lion Baron's children?' asked Guinan.

'Shortly after his marriage, the Lion Baron made it known that Morgana would never be welcome in his home,' said Sir Pinel. 'Disowned by her own family, her crimes must have been great indeed.'

'I don't choose that I and my distinguished band of Travellers should get mixed up in family squabbles,' said Guinan, grandly. 'What of the murders of King Urien, and of Prince Nikolai? Surely they're more to the point? I understood our purpose was to help rid the kingdom of a murderess.'

'Well,' said Sir Pinel uneasily, 'we don't fully know about Urien. His own people have kept quiet about it. And as for Prince Nikolai... some say it was her, and some say it was her daughter, Rose Red, who killed him.'

'Prince Nikolai recovered anyway,' said Kilkenny, one of the undertaker dwarves. 'Snow White restored him to life and Rose Red fed him bread and cheese at our cottage some years ago.'

'Yes, that's right,' said Guinan. 'I remember, we'd not long been in Valerian – and great, greedy six-footer that the prince turned out to be, he ate a whole loaf and more than half a lump of our cheese with never a thought for how hungry his dwarven brethren might be.'

'You know,' said Dagonet, 'the more I hear about how evil Queen Morgana is, the less convinced I am.' And so the same circular arguments began again, with each dwarf trying to convince the others of the unassailable rightness of his own convictions. Meanwhile, Sir Pinel pulled at his hair and consulted his notebook of various poisons, intended one day for publication (though it would be an ancestor of his, Sir Pinel Shakespeare, who would become so renowned for writing plays.) The poisons were written out in his best handwriting: *Hemlock, Nightshade, Snakeroot, Oleander, Narcissus, Foxglove, Bloodroot*. He wondered briefly which would be the best for each of his dwarf companions. But no. He needed their help far too much. Guinan, their chief, was strangely gifted in the art of spells, magick, and time-travel, though he would not reveal how he came by his occult knowledge.

Finally, the dwarf, Voldip, who had been silent so far, took a small blue crystal out of his pocket and held it up to the river-light from the open casement. It shimmered and grew large, until it was the size of the window itself. 'Look what I have here,' he said. 'With this, we can watch scenes from Morgana's life. This will help us decide the true nature of her crimes, and when and if she should be killed.'

Sir Pinel shifted nervously against the solid oak, leather and brocade of his chair. 'T'is too much magick, all at once,' he muttered.

'Where did you get that, Voldip?' asked Guinan.

'Whilst you were stealing the magician's spell book, I was rummaging through his cabinet of curiosities,' said Voldip, not without a touch of pride. He was one of the younger dwarves, but there was a shrewdness about him that belied his youthful appearance. 'It was hidden behind a dragon's skull. But I knew what it was. The rest of you just dig the stones out of the mines, but I made a study of them. This is the Celestine of Avalon, which Morgana once gave to Merlin as a lover's gift. It is still imprinted with her energy, and through its own magical properties, it will provide us with a window into her life.'

'Show us then,' said Sir Pinel, 'show us Morgana on the day she said farewell to her son, Sir Mordred.' For it seemed that Sir Pinel had a perverse grudge against anyone Morgana may have loved who was not him.

'I need the spell,' said Voldip. 'It doesn't work unless you recite the spell over it.'

'Oh, for Valeria's sake,' said Sir Pinel, impatiently and he shoved the stolen volume of spells, heavy, and clad in dark-red leather, towards Guinan. 'You know I can't read those cursed runes.'

For Merlin's book of spells was more-or-less unreadable, besides being three hundred or so pages long. For every page had an ample margin, and every margin enclosed in the middle a rectangle of text, that looked like a little blot, since the words were no larger than the limbs of spiders. And then, in every rectangle, there was an awful charm, written in a bygone language, a language so ancient that it was grandfather to the sphinxes and pyramids. Then too, every margin of this book was scribbled, crossed and crammed with comment, too hard to follow for mind or eye. Sir Pinel remembered Merlin telling him that he had spent long, sleepless nights of his long life poring over this text, but that there were still sections that even he could not read.

'You claim to be the seventh dwarfish son of a seventh son,' Sir Pinel said to Guinan. '*You* find the spell.'

'But it's there in the index,' said Guinan, pointing to the bottom of a dusty page which was actually fairly familiar to him. '*Spell to Activate the Celestine of Avalon.*' Then he turned to the right page, and spoke some ancient words of Avalon sea-magick mixed with a beseeching charm from a Valerian mage:

'Ula, Ula, Ulalume
Lullalume, Ula, may,
Shirra, Shirra, Ula,
Show us Morgana this sorrowful day.'

The great blue vista of celestine grew rugged and shadowed, until it seemed to resemble the crags of a cave cut into a cliff. There sat Morgana, mother and grandmother both, and yet in that moment, and in the sanctuary of the sacred cave, she was ageless and fair. Her face was pale ivory against hair that gleamed red as the setting sun beyond the cave. She was gazing out at the great stretch of sea and the magnificent chalk-white Aiguille towering above the waves. These were blue jewels too, topaz and turquoise, and a flight of seabirds flew across it and across groves of sacred apple-trees, and into the distant, flame-tinged clouds.

She heard then her own name.

'Morgana,' a lilting voice called to her.

'Nimue,' she said as her sister appeared over the horizon, slenderer than Morgana, and clad, as ever, in the white robes which accentuated her pallor. Nimue had once wanted to be a Sister of Valerian, and there was something still of an ascetic look about her. Or perhaps it was because she was more accustomed to her kingdom beneath the sea. For she emerged from the island mist with the flowing undulations of a finny sea-creature, unused to the cliffs and rocks that Morgana favoured.

'Mordred wanted to say goodbye to you,' Nimue said then. 'He has been all day with his cousins, but now he comes to bid you farewell.' Her webbed fingers made a curious gesture to summon him, that, to Morgana, seemed half-welcoming, half-dismissive. But the dark-haired youth was still some distance away, twisting across the cliff paths towards the cave. He had not even passed the spire of the Aiguille yet, rising upwards into the sky.

'So, I am to lose my last child,' said Morgana. 'I've already lost Ywain - and Rose Red.'

'Ywain was very ill,' said Nimue, lowering her eyes. 'His sickness was beyond our ability to heal it. Though at least we could bury him in the sacred grove. But Rose Red... her passing was an even greater sorrow to us because her spirit did not return to this island.'

'Yes,' said Morgana quietly. 'There was no-one at her side to say the Words of Passing to bring her back to us. When my priestesses arrived at the Baron's castle in Astalot, it was too late. The men had already placed her in their chapel tomb. Now she is nothing more than a pile of bones beneath the banner of a lion.'

'It is too late for her,' agreed Nimue, sadly. 'But she left you with three grandchildren. And Mordred goes to take his rightful place with Arthur in Camelot. You cannot deny him this chance.'

'I have no wish to,' Morgana said. 'But you must remember how you felt when Lancelot left your side to take his place in the world of men. I had to use all my powers of persuasion before you would relinquish him.'

'Perhaps I was wrong to keep him beside me for so long,' said Nimue. 'But he was the most beautiful of my foster-children.'

'And the bravest, and the most talented,' said Morgana. 'That is how all mothers feel about their sons. That is how I felt about Ywain, and even Mordred, though he is not the equal of his brother.'

'Mordred does not lack heroic qualities,' said Nimue then, so that Morgana wondered whether she was going to speak in praise or condemnation of her nephew, 'but he struggles to find his path. Perhaps he will do better with his father in Valerian.'

'Then I do right to give him up?' asked Morgana.

'Precious good I would be to the world, otherwise,' said Mordred cheerfully, appearing at the mouth of the cave. Both women wondered if he had heard their spoken doubts and misgivings. But his olive face was smooth and smiling. 'Why would you teach me how to be a king and then deprive me of my birth-right?'

'I would not do that,' said Morgana. 'But Valerian is very different to Avalon. There are many things you will find strange…'

'Enough,' Sir Pinel said then, angrily, from the other side of the celestine vista. 'I don't wish to witness the mewling of naiads and striplings.'

'I thought it was nice,' said the youngest dwarf, Pippin, the only one without a beard. 'I had a mother once. And a spoon for my porridge.'

'We all had mothers, once,' said Guinan, 'but not all of us were lucky enough to have spoons. It was a rare, precious home we once lived in, Pippin.'

The younger dwarf wriggled and turned pink with pleasure.

'I want to see something more to the point,' said Sir Pinel. 'Show us,' he commanded then, 'show us what she did to my own cousin, Lowenhardt of Astalot.'

Now the celestine grew to the size of a church archway, and there, inside it, was a handsome young man of no more than eighteen, standing in a courtyard. He was holding the bridle of a fine, chestnut horse that was arching its neck, and stamping. The youth was wearing sable-grey velvet, and the pallor of his shirt made his skin seem more golden and tanned. Yet to Guinan, there was something rather terrible about this young man's beauty, although it was hard to say where the dreadfulness lay: an imbalance in the symmetry of his chin, his neck, his shoulders perhaps. Then too, the light in his eyes was a little too bright, as if his soul was burning.

And there, too, was Morgana, not as they had last seen her in all her defiant, ageless beauty, but as an elderly beggar-woman, though nonetheless, she bore a proud look that made her recognisable. Yet she was tired to the bone and just for this one night, she could not sustain the effort required for all the magick that she must do. They watched as, through the bars of his gate, she offered the young Baron Lowenhardt a single red rose in exchange for shelter at his castle.

But though he was wealthy, with everything his heart could desire, and though the family at Astalot were renowned for their hospitality, still, there was something spoilt and arrogant in that fire-eaten heart. He sneered at Morgana and tried to turn her from his gates. She warned him then, not to be deceived by appearances. But when he repulsed her a second time, she transformed into her true guise of powerful sorceress. How she gleamed in a gown of forest-green - and light emanated from her until it reached every part of the courtyard.

The youthful Baron tried to apologise, but it was too late. She had seen the true nature of his heart, and as punishment, she transformed him into a lion. The spell could only be broken by a maiden who would accept him as a lion by day and a man by night, thinking not of herself, but only of what was better for him. If the maiden could not do this, then he would be doomed to lion's shape for all remaining time.

'Well now,' said Voldip after a moment's pause from the other side of the celestine vista, 'did he not kind of deserve it?'

'Study has taught me that magick is a double-edged sword,' said Guinan. 'Listen,' he added then, 'all of Valerian knows how she bled our land dry to fund her schools and temples in Avalon – and how she mistreated not only your cousin, Sir Pinel, but also her second husband, King Leopold. But what of her first marriage, to King Urien?'

At his words, the blue celestine twitched and shook and instead of a small, blue stone, suddenly there was a sky-blue arch in front of them. They peered through it into a bright summer's day.

Ravenglass. Caer-Ligualid. And Morgana, called Modron here, was a girl of seventeen, wearing a long, green dress, with a garland of red and blue wildflowers twisted into her dark red hair. There was a pattern of poppies and rose-buds embroidered onto her dress, and it seemed to the spellbound dwarves that she was walking through a field where these flowers bloomed, only the stems were so long that the flowers were as tall as trees. These gave way to an avenue of oaks that led to an arch that had been woven from their branches. Beneath the branches stood King Urien, tanned and lean, battle-ready and resolute, with long hair of a colour half-way between brown and flax. He took Morgana's hands in his own and then they were bound together by six ribbons.

('Why six?' thought Pippin crossly, 'why not seven? Or eight?')

Ah, but it was a beautiful sight, those six ribbons round those fair hands, green, blue and purple for Morgana, red, yellow and orange for Urien. It was as if streaks of rainbows had come to bind them together. And a gentle voice said then, 'May this knot remain tied for as long as love shall last. May this cord draw your hands together in love, never to be used in anger.' Fairer even than the ribbons and the words, was the bride herself, and it was her smile above all that transfixed the dwarves. They could not remember ever having seen someone look so happy before.

'Anyone can look happy on their wedding-day,' said Guinan, sourly. 'It's the marriage afterwards that is important.'

'And what would you know about that?' asked Sir Pinel.

'I was married once,' said Guinan.

'Were you?' said Sir Pinel. 'Very well then. Let us witness the marriage of Queen Morgana and King Urien. Or – no – better yet, let us witness the *death* of King Urien.'

Guinan did not need to mutter the words of the spell again, for now the blue celestine was activated, it showed them Queen Morgana and King Urien, looking not much older than on their wedding day, riding out into Ravenglass's open country. The wind was blowing into their faces and the sounds of the sea rushed in upon the shore far below the towering cliffs.

The dwarves watched as Morgana shaded her eyes from the sun and looked out towards the west. A long strip of moorland lay before them, rough and ragged. At the far end of it, there was a narrow, soggy marsh, where the ducks would fly to feed in stormy weather. At all seasons of the year, the seabirds came, the curlews and gulls and herons.

'This is poor sport indeed,' said King Urien scornfully, but a moment later, he let fly the hood of his falcon and slipped her, putting spurs to his horse upon the gesture.

Within ten seconds, Morgana had done likewise, her grey-winged peregrine soaring into the sun so that its wing-feathers seemed crimson-tipped. Then she and Urien went galloping across the moors towards the marsh, with the two hawks circling above them.

Morgana's horse galloped out in front, then Urien's raced like a mad thing in pursuit; the cries of his wife to the falcons whipping up the speed. The dwarves could see, there was the sun in his eyes, the wind in his face, the horse shifting beneath him, its hooves thundering through the heather whilst the falcons pitched and hovered above, and the sea crashed its cacophony below.

Suddenly, away from the marsh ahead of them, up rose a heron, his great grey wings unfolding. It seemed that both hawks had caught sight of their quarry, for they began to circle above the heron, climbing higher and still higher, circling out in rings. And then Urien and Morgana were galloping abreast, the ground rising steadily towards a circle of stones in the middle of the moor.

The heron was now direct above their heads, and the falcons lost to view. Now the dwarves heard Morgana shout out in triumph: 'My bird has her.' And so it was, for silhouetted against the sun, one of the falcons was locked against the heron, and the two were swinging down to earth.

Urien swerved then to avoid them, but he could not get control of his horse – and it was this, the dwarves realised, that would later lead folk to say that the beast was under an enchantment.

'Which way is the chasm?' Urien shouted out to Morgana, but perhaps she did not hear him above the horses' thundering hooves. At any rate, she did not answer, and on they galloped, towards the circle of stones with the sun shining down, right into their eyes.

Then, out of the darkening sky, there fell the dying heron and the blood-splattered falcon, straight down into the rocky crevice opening out in front of them.

Morgana got control of her own horse.

'Urien!'

Now her cries rang out across the moors as down into the crevice he and his horse fell. She halted her own horse to go after them. But they were lying there broken, splattered against the rocks. It was already too late.

'But who enchanted the horse?' asked Pippin, his piping voice rising a reedy octave as he lay sprawled on the floor of Sir Pinel's turret room.

'It was only Merlin the Magician, or Morgana herself, who would have had sufficient mastery of magick,' said Sir Pinel. 'For some say she became Merlin's lover and his apprentice even before the death of Urien – and that it was a plot between them to kill the king and take over his throne.'

'I saw nothing there that showed Morgana was responsible for his death,' said Guinan firmly.

'And I believe that the Celestine of Avalon only shows the truth,' said Voldip.

'Then let us see her when she has grown thick with magick,' cried Sir Pinel. 'Let us see her when she has become the Magician's Parasite.'

The window of celestine arched and grew to reveal Morgana again, in the same cliff-top cave they had glimpsed previously, near to the Aiguille, on the Isle of Avalon. There she was, muttering over some spells. But now it seemed to the dwarves that Morgana looked sorrowful, for there were lines upon her ivory forehead, and shadows beneath her eyes.

From what Guinan could gather from her incantations, she was trying to use the magician's own magick against him, as if they were enemies now, not lovers. First, she summoned up a plaster wall in which to imprison him, but the plaster would not set and crumbled apart. Then she would capture him in a door, but the magician had an affinity with the forest trees, the oaks and chestnuts, and so the door's beams sprouted leaves and the Magician felt a lightness of heart and laughed among them. So, then she knew she must redouble her efforts, and the scene within the celestine changed once more.

The dwarves saw how, when Merlin travelled again from Camelot to the Isle of Avalon, Morgana appeared on the seat of the boat beside him, wrapped in a cloak only slightly darker than the mists which swirled around them.

Their boat touched upon the Falaise d'Aval, that is to say, Avalon, on Breton sands. Here they disembarked, and then Morgana followed Merlin all the way into the wild woods of Broceliande. As they walked through the forest, she cried out that Merlin was her lord and liege, her seer, her bard, her shining star, even her god. They came to a clearing, and together they sat down on the stump of an oak tree, and he took both her hands in his own.

'Morgana, child,' he said, 'you think you love me. But Urien's death last year has shaken you, and you look for security – and power. You must cease entreating me for the Charm of Captivity.'

'If you will not tell me the charm,' said Morgana, 'tell me at least where it comes from.'

'From an ancient time in Valerian,' he replied, for despite his words, he loved her and wished to please her. 'There was a king who loved a maid so fair it was said that a light came from her when she moved. And then the king called upon a little wild faun to put a charm upon this maid, so that she might see no other man but him. The charm was made, but it was an unhappy time for the maid, who lived as one who had died. So, the faun who had wrought the charm was called back to undo it. But then, when it was undone, the faun vanished back into his old wild, and his spell book passed to me. I found this charm in the margins of its pages.'

'Tell me how it is, my love,' said Morgana then, 'that the women of those times were so meek and mild?'

Merlin gazed on Morgana and half-believed that all her sweet words were true, so tender was her voice, so fair her face, so sweetly gleamed her eyes. Yet still he resisted her.

'Look up into the sky,' he said. 'See – look – there is a single misty star there, which seems the point of a dagger beneath Orion's belt of three.'

'What of it, my love?' asked Morgana, following his pointed hand upwards with her gaze.

'Whenever I look at that star,' the wizard said, 'it seems to me that it was wrought from some powerful charm that could bring about my downfall. And just as I fear that star, so too do I fear you, Morgana, for you might play me false with the power that I should grant you.'

'There can be no love without trust,' she muttered.

He placed his arm around her, for now she seemed so fair and sad. But the moment that his hand touched her, a bolt of lightning ripped through the sky, and struck the stump of giant oak which sheltered them. This sent sparks and splinters of wood scattering into the great forest. The lightning-fork, the cracks and claps of thunder seemed to frighten her, so that she clung to him. She held him close and called him her dear protector. And then his oval face, that in that moment seemed carved from moonstone, grew flushed and rosy.

But as the storm raged on, so too did the furious passion of her eyes. In all that tumult of storm and emotion, Merlin grew exhausted and fell asleep. Morgana wrapped him in her hair as he slept, and in his sleep, she drew the magick words, *'Tirra Lirra,'* from his mouth. This, she realised, was the powerful Charm of Captivity.

She murmured the words three times over whilst the storm spent its passion above their heads. Then she bound the charm fast with woven paces and waving hands and added some water-magick of her own. When the storm finally broke, she seized a slither of glass from the pouch she wore around her neck. When Merlin awoke, there he was, inside that glass. For him, it was like being enclosed in the four grey walls of a hollow tower from which there was no escape.

He lay there, inside that prism of glass, until she could reach her own palace to place him within a magic mirror. This then was to be the dwelling-place of the mighty Merlin, heir to the throne of Ravenglass, the Valerian King's Supreme Magician, and the Fairy Queen's Chief Advisor in Magick at the court of Avalon!

'Imbecile,' Morgana thundered as she paced back through the Broceliande forest. 'Imbecile,' she howled again as the lurid lightning shone in her eyes.

'See,' said Sir Pinel then, 'see what the foul witch is capable of.'

'But why did she do it?' asked Cooey.

'Might it have been from grief at her husband's death?' asked Guinan. 'Or from fear of what the Magician had done – or might do? For you are right about one thing, Sir Pinel, Merlin is the only one with enough power to have enchanted Urien's horse. And, with Urien gone, people would naturally turn to Merlin to lead them, with or without Morgana at his side.'

'That's not what I believe,' said Sir Pinel. 'I believe she had learned enough of Merlin's magick by that time to have killed Urien herself. Her only rival for Ravenglass's throne was Merlin, and so he must be contained. Then she consolidated her power by returning to Avalon, and later, by travelling to Valerian and marrying King Leopold. If Leopold had not seen fit to banish her from his kingdom, he might have become her next victim. As it is, who knows what great evil she is planning to unleash upon us all from her power-seat in Avalon?'

'Is that really what you believe?' asked Guinan. 'For sure, the dwarves have no reason to love Morgana, but mightn't she just be going about her royal business in Avalon, safeguarding its temples, educating its girls…'

'Re-writing prayer-books so the fairy folk can turn their minds to proper worship,' said Dagonet, eagerly.

'Imbeciles,' said Sir Pinel.

'What *does* that word mean?' asked Cooey.

'It means we have wasted too much time already,' snapped Sir Pinel. 'Even if you don't believe that Morgana killed her husband, you all witnessed how she stole magick from the Magician and imprisoned him in the mirror. You have seen how powerful she has become. I believe that we must stop her some short time before she learns the Charm of Captivity.'

'It is true,' said Guinan slowly, 'that at that point in time, she has a son and daughter by Urien yet living. They are niece and nephew to King Arthur. If we take them into our custody and bring them back with us to Camelot, then the Pendragon line of succession is secure.'

'Yes,' said Sir Pinel eagerly. 'It is the perfect moment to strike. For, regardless of whether she killed him or not, Morgana will be in Avalon, mourning Urien's death, and she will be vulnerable.'

'I don't like it,' said Dagonet.

'Nor I,' said Cooey.

'Nor I,' said Pippin.

'And I'm in two minds about it myself,' said Guinan. 'But there are eight of us, so we must vote.'

'Only seven of us now that Clairmont is gone,' said Pippin dolefully. 'Crushed in the mines by the biggest diamond that ever was, that Queen Guinevere threw into the water.'

'He was crushed ever so many years ago,' said Guinan. 'I'm surprised you still remember it. Besides, I didn't mean Clairmont, I meant *him*,' he added, as he pointed to Sir Pinel.

'Well, if you're sure,' said Pippin.

'All in favour of travelling back through time to murder Queen Morgana say, *Ay*. All against it, say *Nay*,' said Guinan.

'*Nay*,' said Dagonet quickly.

'Yes, *nay*,' said Cooey.

'*Ay*,' said Kilkenny.

'*Ay*,' said Fieldung.

'This is ridiculous,' said Sir Pinel. 'Of course, *Ay*. Obviously, *Ay*.'

'*Nay*,' said Pippin.

'I'm not sure,' said Voldip.

'*Ay*,' said Guinan, reluctantly.

'Alright then, *Ay*,' said Voldip. 'Though I wish we could have seen more with the Celestine.'

'That makes five votes to three,' said Guinan, with a sorrow in his heart that he could not quite shake.

'It's not the time for scruples,' said Sir Pinel, 'it's the time for action. The plan is this: we will travel back to a day shortly after Urien's death, to when Morgana is alone and unprotected, and then you, who are strangers to her court, will perform some dance or clownish antics. You should be good at that,' he added.

'What are you implying?' asked Guinan, drawing himself up to his full height of three-foot-one.

'That you dwarves have many talents,' said Sir Pinel, quickly. 'Anyway, at the end of your performance, you will bow and offer her a bowl of fruit that I have poisoned.' He added, almost to himself, 'Morgana has a great liking for apples.'

'Araminta always said they grow the finest apples in the world in Avalon,' said Guinan, also sounding wistful.

'Never mind that,' snapped Sir Pinel. He continued, 'You, dwarves, pick up the bowls from that cabinet, and you, Guinan, find me the Magician's Time Travel Spell in amongst all that scrawl.'

'You know that the spell runs counter to Valerian's Known Laws of Magick, don't you?' said Guinan.

'That isn't my concern,' said Sir Pinel. His eyes narrowed suspiciously. 'But how do *you* know that Guinan?'

'I know a lot of things,' said Guinan, glibly. 'Seventh dwarf of a seventh dwarf, *etcetera*.' He reached for the spell-book again. After a few moments of turning the pages and reading them, he said, 'Actually, it's been a while since I thought about all this, and now I remember, it's not as straightforward as all that. There's a process. First of all, you need to clear me some space so I can draw a compass symbol on the floor.'

The dwarves jumped up to do his bidding with surprising alacrity, for this was not the first time they had embarked on time-travelling adventures with their Chief. Then Guinan took a piece of chalk out of his pocket and drew the largest and most even circle he could manage, though the chalk kept crumbling against the flagstones. He gazed out of the casement for a moment before muttering, 'North as the crow flies.' Then he wrote, N for *North*, S for *South*, W for *West*, and E for *East* on the corresponding points of the chalk compass.

'What next?' asked Sir Pinel.

'I'm going to need a Symbol of Wisdom for North, a Symbol of Courage for East, a Symbol of Love for South, and a Symbol of Innocence for West,' said Guinan, 'and then we must place all our symbols on the corresponding letters and stand inside the circle whilst I recite the words of the spell. So, what do we have for Wisdom?'

The dwarves looked at each other and scratched their heads and chins, pulled on their beards and emptied out their pockets, to no avail.

'You could have had my spectacles if I hadn't broken them,' said Kilkenny, sorrowfully.

Silence reigned. Then, finally, 'What about this?' asked Voldip, holding up the blue celestine he had purloined from Merlin's cabinet of curiosities.

'I think that's our best, and in fact, our only option,' said Guinan, and he carefully took the celestine from Voldip and placed it on the letter N. 'And for Courage?'

'We dwarves don't lack courage, father,' said Pippin stoutly, and he took a sprig of thyme from the pouch he wore around his neck. 'If we ever made it to Avalon, I was going to burn some thyme in one of their temples, to grant us further bravery. But it might do us more good here than there.'

'Sometimes, Pippin, you make me proud,' said Guinan, and he placed the sprig of thyme on the letter E. 'And for Love?'

'I still have a lock of my lost Suzanna's hair,' said Sir Pinel then, reaching into his desk-drawer and unwrapping a coil of black hair from a twist of paper. He handed it to Guinan, who glared at it and seemed not to want to touch it.

'It's a shame she was turned into a hog,' said the dwarf at last. 'But are you sure you truly loved her? For the spell won't work otherwise.'

'Oh yes,' said Sir Pinel, with a rare moment of grace, 'she meant all the world to me.'

'Very well then,' said Guinan, and he placed Suszanna's lock of hair on the letter S. 'And finally, for Innocence, who has the clockwork mouse this week?'

'It's me,' said Cooey reluctantly. 'But I had to wash all those dishes to have it. Can't we use something else?'

'You'll get it back,' said Guinan. 'I would have asked Kilkenny for his dear little rat otherwise, but it wouldn't have sat still long enough. Whereas this fellow,' he said, as Cooey handed him the clockwork mouse, 'he'll settle quite happily on the W as long as none of us wind him up.'

He placed the cherished toy on the chalk letter.

'And the magick words?' said Sir Pinel, then.

'Patience,' said Guinan, with such natural authority that for a moment he seemed to tower over Sir Pinel. 'Get your poisons together, and then everyone stand in the compass circle with me whilst I say the spell.'

Sir Pinel and the dwarves hauled themselves into the centre of the drawn chalk compass where they were joined by Guinan and the Magician's red leather volume. He opened it and recited the magick words:

'In sigli sela
Monis Morgana
Sonor doni
Ex fugit sela.'

'Oh yes, I remember now,' said Pippin. 'This is the part that always makes me diz-'

Where there had been eight beings of various shapes, sizes, and dispositions, now Sir Pinel's turret room was empty. Now in a field, Pippin was shaking his head, trying to make his ears pop, whilst his six companions and Sir Pinel walked beside him.

It was a rich, ripe field that had no need of ploughing. Ahead of them lay a white path than ran through a green grove where daisies grew. On either side of the path, there were clumps of apple trees, with vines that entwined their trunks with jewel-like grapes. When they stepped onto the path, they could see the clusters of starry fruit hanging down from the branches.

Beyond the green grove were the columns, pagodas, and archways of Queen Morgana's palace, reaching up into the sky above them, and reflected in the lakes beneath them. It was all so lovely, and ethereal, that several stout hearts began to regret the course of action upon which they had embarked.

Not so Sir Pinel, who had no qualms about raising his sword up into the branches of the trees and knocking down ripe apples, to fall into bowls held up by the dwarves. Soon, the knight had laced the fruit with slow-acting poisons, aconite, and hemlock, then he and his companions passed through the palace gates.

Sir Pinel, with that streak of cowardly superstition that was innate to him, gave the fruit back to the dwarves whilst he went to lurk among the horses in the stables. For Morgana of the future knew him well, and with all the magick she was learning, might she not experience some strange pre-cognition of his craven soul?

The palace was in mourning for the death of King Urien of Ravenglass, and the dwarves found the abode of the great six-foot faes, the tiny fire fairies, the naiads and the witchlings, very strange. The dark, wood-panelled gallery was dotted with garlands of yew berries and made darker yet by swathes of black and charcoal velvet draped over many of the fine tapestries. The candles in chandeliers wrought from oak branches were flickering down into extinguishment, and a raven had made his perch in the neighbouring beams.

Queen Morgana herself sat on a throne hewn out of a stump of massive oak, once blasted by lightning. Its dark tangle of branches threw into relief her pale, oval face which just now appeared wan, and her once bright halo of hair was lank against her cheeks. Her children, a fine boy and girl of eight or nine, both with brown hair tinged with gold, and clear, bright eyes, were sitting beside her on the throne's raised dais. They were playing a game with golden acorns that was a bit like jacks.

At their approach, Morgana raised her head sharply from the listless contemplation of her embroidered belt.

'Who are you?' she asked, surveying them all, 'why have you come?'

'We have come, my lady, to bring solace to your sad hours,' Guinan replied. Just in that moment, standing with his friends below the dais, in darkness except for the light from the chandelier, he felt it to be true. He took out a small harp from his knapsack and played a few tentative chords. His hands on the strings seemed to be plucking the notes out of the air.

The sound was sweet enough that all eyes turned to the dwarf's strange, intense face and his sharp, compelling eyes. And when he began to sing, his voice was marvellous and deep, resonant as an oboe, and light as birdsong.

In the darkening room, the figures on the few uncovered tapestries began to move in step to his singing. All around him, the gathered court listened spellbound as a magick circle of dancers wove in and out of the flowering walls. Morgana was not the only one who sighed in the near darkness as he sang:

'Take care, fair maiden, to guard your best wine,
Be cautious of knights and their soft-spoken rhyme,
They'll promise you all, the sun, moon and stars,
Then swiftly forsake you, leaving broken glass.
Ah-oh-oh-oh, broken glass.

With rubied words and liquid touch,
He offers so little and asks for so much,
He makes all his promises under cover of night,
But the flagon is empty in the cool morning light.
Ah-oh-oh-oh, the cool morning light.'

Guinan's voice and the harp notes swept up-and-down the gallery like wings, then faded away as the song came to an end. He gave a graceful bow and then Cooey stepped forwards and presented Morgana with the bowl of apples that were laced with aconite and hemlock.

She bit into one, her coral mouth leaving a perfect crescent moon circlet in the apple's pale flesh.

Meanwhile, her son Ywain had caught sight of the little rat peeping out of the dwarf Kilkenny's frayed shirt pocket.

'Show me, show me,' he said, so that Kilkenny had no choice but to obey the royal command. He knew, besides, that Guinan still had some notion about taking the boy into his custody and returning with him to Camelot. To this end, Kilkenny showed Ywain and Morfydd the tricks that the little rat could perform. But they seemed fascinated by quite ordinary things, like the way the rat stood upon its hind legs to eat a morsel of bread-and-cheese, and how daintily it washed its paws afterwards.

Since they had managed to cheer the queen and her children, the dwarves were granted fine quarters in the palace for the night. It was true, Voldip and Kilkenny were anxious to be away as quickly as possible, but Guinan wanted to see the results of their actions.

In the middle of the night, Morgana woke up sick, after dreaming that she had been buried alive. The feeling of suffocation persisted even when she opened her eyes. Her chest felt heavy, and she couldn't breathe. She shut her eyes and lay there without moving for a few seconds. When she opened her eyes again, she could see, through the gap in the doorway, that the candles had burned down even lower in the chandeliers. Then she knew where she was. But it was very early still, before dawn. And she was cold, deathly cold, sick and in pain.

She got out of bed and staggered into her dressing-room. There she saw herself in the glass, her pale skin tinged citrine. She turned away at once. She could not vomit. She only retched painfully.

The great cheval looking glass showed her what she already knew. She had been poisoned. But it was a dull thought, like spelling over runestones she could not read. Now she was too giddy to stand. She went back into her room and collapsed on the bed. The blanket loomed out at her in strange shades of pink and red.

After gazing at it for some time, she was able to stand up, find the pitcher and vomit. It seemed like hours before the vomiting stopped. She would lean against the wall, then the retching and sickness would start again. When it was over, she returned to bed, too weak to move.

Yet she knew she had never made a greater effort in all her life. She wanted to lie still and sleep, but she forced herself to get up. She was still weak and giddy, but no longer so sick or in pain. She pulled on her morning-robe and splashed cold water from the basin onto her face. Then she walked down the corridor towards the dwarves' quarters.

They were sleeping haphazardly in their beds, pulled crookedly into different corners of the room. The dwarf who had sung to her, and who seemed to be their Chief, was now snoring. Their bowls of apples were still on the dresser beside him. She took one of the apples, a russet from the sacred grove, and sniffed it.

It smelt bitter, not sweet.

So, the dwarves had taken her own sacred apples and, foolishly, tried to use them against her. The apples were Avalon. She was Avalon. They could cause her no real harm.

Then she noticed something else. The red-bound leather spell-book. Merlin's spell-book, that she had glimpsed previously in his chambers, that he would never let her see, that he kept under lock-and-key. Had he given it to these dwarves to bring about her downfall?

She shook her head. The Merlin she knew loved her. He did not want her dead. At court, it was already rumoured that he had killed Urien to rule by her side.

But Merlin in the future might feel differently about her. He might have suborned these demon-dwarves into his service and sent them back to destroy her. And the dwarf who could sing, who seemed shrewd and wise, might well be the trusted heir and apprentice to Merlin's magick.

This must not be, she thought, and she reached for the spell-book and placed it in the folds of her robe. Then it was as if her mind and gaze were flooded with a pool of black ink. Her last clear thought before she lost consciousness and slid to the floor was that Merlin and the dwarves were now her implacable foes.

The first thing that Pippin saw when he opened his sky-blue eyes was the crumpled heap of the queen on the floor. He had the presence of mind to get up, tiptoe over to Guinan and shake him awake.

'What do we do?' he asked.

'If she's alive and she's here, she knows it was us,' said Guinan, 'so we should go. And if she's dead and she's here, everyone will soon work out it was us. So, we should also go. Quickly, son,' he added, as he and Pippin began to shake the other dwarves awake. Then they quit their chamber to join Sir Pinel, who had spent the night in the courtyard stables.

'Morgana?' inquired the knight.

'Dead – we think,' replied Guinan, 'but we must hurry.'

Once again, Guinan drew a chalk compass on the floor and readied them for the Spell of Return. He recited the necessary words, for his previous experience as wizard's apprentice had rendered him an adept spellcaster:

'In sigli sela
Ex Morgana

*Sui dona
Sorres Camelot.'*

It was only after they had returned to Sir Pinel's crowded turret toom in Camelot that they realised two precious things were missing: Merlin's spell-book and Kilkenny's pet rat. It was hard to tell which loss they felt most keenly, or which would wreak greater havoc.

'But we still have the Celestine,' said Sir Pinel, 'and we can use it to ascertain whether Morgana is alive – or dead.'

Voldip picked up the Celestine crystal from the North point of the chalk compass.

'Show us Morgana,' he said, 'in the aftermath of our visit.'

Again, the Celestine grew to the size and shape of an arch, and through it, the dwarves glimpsed men in dark cloaks wearing strange, metallic masks. They were hurrying through the gloomy corridors of Morgana's summer palace.

'Are they undertakers?' asked Fieldung.

'The doctors, most likely,' said Sir Pinel.

'Then she's dead?' said Kilkenny, peering forwards as best he could without his glasses.

But the Celestine shimmered once more and the archway grew larger yet, to reveal Morgana tending to her two sick children, Morfydd and Ywain. Unbeknownst to the dwarves, Kilkenny's rat had carried a sickness against which these half-fairy children had no natural immunity. However, it was only the girl who was able to fix her gaze on her mother's mouth and follow the waving of her hands that signified the healing spells of Avalon. She heard the incantations, swallowed the broth and the herbal tisanes. Her twin brother, Ywain, did not.

So then, the girl recovered and began a regime of echinacea and rose-hips. She sat reading in her chair, her face pallid, her cheeks devoid of their customary roses, but still, her eyes were bright and alert.

However, the boy did not recover. His body had become its own hell. The flesh prison writhed and strained, buckled and twisted.

The dwarves saw that Morgana was slight, but she was strong. They watched as she held Ywain down by the shoulders, the chest. She wanted to keep him in place, keep him safe, keep him still. But she was already starting to despair that there was nothing more she could do. She could stay beside him and make him feel as comfortable as she could, but this strange sickness that the dwarves had brought with them was too great, too vicious.

Morgana knew she had incurred the wrath of many enemies over the course of her life. It seemed to her now that this sickness was the one who hated her most. This pestilence, that had taken hold of her boy, just as her courtiers whispered that the demon enchanter, Merlin, had taken control of her. Or she of him – for now, she and the Magician were locked in some kind of fierce struggle on a battleplane of love and hate. But she would not surrender. No, she would not surrender. And so, she willed it that her son would likewise not surrender to his own death.

But the scent of death remained strong, like rotting apples.

Morgana did not leave Ywain's side. She swabbed his brows and limbs with a damp flannel. She packed salt into the bed with him. She laid a posy of valerian and duck feathers on his chest and bathed his eyes with feverfew.

But still, his fever rose higher and higher, and the glands in his neck swelled tighter. She raised his hand, veined blue and pale, and pressed it against her cheek. She would do anything now to save her boy. She would try anything. She would sell her soul to the devil – except she had done that once before. But she had given Ywain everything – could she not do the same again? – for look, here, were her veins, her blood, her heart. What must she sacrifice to make it right again?

Ywain knew she was there. He wanted to say something to comfort her, only just now there was a great weight upon his tongue, and he could not speak. Or was it that he was somewhere else entirely? Somewhere where the snow was falling, where it was still and cold and quiet. Perhaps he would pile up the snow and make a castle with his sister. If he could only move his limbs. Or perhaps, instead, he would just lie down and rest his tired legs and aching arms beneath this thick, white blanket. The light was very beautiful here, slanting silver between the trees. He did not want to leave.

But his mother was calling him. Over-and-over. She would not let him sleep. She was trying to apply the poultice to the swellings in his neck and armpits. But he was trembling so much that they would not stay in place.

The mother felt as if she were fighting with his trembling frame. And yet it was not her son she was fighting, but death itself.

And then, all at once, he was still. His dark eyes were somewhere else entirely, focussed somewhere else, on the snow, perfect and crystalline, yet so soft when he laid his cheek upon it. It would not be wrong to rest here a while. It would not be wrong to close his eyes. For a little while.

She could call him when it was time to wake up.

Morgana bent forwards to touch her lips to her son's forehead. There, on his pallet bed by the great fireplace, he breathed for the last time. She did not know that it was his last breath, but there came nothing after.

Darkness clouded the Celestine vision.

'You failed then,' Sir Pinel sneered at the dwarves in the turret room. 'The boy died but his mother did not. You need to return to Avalon and carry out the murder, properly, this time.'

'It's your poisons that failed,' said Guinan, 'and besides, Morgana must now have the Magician's spell-book. If she has learned to read it, she will be more powerful than ever.'

'Coward,' said Sir Pinel then, so that the Celestine obligingly twitched and shimmered in Voldip's hand. Now it showed another shadowy being, not in Morgana's summer palace this time, but at a feast in King Leopold's banqueting-hall in Valerian, some twenty years ago. Here was a familiar, slender, masculine hand with a striking ring at the knuckle, reaching out from the sleeve of a dark cloak to slip a vial of deadly nightshade into a goblet of red wine.

And here was Prince Nikolai, taking a right good gulp of it, so that his blue eyes gleamed and his pale face became ruddy and handsome. But a few moments later, down he slipped upon the floor, his eyes bulging in his head, his neck veins writhing. Someone screamed and then, a moment later, a similar scene played out.

Now that same hand with its striking ring was lacing an apple with a tincture of wolfbane and belladonna. And then a raven-haired girl took a bite from that apple, and, with a single, piercing cry, fell to the ground.

The dwarves knew that hand, knew that ring with the gryphon and the serpent devouring each other in the shape of a circular PS. Those that could read knew those initials stood for Pinel Le Savage.

'*You!*' they said, turning on him. 'You poisoned Prince Nikolai and Snow White. But why?'

Sir Pinel edged back nervously until he stood against the circular tower wall. 'To discredit Morgana,' he confessed, 'I knew she would be blamed. Besides, I judged Snow White too weak to rule. Is Valerian not better under the Pendragon banner?'

Guinan spoke then, and it was a wonder how a voice so quiet could sound so menacing.

'But you wanted us to murder Morgana for crimes that you yourself had committed.'

'That doesn't sit well with me,' said Voldip.

'Nor me,' said Pippin.

'Nor me,' said Cooey.

'Nor me,' said Dagonet.

'Let's get him, lads,' said Fieldung, and Guinan and Kilkenny nodded, so that they all charged forwards. The seven savage dwarves set upon Sir Pinel and killed him with tooth, claw, pickaxe, and penknife. And then, when he was good and dead, Fieldung drove a wooden stake through his heart. Such was the force with which he impaled the corpse that its handsome head tipped right back, and its mouth lolled open to reveal a perfect set of vampire fangs.

'Well,' said Guinan, slowly, 'that certainly explains a few things. But how did you know to set a stake through his heart?'

'We undertaker dwarves hear many strange things,' said Fieldung. 'You remember how it is the custom in Novgorod to dismember the body so that it cannot come back as a ghoul – or a vampire? In fact,…' He paused a moment to set a piece of garlic in the corpse's mouth. 'That will stop his soul from re-entering his body – and it will block wandering evil spirits from reanimating his corpse,' he added.

'Yes, the last thing we need on our hands is a zombie vampire,' said Guinan.

'When I'm dealing with the deceased, I do like to be extra careful,' said Fieldung. 'Besides, you can't deny that Sir Pinel was always a strange one.'

'I've travelled through many times, and lived many lives, and I can safely say, of everyone I've ever known, he was the strangest,' agreed Guinan.

The dwarf's gaze dropped once more to the ring on the thickening hand of the corpse, with its emerald serpent slowly devouring the ebony gryphon.

Un Beau Rêve Rose

Arabella De Lys,
Crowcroft Grange,
VALERIAN,
Le dix septembre, 1888

Ma chère Madame Riven,
You asked me to write and let you know how I fared in this so-strange land with this so-strange man who once told me he was my father, and now I am keeping my promise to you. If my handwriting is not so neat as you once taught me, it is because this letter is a secret and I am having to write to you at night, by the light of a lantern. *La Reine* has left it here for me, on the table beside my bed, but still, it is very dark. I want to stretch out my hands, to warm them at its glow, but the heat is more like breath, the breath of someone very close, keeping me company, here in the dark.

You remember, Madame Riven, you thought that the man who said he was my father was very grim and very odd, and so did I. Indeed, I did not care for the news.

'Madame Riven's dog, Chevron, is more like you than I am,' I told him.

At that, he gave a great, uproarious laugh, and it was then I began to like him.

Before that, I had known him as Lord Édouard Darvell. That was when Maman, whom you told me was far too pretty to be sensible, was still alive. I wish she were here now, *chère Madame*, to share this bed with me. She used to before, although not too often, since sometimes there were others who wished to take my place. Gentlemen, I suppose, judging by the sounds of voices and Maman's tinkling laughter and the remnants of dainty suppers and glasses of champagne.

One of these gentlemen was Lord Édouard Darvell, whom you seemed not to like, Madame. But he used to visit us often in the *appartement* we rented from you, swinging me in his arms so that the tip of my head almost collided with the chandelier.

'Be careful with the child, Édouard,' my mother would say, scolding him prettily, wringing her lovely, white hands.

'I am always careful, of what is mine,' he replied, returning me to the ground. That was when he told me he was my father.

And so, when Maman had gone to the Holy Virgin, and Lord Darvell asked me to live with him in Valerian instead, I said yes. I know, Madame Riven, that you said I could stay with you, but you only had a little, three-storey *appartement*, and Lord Darvell said he had a house that was like a *château*, with stables for his horses, and the new pony he would buy me.

Though, sometimes, I wish I had stayed with you, Madame Riven. You would have taken me to church on Sunday. But this Lord Darvell, he does not go to church; I do not know if he believes in God; it seems to me he does believe in anything except himself.

The lantern is flickering now. I wonder if the light will last long enough for me to finish my letter to you? I stretch out my hand to steady it. One Two Three Four Five fingers, counting the thumb. And did you know, Madame Riven, I have had five mothers? The first finger, the index finger, is for *ma vraie mère, so beautiful, so charming, la belle dame qui ne retournera jamais* - Delphine De Lys. I remember her perfume too, *Caresse,* I think it was called, a blend of musk and jasmine. But she was just like that. A spray of perfume, a moment of something beautiful, and then she was gone.

Next to the index finger is the thumb: short, squat Clara, the dressmaker, with her thimble. She liked to dress me up in clothes she had sewn herself, and curl my hair in ringlets, as if I were a doll. She cosseted me, fussed over me, and fed me many dumplings. But that was because Clara had once had her own daughter, who had died. And sometimes, when I was half asleep, she would cry over me and call me by another child's name. *Bah* - when Lord Darvell broke with her, I think it was me she wept for, not him.

As for me, Madame Riven, I am glad that I am his daughter and not his mistress, and that I shall live to break hearts, not have my own broken.

His next mistress was Giacinta, the little finger, vapid, slight in person; she hated me when she had the energy. She used to give me sly nips and shakes when she thought he couldn't see. She was pretty in her own way, with her tawny hair and sulking mouth, and she slunk around gracefully enough, like a cat, but then she had a cat's manners and morals, and the same poor mothering instinct, Lord Darvell said. I am glad we only stayed a few weeks with her.

For finally we came to Valerian, crossing over the sea in a great ship with a chimney that smoked – how it smoked, even more than my father used to! I was sick and so was he. He lay down on a sofa in a room called the salon. I had a little bed in another place, but I nearly fell out of it every time the ship tipped and heaved.

My bed was like a shelf, and I could not sleep in it. I wanted a hammock instead. But I went and sat down on another sofa in the salon. I looked up at the ceiling and there was a chandelier which swayed backwards and forwards with the motion of the ship. It reminded me of the chandelier in my mother's *appartement*, which nearly struck against my head when Lord Darvell threw me up towards it. Then, all the glass drops were sparkling and gleaming, like diamonds and champagne, pouring their light all over me. But now I gazed up at this chandelier and thought that all the broken bits of my life were sparkling there.

Then the chandelier's glass drops chinked together. It sounded like when Maman chinked the champagne glasses with us. 'Remember Arabella,' she used to say, raising her glass to me, too intoxicated to be discreet, 'Always use champagne flutes. The bubbles evaporate in the round glasses.' Then she turned to my father and said, 'Did you know, they were modelled on Marie Antoinette's *poitrine?*' And she stole a sly, sidelong glance at him to judge his reaction.

But his full mouth compressed into a thin line, and he said nothing.

After that, Maman clasped her hands together so that they just rested on her diamond necklace. Then she closed her eyes and began to sing. Her plaintive voice became discordant as she tried to reach the higher notes, but still she warbled out the words to *Le Beau Rêve Rose*: '*Ne pleure pas, petite chose.*'

As I looked up at the ship salon's chandelier now, I tried to remember, and sing, the rest of the words. But instead, I found I was crying. Tears pouring down my cheeks; tears tipping and swaying above me.

Was it then that the scowl took up permanent residence on my father's forehead or did that come later? He said he was still seasick, and he groaned and turned his face to the wall. But I think, on that sea-voyage to Valerian, we somehow lost our way, for he began to mutter that my mother's songs were in poor taste.

The ship stopped in the morning, before it was quite daylight, at a huge, fog-filled city with very dark houses. Madame Riven, it was not at all like our clean, pretty town in Ile-Grande. Lord Darvell looked sorry for the previous day, or perhaps he was still feeling sea-sick, but he carried me in his arms over a plank to the land. Then we climbed inside a coach, which took us to a beautiful, large house, called a hotel. And there was another chandelier in the lobby, but now chandeliers were no longer special to me, and I would not look up at it, no, not even when he pointed and exclaimed.

But every morning that we stayed at the hotel, he would take me for a walk in a great, green park full of trees. There were many children there besides me, and a pond with beautiful birds in it, that I fed with crumbs. I liked them because even though they could fly away at any time, they chose to remain. No-one else did, not even the children, running about, laughing, and screaming. But then, Lord Darvell would call me back to him and take my hand and we would walk in this park, oh so slowly and sedately, very properly, very Valerian.

And though I had sometimes seen him merry and not quite sober himself, he said that I must not laugh and scream with the other children, that despite my disadvantages of birth and upbringing, I must learn to behave like a good little Valerian girl, his own Arabella, the name he had chosen for me. If I could do that, then he would be proud of me. Then he would have a photographic portrait taken of me with his ward, Arthur. For he had met a lady photographer just before he came to Ile-Grande that last time to collect me. He said her name was Miss Violetta.

I nodded and agreed, because I thought it would be very exciting to have my photograph taken in a studio. If the portrait turns out a good one, Madame Riven, I promise to send a copy to you.

After a few more days, we travelled on from the hotel until we came to this great, dark, fine house they call Crowcroft Grange. It is not, after all, a *chateau,* but it was the home of Lord Darvell's father and his grandfather before him, his ancestors he said, who, I suppose, are also mine. But the very day that we arrived back, when I was still wanting to explore, Lord Darvell placed an advertisement in a newspaper he called *The Valerian Times,* and in this way, he engaged a governess for me.

The governess, the ring finger, the one who wants to marry him. Mademoiselle Sibylla Dulcetta, neither as kind as Clara, nor as spiteful as Giacinta. And yet, Madame Riven, you will be surprised to learn this, but I am not so sure she likes me. Her eyes narrowed when I sang my mother's song so that now the words catch and scramble in my throat, and I no longer like to sing them.

And with this not liking comes a feeling of shame, as if my mother had not been so very beautiful after all, as if all her charm had come from the pots of rouge on her dressing-table.

'Everyone is beautiful when you drink champagne,' she once said to me, starting to spill it everywhere, so that even the pots of rouge became frothing, bloody messes.

'For God's sake, Delphine,' said my father. 'Think of the child.' But it is the governess who thinks of me now, and after all, I am not sure I am such a source of pleasure, for she is always frowning when she looks at me, and then nothing, neither rouge nor champagne, could make her pretty.

The other night, I dreamed of the statue of the Holy Virgin in our church at Ile-Grande. She had roses in the holes in her feet. Her robe was very blue, her mouth scarlet, her eyes mild yet transfigured by her halo. But the beautiful, rosy dream glow started to fade. Then tongues of flame flickered round the statue of the Virgin, and she became charred and blackened. Yet still she held her arms out to me in mute entreaty.

'Maman,' I said, and then I woke up, sweating, as much as if someone had thrown water over me. Just like Mademoiselle Dulcetta had to do a few weeks ago when she was passing by Lord Darvell's chamber, and there he was, burning in his bed.

At first, for a joke, he said it must have been the ghost of the house that did it, but we did not think that was very funny. So, then he said that he had started smoking again, and that he must have fallen asleep, and that the ash had fallen from his cigar and set alight the sheets. How quickly Mademoiselle Dulcetta rushed to his side with her chamber-pot, and how quickly, indeed, he turned her out again!

Although he said it for a joke, I do think there is a ghost in this house, Madame Riven, but I do not think she tried to burn him alive. He is a very odd man, who gives thistles instead of *bon-bons,* but he does not deserve to perish in flames. I think, in her own way, the ghost is trying to protect him, and all of us. And so, she is the final finger, slender, stately, a queen compared to all the others.

For if he will not marry Mademoiselle Dulcetta, for which I cannot blame him, there is still *La Reine,* this mysterious lady of the night, this dark phantom who hangs over my bed when I wake, calling for Maman.

La Reine is there for me when I wake from dreams red as blood, and she smiles at me, and tells me the tales of *enfance* to comfort me. Sometimes, she leaves me a candle or a lantern, as she did tonight so that I can write her stories down – or else, write you this letter, *chère* Madame Riven.

When she smiles at me, I no longer think that my room is the chamber of Barbe-Bleue, and I am no longer afraid. She tells me that she is Morgana le Fay, *La Reine, la revenante* who always returns. She is near to me now; I can feel her breath upon my cheek.

But what do you think of all this, Madame Riven? Write and tell me please, for I will be so lonely here until Arthur returns from boarding-school. They have given him his very own holiday. Until then, my dearest friend is a ghost and there is no-one else with any sense in whom I can confide.

Amitiés et bisous,
Ton,
Arabella

Violetta *or* The Titrations
Part II

On the centenary ride from East Grinstead to London, Aurélie had read all the fairytales thus far, but she started to doze over the child's, Arabella's, letter. A sudden jolt from the train carriage woke her.

The child's surname, De Lys, was her own, but that was a very common surname in Avalon and its surrounding islands, as common as Smith or Jones in Valerian. And yet certain words and phrases, certain incidents reverberated like wind chimes in the interstices of her mind. She tried to think back over her own family's history, but she had been estranged from her mother, Catherine, for a year or so now, and besides, her mother was resolutely modern, and hadn't told her much about the past.

Aurélie reached out for the ivory handle of the parasol opposite her, as if something real and tangible could dispel the fog of her strange dreams and scattered memories.

However, when Aurélie clasped the handle, she could feel the gentle pressure of a gloved hand around her own. She shut her eyes again, and in her mind's eye, she glimpsed ivory gloves, which stopped just short of parchment pale wrists, with their skeins of veins lacing delicately through them, like bluebells in forests of snow. Aurélie shook her head. If she were not careful, in another moment, she would be swearing that Violetta was dusting the leather seat beside her with her handkerchief and sitting down.

Aurélie almost thought she could see her now, peeling back her glove and baring her wrist to her mouth so that she could chew daintily on one of her veins. Was it Aurélie or Violetta who was dizzy now, as the taste of refined metal sent her soaring?

Savouring the sweet intoxication of herself, Aurélie laid down the parasol. The watery sunlight of the dying day would not freckle her skin through the carriage window. Though was it sunlight, or the heat of Violetta's breath on her arm and nape?

Perhaps it was all just her imagination. Or perhaps Violetta was a more powerful vampire than she had realized, and really could take psychic possession of her first female reader. But Aurélie did not think that Violetta, reaching out to her from the pages of the journal, meant any harm. Besides, the vampire's intrepid spirit, and the journal's account of her adventures, *was* inspiring. What Aurélie had told her friend Harmony was true. She did want to run away, run away to the circus, run away *somewhere*, anywhere, leave it all behind.

Aurélie placed the fallen bundle of papers back inside the journal and found the place in its pages where Violetta's narrative began again.

I, Violetta Valhallah, of the House of Vladimir of the Sabre, continue to set down a faithful and accurate account of my life thus far, as I journey towards my perilous destiny. I was born human, then became immortal but now I long to die a human once more. I pursue my lover, Lord Darvell, through the forest, through the snow; over land, by rail; over sea, by ship. Cruel and bitter Fate, alas, has caused him to forsake me. Then too, he condemns me for my past misdeeds, although for his sake, I have renounced the taste of human blood, choosing to feast instead upon vermin or myself, in a perfect circle of uborobus-like splendour.

Aurélie realised she had turned over too many pages at once. She turned back the pages more carefully, found the right place, and began to read.

When I first woke up, on what should have been my long sea-voyage from Kief's harbour, it was very strange, for now there was no sea-voyage at all. I missed the rocking of the ship and the lulling of the sea. And where was the light from the stars? For now, it was completely dark, with no stars – no stars! -

and no sense of the sky above me. I reached upwards and my fingertips touched a wooden beam.

Then I knew what had happened. On board ship, they had not been able to rouse me from my slumbers and had presumed me dead. They had buried me, and now I had awoken. Inside my own coffin.

My first task was to escape. Such a long sleep it must have been, for now my nails were long and claw-like. But the lid of the coffin would not yield to my efforts, not even when I pushed against it with all my force. So, then I lay quite still in the dark, wondering what to do next, when, all at once something metallic hit against the coffin's top. I held my breath. Was I being dug out of the earth?

A few minutes later and the lid of the coffin was prised back. Sudden, cool night air cascaded round my face. Then I opened my eyes.

Two grave-robbers screamed; one dropped his spade. It gave a hollow, metallic clang against a neighbouring grave.

I sprang out.

Snarling, my eyes ranged over them. Then I reached out and pulled the shorter of the two towards me and broke his neck. His companion seemed immobilised with fear. I ignored him and found the vein in his friend's neck, then drained him of the necessary blood. It spilled down my lips, onto my chin, and stained the purity of my white death-robe. Blood to me was like wine to another: I had not fed in such a long time, and now it sent me soaring.

I reached out voluptuously to the living grave robber and said in Valerian, 'My arms are hungry for you. Come, lie with me.' Even to my own ears, my voice sounded diabolically sweet.

The grave-robber gave two or three entranced steps towards me, then suddenly reached for the little silver crucifix round his neck and thrust it at me.

I shrugged, gave a *mou* of disdain.

'Go then,' I said. 'If you have no desire to become my immortal companion, then I have no further need of you.

The grave-robber seized the lantern he had set down and fled into the night.

I turned back to his companion and reached inside his trouser pockets for his money. There were a few coins, a few notes clipped together, and something I later learned was a bottle-opener. I made a tear inside my dress and stowed these things away. Then, with the blood feast's remnants of weary strength and exhilaration still coursing through my veins, I dragged my coffin out of the ground towards a stone tomb with a wooden door and a metal padlock.

Along with their spade, the grave-robbers had dropped a metal implement with a twisted head. It was the work of a few moments to pick the padlock using this implement, push open the door and haul my coffin inside the tomb. Now I had shelter for the night. I laid down inside the coffin and slept until morning.

In the morning, of course, I felt differently. I had intended to present myself at the Valerian court, and now here I was, lying in a coffin in a blood-splattered gown. I groped around the coffin's interior. Fortunately, there was enough black silk grave-cloth to tie round my waist as a makeshift apron until I could contrive something better. Then, too, they seemed to have buried me with this, my journal. I removed it from a fold in the grave-cloth and examined it carefully. Miraculously, the leather covers and fine parchment had survived the centuries with scarcely a mark upon them.

The centuries – but which century was it? Was I even in Valerian? I resolved to leave the churchyard and make enquiries of the denizens of this place. I was a stranger in a strange land, so I hoped that what I asked would not seem too odd.

I walked out of the gate of the churchyard. The sign in front of the church named it as St. Swithin's, in a language that did seem to be High Valerian. Then I walked a long way down a quiet road towards an outbuilding with a sign on it that read, 'Lostwithiel,' again, in Valerian. I was glad then that

I had insisted on lessons in both written and spoken Valerian, from the finest tutors, in case Oleg and I should ever go to visit his relative, Prince Nikolai, at the foreign court.

Suddenly, some manner of creature hissed and shuddered before my eyes, then came to a halt: doors swung open, and many, many human beings spilled out. The hissing was overwhelmed by a cacophony of voices as people were caught up in trying to retrieve their bags. In my makeshift attire of a rumpled white dress and a black silk apron, I could not help but admire the bright skirts of women swirling through the lurch of bags and baggage.

I turned my back on the commotion and walked towards a man with a chestnut beard and whiskers, sitting behind a wall of transparent glass. He seemed to be offering advice to the bewildered.

'How can I get to Valerian's royal court?' I asked him.

'Do you mean Buckingham Palace, in London?' said the man behind the counter.

'Is that where the king lives?' I replied.

'You're not from Valerian, are you?' he asked.

I shook my head.

'I didn't think so, see, not with that accent. There's no king on the throne, see. It's Queen Victoria and her husband, Prince Albert.'

'A woman ruler? But that's wonderful,' I cried.

'Yes, she's right enough, and her son Bertie is to reign after her, if nothing happens to him, so then Valerian will have a king again.'

Bertie wasn't a very regal name, I thought. Still, I should like to go to Buckingham Palace.

'Can you direct me to London, please?' I asked.

'Well, you'll need a ticket for the Penzance line,' he said.

'A ticket?'

'For the train,' said the man. 'Don't they have them where you're from?'

I thought it safest to shake my head again.

'You can take the train from Lostwithiel through to London,' he said. 'Do you have friends in the city?'

Now I thought it safest to nod, for what are friends after all, but people we haven't met yet?

The man behind the counter looked me up-and-down.

'No third class compartments on the Penzance line,' he cautioned me.

I produced a crisp banknote from the tear in my dress. 'Is this enough to travel?' I said, smiling, excited by the novelty of my adventure.

The man paused for a moment as if he were wondering how someone so poorly attired could be in possession of so much money. But, by now, there were other people behind me in the queue, and I suppose he decided to give me the benefit of the doubt.

'More than enough,' he said. 'Return?'

What little I had seen so far of Lostwithiel had not impressed me and I was about to shake my head. But then, with a pang, I thought of the sanctuary of tomb and coffin in the churchyard, and I nodded.

The man chewed his bottom lip as he prepared the ticket with his fountain pen.

'Seventeen past eleven, Platform Seven,' he said.

I took the slip of paper in my hands and began to weave carefully through the crowds. On Platform Seven, a man sporting some manner of headgear was ushering people onto the train, gripping the clapper of his bell, and pointing with the handle.

'All aboard,' he cried.

I entered my carriage, something like a stable on wheels, and found somewhere to sit. The seats were wooden, just like in church, but without the fine, embroidered upholstery. My fellow passengers were a young woman with a child leaning against her arm, asleep, and an old man, though in truth I could only see the top of his face and the beginnings of a grey beard just above a very thin sheet of parchment.

'Any person not intending to travel on the train please disembark now,' called a voice from outside.

And then the train hissed, shuddered, and rolled into motion. I held my breath for a moment, wondering if I would fall off my seat now that we were flying. I glanced out of the window to see the platform rolling by before my attention was irresistibly drawn back to the gentleman's sheet of parchment. Beneath a bold title 'THE NORTHERN STAR,' there was a vital piece of information which I had not wanted to ask the man at the ticket office – the date. SATURDAY, MARCH 20, 1888 – some nine hundred years, then, since I had set sail from Kief.

Another piece of bold writing further down the sheet of parchment arrested my attention. 'MURDER IN SHOREDITCH' followed by some smaller lettering: '*About half-past ten o' clock on Wednesday night, a fearful murder was committed by a man named Thomas Brooks, an umbrella-rib-maker, upon Wil. Gilbert, who at the time was living with the sister of the former. The prisoner, when conveyed to the stationhouse, at once confessed the crime, merely assigning as a reason for its commission that had he not shot the deceased, the latter would have shot him.*' Beneath the lettering, there was a picture of the murderer, a smooth-faced, young man with startled eyes and a black bowtie.

'But this is wonderful,' I cried out.

'I beg your pardon?' said the elderly gentleman, lowering his sheet of parchment. I wondered then if it were not quite polite to peruse someone else's reading material. There were so many matters of etiquette I had still to learn. Nevertheless, I pointed to the image towards the bottom of the sheet of parchment.

'To capture the likeness of a human soul and thereby render it immortal without the need for brush, paint or palette,' I said. 'Where can I go to learn more of this curious and beguiling art?'

'Oh, you mean the photograph?' said the elderly man. 'Well really, I'm sure I couldn't say.'

'My sister and her intended had their portraits taken by a photographer,' volunteered the young woman sitting opposite me. 'Half a mo and I'll remember the name.' She blinked, then said, 'Hawkins, that's it. On Preston Street, near the night-market.'

'Thank you so much,' I said. 'You've been exceedingly helpful.' And I decided that Queen Victoria and Buckingham Palace could wait for another day, until I had grown a little more accustomed to the manners of polite society. In the meantime, I was ready to venture forth on a new quest, in the Pursuit of Photographer's Art. I shut my eyes and dozed a little, wondering what adventures awaited me when I reached the end of the line.

As the young woman on the train had told me, the photographers' studio proved to be situated on the first floor of a three-storey building in Preston Street, not so far away, as the crow flies, from the marketplace. The bronze plaque outside the door read *C. Hawkins (A.R.S.A) Photographer & Artist*. Half-way up the building's brown, floral carpeted stairway hung a black-and-white framed photographic portrait of a plaster angel beside a bunch of gardenias. *'Inquire Within'* explained the discreet description beneath it.

Within, I was greeted by a tall gentleman with a flamboyant wig and a purple frockcoat.

'Good day, Miss,' he said.

The walls were crowded with framed photographs of men, women, and children, singly and in family groups. There was also one quite beautiful painting of a very pale young girl, although there were cracks in the paintwork spreading out across her skin. In one corner, superimposed on her lacey sleeve, was the signature, *C. Hawkins, 1885.*

'I see you are admiring my daughter, Ophelia,' said the gentleman. 'But I forsook my first love, Painting, and abundant commissions besides, to champion the Art of Photography.'

He stepped forwards then so that I could see, through the opening reception room-door, a small, bird-boned woman in a lilac robe pouring a colourless fluid from a small bottle into a larger one. She glanced up then and gave me a wry smile.

'You permit women to help you in your Great Work?' I asked in excitement, at which the woman's smile became an outright grin.

'Only my wife,' said the gentleman. 'Come here, Ramona. Miss – er…'

'Violetta,' I replied, as the woman stepped forwards.

'Miss Violetta wishes to learn of our noble calling.'

'No, I wish to *assist* you in your noble calling,' I said firmly. As expressions of doubt crossed their faces, I added, 'I'm strong, diligent and I learn fast. Besides, I have often been told that I have an artistic eye and a… certain something. If you will provide me with bread and board, and teach me everything you know, I will work in your shop and studio every day. And then, if I became proficient in this noble art, I would grant you forty per cent commission on every portrait I make.'

'Why, my dear, you have it all worked out,' said Mr. Hawkins. 'I am lost in admiration.'

'Fifty per cent commission,' said Ramona Hawkins, suddenly.

'Forty-five,' I said.

'Done,' said Ramona.

'Wonderful, wonderful,' said Mr. Hawkins. 'And if we are all to be under one roof, as it were, you must call me Clive. And now Ramona will show you to your room.'

Ramona raised a quizzical eyebrow, to which Clive responded, 'The white-washed attic, of course, my dear.'

'How clever you are, my love,' responded Ramona then.

'Oh, and Miss Violetta,' said Clive, 'you will forgive me for saying this, but you must remember to keep your bedroom door bolted at night. Some of our bohemian friends and their nocturnal habits are a little, how shall we say, *louche*.'

159

'Already I feel quite at home,' I said, tugging at the creases between the splayed fingers of my glove.

'Tell me my dear,' said Ramona as I followed her up another two flights of stairs towards the attic, taking care not to tread on the folds of her lilac dress, 'are you fond of children? We sometimes require a chaperone for our daughter, Ophelia.'

Yet alone at night in my attic room, I felt all too keenly the incongruity of my situation. I even wondered whether I should travel back to the churchyard, and to my peaceful coffin within the tomb. I tried to pray to the moon goddess Selene, but the words stuck in my throat. Then I tried to pray to the Christian God, but I found myself repeating the same phrase, *Pater noster, Pater noster,* over and over, until the words lost their meaning. I remember calling out loudly, who then can I pray to, and still I had no answer by the time I fell asleep. But my dreams seemed to grant me a truth which my waking life could not provide.

In my dream, I saw nine planets, sharply delineated from each other. Three were in a circle of luminous fire, three in a circle of black fire beneath them, whilst another three were below, in a circle of pure ether. All these circles were filled with stars which shone their rays into the clouds, rays that were brighter than the brightest day.

Beneath these planets, at the centre of a giant wheel, was a goddess. Her hair was flame-red, and her skin was ivory and pink. Her head was raised proudly towards the sun, and how she gleamed in its lambent fire. The fingertips of her right hand were stretched out to the right, and those of her left hand were reaching out to the left, forming a cross which extended to the circumference of a circle. Her arms were outstretched in a gesture of power and strength in the white and luminous air. She was riding on a leopard with red eyes, and a mouth that exhaled flame. Beside the leopard, there paced a wolf, a lion, and a bear, alike radiant and gleaming.

I knew her then to be the visionary woman of my dreams in Kief. But how much mightier and more powerful did she seem to me now! She seemed nearer too, as if sailing nine hundred years from Kief to Valerian was bringing me into her orbit.

The fire around her became a sudden, red explosion, clouded with fangs and dark, vampiric eyes. And there was the shape and form of the photographer, Hawkins. Lilac smoke wreathed its way through the fire, and I glimpsed purple eyes and sharper teeth. And that was his wife. And then the lilac smoke drifted into purest white, and at its heart was a very pale young girl, with cracks appearing all over her. And that was their daughter, in the process of Turning. I knew then that the visionary woman of flame was showing me that my new companions were also vampires. My eyes flew open.

I realised that my pillow was red; my bedsheet was purple, and my mattress was white beneath it. These were the very colours of my vision. I decided then not to tell the Hawkins family that I was a vampire too, since their modes of being might not be my own. Better that they think me mortal and weak, than be aware of all that I could do – and then, perhaps, fear me, or threaten me, or deny me the knowledge that I sought.

I would watch and learn all that I could from them, but I would not become part of them. For I was still trying to become all that I could be, and I would not be hindered in any way.

Despite my misgivings, I settled readily enough into the rhythm and ways of the Hawkins household. I knew that Ramona Hawkins had taken a fancy to me when she began to request my attendance at her celebrated Tuesday At-Homes. Quite often, I didn't go, but sometimes I did, and sometimes it proved worthwhile. One week, she informed me, in that brisk way of hers, that there would be a reading of spiritualist poetry from the members of the Dalston Association of Enquirers into Spiritualism. My longstanding correspondence with the Moravian scholars had given me a passing interest in the subject, so I agreed to attend.

However, as one spiritualist poet after another took to the makeshift podium in the newly decorated parlour, my handclapping became less and less enthusiastic. As my own journal entries prove, my standards for literary composition are extremely high. *Trite, pretentious,* and *derivative* were a few of the more flattering adjectives that occurred to me. I was on the point of slipping out of the parlour on the pretext of searching for more cups or saucers, when I noticed, thank Selene, someone who appeared to be as bored by it all as I.

I recognised him. It was the artist and poet, Dante Gabriel Rossetti, whom I had met a few weeks ago when the subject of the gathering had been watercolour painting. Now he was seated at a little occasional table beside the fireplace, entirely ignoring the assembled company, instead scribbling away in a foolscap notebook.

Stealthily, I crept towards him.

'It nearly looks like you are making notes on the recital,' I whispered over his shoulder, so that my breath grazed his cheek 'Nearly, but not quite.'

His dark eyes looked up then, startled, but their expression relaxed into one of warmth and amusement when he realised that it was me. He gave a sheepish smile and angled the notebook so that, over his shoulder, I could more easily read his writing. It appeared to be the draft of a poem, quite beautiful in fact, which he had entitled, 'The Blessed Damozel.'

'Your spelling is appalling,' I told him in the interval when we could converse more freely. 'Unless it's meant to be like that, deliberately pseudo-medieval?'

'No, no, you were right the first time,' he agreed, cheerfully. 'My spelling is atrocious. Family trait. Even though my Father was a Professor of Italian Literature at King's College, he was always writing his letters and numbers back-to-front.'

'That is no reflection on his intelligence – or yours,' I said.

'It does lead to some entertaining errors though,' he continued. 'In the official parish records, my father put a *2* when he meant a *5* for the year of my birth. With one stroke of the pen, he aged me by thirty years!'

Upon occasion, I have a mind for mental arithmetic. 'So, you are actually thirty, then?' I inquired of this personable young man.

'Well, nearly thirty-one,' he said, modestly.

'Would you believe it if I told you my years numbered more than nine-hundred and ninety-nine?' I said, archly.

'Really?' he said. 'You look very well on it. What is your secret?'

'Oh, I'm sure we all have our secrets, Mr. Rossetti,' I replied. 'Unfortunately, it is far too early in our acquaintance for me to share that information with you.'

He bowed slightly from where he was sat. 'Then all I can say, Miss Valhallah, is that I hope to get to know you, much, much better.'

'Hush,' I said, glancing at my programme notes. 'Madame Zozostra is just now beginning her *Ode to Her Resurrected Canary*.'

And indeed, Madame Zozostra, a small, energetic woman wearing a turquoise and crocus-coloured turban and a purple tunic embroidered all over with golden tulips, was even now reciting:

'Hail! Hail! Bright, feathered friend,
Canary Esteemed, beyond compare,
That from Heaven, or near it,
Pourest thy song into the still air.
This is not the moment of thy life's end.'

'I'd pay good money not to hear the rest of it,' Mr Rossetti whispered then. 'Shall we leave this fine, artistic, venue and all these good people, and find somewhere else to be?'

However, what my answer might have been must remain unrecorded, since at that moment, Madame Zozostra began declaiming, even more loudly:

'Ah me! Ah no! In this tranquil even,
You are once more restored to flight,
So, levitate, my love-laden daffodil,
Let us hear again thy shrill delight –
Fly! Fly! Fleet, feathered, Star of Heaven.'

And presumably to create poetic verisimilitude, or at the very least, a Sensation, Madame Zozostra raised aloft her birdcage so that we, the audience, could see that the tiny canary inside was indeed levitating (rather than flying) from its perch. Then, just at the moment when she started to say, 'Fly! Fly!' she unhooked the door to the cage and set the newly resurrected bird free.

Madame Zozostra had not considered that although Ramona Hawkins was all agog for the latest Sensation, she did not want a levitating canary flapping round her fine (and newly decorated) parlour. In fact, Ramona gestured to me that we should try to catch it. And in the midst of the general hubbub, the ensuing squawks and flaps, Mr Rossetti made his departure.

Really, I cannot say that I blamed him, for I knew all too well that young men will do as they please, yet nonetheless, I hoped ardently to see him again. However, since I did not, for some considerable time, I was left to conjecture that it was bird shit rather than my antiquity which had disconcerted him. Instead, in the ensuing weeks, I made the acquaintance of another gentleman, a term I cannot apply to many of the other men I encountered at the Hawkins' photography studio.

As it was, one afternoon, a few weeks later in April, when I was happily ensconced in the photographic studio, rearranging its props, and entirely minding my own business, I first met Lord Edward Darvell.

The studio was not very large, about twice the size of my attic room, but it was ingeniously contrived. Three of its walls were made up of backdrops: one of forests, mountains, and a brooding sky, one of a modern Valerian sitting room complete with striped wallpaper and lined with bookcases, and one, a country cottage window decorated with lace curtains. Then too, there were props to be arranged in endless combinations: leather-bound books, a rocking horse, a dolls' house, a toy locomotive, a mountaineer's walking staff, a bundle of keys, various clocks, a peacock feather, and a small bottle of purple ink.

I had just finished positioning a great golden crucifix above a sword studded with red paste rubies. Now I was standing on a footstool, trying to hang a stuffed raven from some hooks in the ceiling when I heard the footsteps of someone coming up the stairs. A moment later, the door scraped across the floor, and a person entered the studio.

'That's a fine tableau,' a deep, rich, male voice said from behind me. 'It wants but a rose-bush writhing in agony, as if the flowers themselves were gaping, bloody wounds, to complete it.'

'Alas sir,' I said, turning in the direction of the voice. 'I fear I am of a melancholy, nay, morbid disposition.' But then, when I saw the gentleman for the first time, I stood stock still. This handsome man with the saturnine expression and dark frock coat was the very image of my lost Daedalus. See – there were the same eyes, blue as the seas after a storm, there was the same olive-tanned skin and dark, craggy hairline. Only, judging by the few grey hairs in that dark peak, he was some twenty-five years older than Daedalus when he Turned. But otherwise, the resemblance was remarkable.

'Is Hawkins about?' the man said then, adding abruptly, 'must you stare so?'

'My eyes are finely attuned to the Aesthetic,' I told him. 'And no,' I continued, 'he's gone to Smithfield for the afternoon.'

'That's annoying,' he said. 'I wanted to commission him to make a portrait of my daughter, Arabella – and Arthur too, if he wishes, when I return from the Continent.'

'Child photography is considered to be my forte,' I said then. 'Both Mr and Mrs Hawkins believe I am quite accomplished.'

'A female photographer?' he said, 'I took you for one of Hawkin's models, not an artiste. But then, it might answer well enough. The girl is more used to petticoat rule.' And so that was how I came to be hired by Lord Edward Darvell to take photographic portraits of the children, Arthur, and Arabella.

Some months went by. On an appointed Tuesday in the first week of October, I crouched beneath a camera hood in the photographer's studio and stared through the lens, adjusting it slightly, whilst Lord Darvell stood in front of a painted skyline and gazed into what I referred to as 'the distance.' The exposure being made, he was then persuaded to stand in front of the bookcase holding a copy of *Middlemarch* in his hands.

'Ah yes, that infamous chapter,' I said, so that Lord Darvell's glassy expression suddenly grew sharp as he began to read in earnest. Quickly, I made the exposure. 'Just a joke,' I added.

'And now for the charming children,' I said and removed the other props from in front of the backdrops until only the toys remained. Then I unhooked the front of the dolls' house and encouraged the girl, Arabella, dainty enough today in her primrose-coloured frock, to kneel in front of it and arrange the furniture at her whim.

'*Ah, c'est mignonne,*' she said.

'Arabella was born in Ile-Grande, just off Avalon,' Lord Darvell said then. 'Valerian, Arabella, Valerian. Then we can all understand you.'

'I forget,' she said but she smiled, her dimples came out, and the exposure was swiftly made. However, the boy, Arthur, thirteen or so, scowling beneath a dark fringe and skulking next to the governess, proved to be more of a challenge. Finally, I persuaded him to pose beside a spindly table. Then I made the exposure, reassuring Lord Darvell that it need not be paid for or enlarged unless it gave complete satisfaction.

There was a moment's awkwardness for the group photograph. For some reason, the chaperone or governess or whatever she was, Miss Dulcetta, thought she was to be included in the picture. I had to ask her to vacate the elegant chair in which she had placed herself. She shot me a look of such pure venom that I found it hard to believe that an ordinary, insignificant woman could suddenly look quite so evil.

Nevertheless, I posed Lord Darvell, Arthur, and Arabella in the simulacrum of the sitting-room: Lord Darvell stood in the centre, Arabella took the chair in front of him, and then, slightly to the left, his head reaching his lordship's watch-chain and fob watch, stood Arthur.

'Oh, but surely Arthur shouldn't stand *there*,' called out Miss Dulcetta from her seat beside me, 'he will spoil the entire composition.'

'On the contrary,' I said, though it is difficult to be polite when others are not, 'they will form a pyramid, more or less, which will be very pleasing.'

Miss Dulcetta sat there, her hands folded in her white-striped lap, her shoulders ramrod straight, her eyes darting daggers. But I continued to ignore her and dived beneath the hood of the camera to take the picture of the three carefully arranged human beings. A pyramid they formed indeed, with Lord Darvell's head at its apex and the skirts of Miss De Lys and the boots of the boy making up the base.

'Perfect,' I called out then, deliberately.

I remember thinking then that the photographer was also part of the picture, since beyond the essential requirements of talent or creativity or technical skill, it was a little of her soul, energy or essence that helped to make it. But Miss Dulcetta was excluded, not only from the family group, but also from the entire photographic process. Just in that moment, the fire of my annoyance died down and I could not help but feel sorry for her.

Although I had not mentioned it to him, Lord Darvell's portraits were my first big commission, and I was anxious to succeed. Clive Hawkins had in fact wondered whether the commission might be beyond my capabilities. However, I persuaded him to let me have unlimited access to the dark room for a few hours that night. I was determined to do well.

By three o' clock in the morning, there hung suspended from the dark-room's wire the results of my night's labours: a fine photograph of Lord Darvell gazing into the Romantic mists of a mountain summit; a fine photograph of Lord Darvell engrossed in the study of a book; a fine photograph of Arthur, standing beside a table, and a most pleasing composition of the entire family together. However, the photograph of the little girl was an abysmal failure. When her features began to materialise in the tray of solution in front of me, I realised there was a problem. Then, as she twisted before my eyes, she seemed a half-formed spectre, preternaturally radiant. I suspected the problem was with the lighting rather than the development process itself. Nevertheless, this was a disappointing result to set before his lordship.

In the end, I decided that I would take my camera, tripod, and other equipment to Crowcroft Grange later in the day and obtain his permission to make new photographs of his ward. Perhaps, in any case, she would prefer to be out of the studio setting.

I had just locked the dark-room door and was about to climb the back stairs to my attic room when I heard the most horrible commotion from outside. Banging, crashing, bricks being knocked over, bottles being smashed and then a savage snarl. For a moment, I wondered whether these were the Hawkins's hedonist friends, whom I suspected were also vampires. But, in my experience, vampires were silent and stealthy: it was only their victims who screamed. Besides, this noise sounded more like a stray dog or wolf, or perhaps even a bear, let loose in the city. I thought then, unaccountably, of my childhood companion from the Neuri tribe, who changed once a year, without fail, into a wolf.

I drew the lantern up to my eyes, and tentatively unlocked and opened the back door. I shone the light out into the alley. Its flickering rays picked out some familiar, yet dazzled and bewildered features beneath a shock of dark hair.

'Master Arthur!' I said.

His eyes stopped sifting vacantly through the night but widened in surprise when they landed on my face.

'Miss Violetta!' he said, in equal astonishment. A look of confusion crossed his face. 'Has it happened again?'

'Has what happened again?' I asked.

'The sleepwalking,' he replied. 'But to have come this far…'

'There is certainly something strange in all of this,' I agreed. 'I was intending to travel to Crowcroft Grange later today anyway. You can sleep on the settle in the studio for the night, and we can take a train there together in the morning.'

'Thank you,' muttered the boy.

'You're welcome,' I said, then added, 'if you would be so kind, you can help me carry my camera equipment, and I will speak to Lord Darvell on your behalf.'

In the morning, Arthur helped me to pack up my camera equipment and then, heavily laden down, we made our way to Fenchurch Street station, passing the bustling food market, the pretty church of St. Dunstan, and even the Tower of London. But this was no time to play tourist. We soon reached the station with its dome-shaped roof and miniscule clock. Then we found a gentleman called a porter who secured my camera equipment inside the train carriage and gave Arthur a wink.

'Run away from school, have you, young man?'

'Not q-q-quite like that,' stammered Arthur.

'Not like that at all,' I said, frowning at the porter, who tipped his hat to me then made his way back down the platform.

We made ourselves comfortable inside the carriage with its plush burgundy upholstered interior. Arthur sat oppose me, on the other side of a burnished mahogany table. He seemed to want to apologise for the events of the previous night, but he was too sleepy to make much sense. I advised him instead to rest while we travelled the fifteen miles or so to Crowcroft Grange.

I had lived in London a few months now, but it still seemed very strange to be journeying on in this way without any visible cause of progress other than this magical machine, with its soaring, white breath, and its rhythmical, unvarying pace.

'It's an enchanted age we're living in,' I said then to Arthur, 'when steam-propelled dragons run on rails.' He nodded, but presently I saw his hooded eyelids start to close. I settled back into my seat to enjoy the rest of the train journey.

We passed through a built-up area of houses, then there were some raised embankments ten or twelve feet high, then we crossed over an area that was something like moss, or a swamp, upon which no human foot might step without sinking – and yet it bore the tracks which bore us.

Next we passed by a magnificent viaduct of nine arches, the middle one of which must have been quite seventy feet high, until we came out into an entire, beautiful valley. The engine must have been travelling at quite thirty-five miles an hour, Arthur later told me, that is, faster than a crow flies. It was a wondrous sensation, like gliding through air. The motion was as smooth as possible too, and even allowed me a few moments' respite to write up recent events in my journal.

Just as our train pulled in at the station that served Crowcroft Village and its environs, a thunderstorm hit. The bruise-coloured clouds were suddenly lit up and livid with lightning as the heavens opened. We sheltered from the worst of it in the station waiting-room, but still, it was an uncomfortably muddy and rain-sodden walk through the village, whose roofs mingled with trees, straggling up the side of the hills. We paused briefly in front of the church, with its old tower-top that overlooked the fields and pastures that lay in front of Crowcroft Grange.

'Thank you, Arthur, for helping me,' I said then, 'it's very chivalrous of you.' But my words only made him scowl, and we proceeded towards the Grange in silence. Finally, though, he stopped and pointed towards an imposing manor house appearing through the bushes.

'There it is,' he said.

'It's very fine,' I said, admiring the battlements, and then the ivy that shawled the three-storeyed gabled manor house. Its cream front stood out well from the background of a rookery, filled with the cawing tenants that gave the place its name. I watched as crows flew over the lawn to land in a vast meadow, which was separated from the house's grounds by a sunken fence and a line of gnarled oak trees. 'When did you come to live here?'

'Three years ago,' said Arthur shortly. 'I was ten and I came here to live with my sister, who died the following year.'

'I'm sorry for your loss,' I said then. 'That's very sad. My husband died a long time ago, but it feels far more recent to me. Sometimes, I catch myself talking to him, you know, in my mind, as if he were still here.' When Arthur didn't reply, I added, 'I expect you think me very strange.'

'No more than anyone else,' Arthur said, and after a moment he added, 'you're not as bad as that governess. I swear she doesn't like me.'

'Unhappy people don't like anybody,' I said. 'And, sometimes, if they think you are unhappy too, it makes them behave worse. Not everyone likes a mirror.'

Arthur stood still as if to think about what I had said. Then he mumbled, 'I'm sorry for your loss, too.'

He led me forwards, up the shrubbery path, towards the house, but he was much swifter than I. The way was unfamiliar to me, and despite his help, I was overloaded with photography equipment. Then too, the path was wet and slippery with the recent rain, and I was none too steady on my heels.

Arthur reached the house a few paces ahead of me. The door swung open to his tentative knock, revealing Miss Dulcetta, who indulged in much tedious, dramatic handwringing and headshaking before she would let him inside.

'No pudding for *you* today,' I heard her say to him.

'Dr Helton wants me to eat as much as possible,' said Arthur, and really, I thought that was quite a restrained response given the provocation. He turned and grinned at me, then went into the house. I remember, Miss Dulcetta stood there in the doorway, waiting for me as I thought, so I waved at her. But she didn't wave back.

A moment later, I stumbled and down I fell, into the rain and ooze, grazing my leg and quite twisting my ankle, the ankle that had never entirely healed from having the mastiff hound's jaws clamped round it. And well I remember Miss Dulcetta standing there in the doorway of Crowcroft Grange, watching me as I scrambled upright, wincing in pain. Why, I could scarce place my foot upon the ground. Well I remember too, that not a single step did she take to aid me as I rescued my equipment and hobbled towards her.

Ah, it is hard indeed to forget her look of cruel disdain as I lurched along the sodden path. I knew then that as long as we two lived, there would never be any help or kindness from her. But such a one indeed was Miss Dulcetta.

When I reached her standing at the door, I remembered that I had once been the Regent of all of Kief, and I said, as grandly as I could, 'I should like to see Lord Darvell.'

She sniffed and turned her head away from me, but since it was a matter of business, and I was carrying my professional apparatus besides, she could not actively refuse me entrance.

'Follow me,' she said, and she moved forwards and descended some oak steps. I hobbled my way down them more awkwardly, still laden down with the photographic equipment. But then she proceeded to march ahead at such great speed along a lengthy, matted gallery that I could not keep apace with her. So I stopped and sat in a comfortable chair in the great hallway – now I was decided that they should all come to me.

Whilst I waited, I wondered whether I might ever converse with Miss Dulcetta about Russian history. I might advise her to look up the reign of Violetta of Kief, whom I would describe as a distant (and bloodthirsty) ancestress of mine. For Miss Dulcetta's sour, jealous demeanour, particularly in these circumstance, was rather more than I could bear. I am not patient by nature, not docile or placid. And her disposition was something like hartshorn or vinegar-water, when, if she had only yielded a little, we might have been friends. For we were both quick-witted, intelligent women, both accomplished, both attractive, she the fair, red moon to my darker sun.

Now I began to glance at some pictures on the oak-panelled walls. There was one which represented a grim man with a tricorne hat, and another, a lady with a powdered wig and a burgundy velvet dress. A bronze lamp hung from the ceiling, illuminating a great clock at the other end of the hallway, which was ebon black with the passing of the years. The hall-door, which was partly made of glass, was half ajar; a moment later, Lord Darvell had pushed it open and entered the hall.

Then Miss Dulcetta suddenly reappeared, and the way that she darted at him and fussed over him where previously she had been nowhere, made me reflect that he was the reason for her entirely tiresome behaviour. He nodded, not unkindly, to her, then said to me:

'You wished to see me?'

'Yes,' I replied, 'I brought the photographs with me – but I think the one of Miss De Lys will need doing again.'

'You had better come with me and show me your pictures in the study,' said Lord Darvell.

'Yes,' I said, 'though there's also the matter of Master Arthur arriving, somewhat distressed, at my door last night.'

A look of consternation crossed Lord Darvell's face.

'And you brought him back with you? Then I owe you both apologies and thanks, Miss Violetta. But do let us proceed into the study.'

Miss Dulcetta made as if to follow, but Lord Darvell held up an admonishing hand. 'No -no,' he said, 'I'm sure there's plenty to occupy you in the schoolroom. Maybe geography this morning. The new globes have just been delivered.'

'Very good sir,' said Miss Dulcetta in a colourless tone.

'Oh, and Miss Dulcetta,' he said, to her fawn-coloured retreating back, 'if you wouldn't mind just popping down to the kitchens first and telling Cook to organise something substantial for Master Arthur's dinner. He'll be needing it, after venturing so far.'

She briefly turned and nodded, so that I saw a dull pink flush crawl across her neck and cheekbones. A moment later, I stood up and followed slowly after Lord Darvell. I left my camera equipment by my chair and tried to ignore the ache in my heart because his lordship's gait was indeed that of Daedalus.

Lord Darvell's study surprised me because it was both masculine and comfortable. The wallpaper was covered in green vines, and, to my delight, there was a Rossetti painting on the wall beside the door. It depicted one of his models as Proserpine, Queen of the Underworld, with her thick, dark hair, her sullen mouth, her green silk dress, and her pomegranates. Over by the fireplace, there were some sketches in ornate gold frames, and a bust of Beethoven on one of the many bookcases. The shelves were handsome, and replete with books, as well as a fine candleholder of a Chinese dragon.

On the low table in front of the plum-coloured sofa, there was a card-game laid out. Lord Darvell flung himself into a leather armchair beside the hearth.

'Sit,' he said to me, gesturing to the sofa.

'I'm not a dog,' I replied.

He looked startled for a moment and then gave the first genuine smile I had seen since the start of our acquaintance.

'I'm sorry, Miss Violetta. These days, I am more accustomed to speaking to children and servants. It's some months since I was last in polite society, and my manners are a little rusty. What I meant to say was, please sit yourself down.'

I sank gratefully onto the sofa, wincing at the pain in my ankle. But Lord Darvell, so dismissive at first, now looked genuinely concerned.

'An old injury,' I said, 'but I might have to trouble you for a bandage before I leave.'

'A bandage – and a carriage home, Cinderella,' he said. 'What a lot of trouble my household seems to have caused you. But if you would be so kind as to put those cards to one side, you can show me the photographs.'

I did as he asked, then laid the photographs down on the table. 'Good, good,' he said of his own portraits, and 'surprisingly good,' of the group portrait, and then, 'oh dear,' of the picture of Arabella. 'She looks like what she claims she is,' he added, 'haunted.'

'I beg your pardon?' I said.

Lord Darvell sighed heavily. 'Miss Violetta,' he said, 'do you suppose this is a happy household?'

'I hadn't presumed to give the matter much thought,' I replied.

'Oh, by all means, presume,' he said then. 'Whatever you imagine can't be much worse than the truth.'

'But I believe I already told you I was of a morbid disposition.'

'Yes, and I first caught sight of you hanging a raven from the ceiling. I wonder if there is much that would surprise you?'

'You'd be surprised,' I said.

He paused for a moment, as if he were wondering whether he was disconcerted or not. I smiled demurely, which was difficult with my fangs, but not impossible.

'Very well then, Miss Violetta,' he continued. 'Suffice to say, this is not a happy household. My wife Morgana died three years ago, and her brother, Arthur, my young ward, spends all his spare time and all his holidays home from school searching for his missing foster-father. In fact, his school have granted him a holiday now and they don't want him to return until he can sleep through the night without wandering.'

'What about his real father – and mother?'

'I was told that they had both died, and that he was looked after by an elderly friend of the family, whilst my wife was sent away to a school in Avalon. And all Arthur wants now is to find that old man who used to care for him.'

'But don't you care for him, too?' I said.

'Arthur doesn't see it that way,' said Lord Darvell. 'He says only my late wife, or this old man can help him fulfil some mysterious destiny he has in mind. Besides, he blames me for her death.'

'I doubt you're a murderer,' I said, and I remembered how Daedalus could not take a human life but hunted instead the creatures of the forest.

'No, but my wife died expecting our first child.'

'I'm very sorry to hear that,' I said. 'But Arthur is young still, and doubtless still grieving.'

'And not just Arthur,' said Lord Darvell. 'Arabella also lost her own mother, and now, bizarrely, she claims to be haunted by my late wife, whom, by-the-by, she never met.'

'Children have odd fantasies,' I said, but my heart was heavy.

'I thought the governess would be some sort of companionship for her,' said Lord Darvell, 'but they don't exactly seem to get on. Tell me, Miss Violetta, what would you do in my situation?'

I thought very carefully before I made any kind of answer. Though I had the appearance of a young woman of five-and-twenty, it was many centuries since I had been a child.

'I believe Arthur is a good boy at heart,' I said at last. 'He helped me carry my heavy camera equipment here without a word of complaint. Perhaps you should ask the doctor to look at him again and see if he can discern a cause for the sleepwalking beyond what you have told me – or even prescribe a sleeping draught.' I added, almost to myself, 'Just as you can't force a physical wound to heal, neither can you force one of the heart and emotions to heal either.' Then I said, 'As for the girl, well, I would provide rest, exercise, fresh air – and maybe a more congenial companion than the governess.'

'Miss Dulcetta's references were excellent,' said Lord Darvell then, with a sudden touch of testy pride. 'And I'm not in the habit of spoiling children. It won't do for Arabella to get it into her head that the servants are hers – or yours - to dismiss. But yes, as to the exercise and the fresh air and so forth – capital ideas.' He sighed again. 'Do you know, I have no more idea of what children want than I have of reading Hindustani?'

'You could learn,' I said, 'or else you could just ask them.'

He nodded then to a soft pencil portrait hanging near him beside the fireplace. 'I wonder what Morgana would have made of all this.'

I took in the oval frame, and the portrait of the woman with the clear brow, the luxuriant hair, and the expression in her eyes that was both fierce and tender.

'I know her,' I said, before I could stop myself.

'I beg your pardon?'

'I saw a face like hers in my dreams,' I said then. 'In several dreams. Only she was more like a goddess.'

'Part goddess, part harridan, that was Morgana,' said Lord Darvell. 'She would ride roughshod over anyone to get what she wanted. But I admired her for that. There was a directness about her too, that I liked, an unflinching honesty. You have that quality as well, Miss Violetta.'

'Don't bestow her qualities upon me,' I said. 'Lest you be disappointed. I've done enough wrong in my time.'

'You dropped your hymnbook on purpose in church to give your admirer the chance to pick it up? But your one great sin was actually an act of kindness, Miss Violetta.'

'I've done worse than that,' I said shortly, 'and would again, if I had to.'

'One day,' said Lord Darvell, 'perhaps one day very soon, you will tell me all your sins, very slowly, and I will see if I can absolve you of them.'

'I would rather confess to a priest in church,' I replied.

'As you wish,' he said, and with sudden, strange abruptness, he changed the subject. 'Fresh air, sunshine, exercise, excellent. The storm has passed, Miss Violetta, and the sun is just now breaking through the clouds. If you will go and wait in the hallway, I will send Arabella to you and together you can find a congenial spot in the grounds for another photograph.'

'I shouldn't like to disrupt Miss Dulcetta's geography lesson,' I said.

'Nonsense. It's break-time,' he said, gesturing to his fob-watch, the hands of which were pointing to eleven. I had been an hour in his company, and it had only seemed like moments.

Today, the girl, Arabella, seemed a funny, sallow little thing, of eight or nine, with hair the colour of buttermilk. Someone had dressed her in a white dress and coat, and placed a white ribbon in her hair, which did nothing to ease my overall impression of her pallor and discomfort, but would, I supposed, show up well enough in a photograph. The nurse who had brought the child to me gave me a curtsey, and after a moment, Arabella copied her, awkwardly.

'Thank you,' I said, 'but not necessary. Now, Miss De Lys, or may I call you Arabella, you need to help me find a good place where I can photograph you.'

'*Il y a le jardin perdu*,' she said then, in her musical accent that was not the clipped tones of Valerian.

'You're still speaking Avalon?' I said. 'Valerian is not my native tongue, and I only know a few words of Avalon.'

'I will try to speak more properly, Mademoiselle,' promised the little girl.

'Miss Arabella calls it the lost garden,' the servant interposed, 'It's where Madame Morgana used to grow roses.'

'Oh,' I said doubtfully. 'I'm sorry, I don't know your name.'

'I'm Martha, Miss,' said the stout, good-natured woman.

'I'm Violetta. Now we are all acquainted.' I added, 'I had a crimson rosebush once, right outside my bedroom window. Tell me, are there still flowers in the lost garden?'

The child nodded, but uncertainly.

'Very well then,' I said. 'Let us go there.' And to Martha, I said, 'Please, would you mind helping me carry the camera equipment?'

She nodded in agreement and then the child led us out into the grounds and onto a walkway at the back of the mansion. It was covered by a wooden architrave where vines and ivy tangled together in thick and shining clusters. At the end of the walkway was a gap and then there were some steps which led down to a wall, where another cluster of ivy hung, loose as a curtain.

Spots of bright colour crept onto the child's cheeks as she held back this curtain and pushed open the little wooden door behind it.

It opened slowly – slowly – and suddenly we were standing inside the Lost Garden.

It was a strange place, and now in Autumn, there were no roses there, so that I wondered at the child's fascination. But she seemed happy enough gazing up at the palm trees and then the leafless stems which climbed thickly up the high walls. The ground was covered in brown grass, and there were other trees sprouting here and there with tendrils of rosebushes forming a hazy mantle all over them.

'How still it is,' I said, and Martha smiled.

Some early October sun was shining down, and the sky seemed midway between honey-blue and approaching cloud. I thought then that I should get the pictures taken before another storm came. But the child was walking round the garden now, looking in old border-beds and among the grasses.

'What are you doing, Arabella?' I asked.

'Trying to see what's living and what is, *morte*, dead,' she said, in a funny, cross voice. Then she added, more gently, 'if I clear some, some *espace*, there will be room for seeds and bulbs.'

'I could help you,' I said eagerly, before I could stop myself. She smiled, for the first time that day. 'But pictures first,' I said. 'How about over there, under the arch?' And I pointed to a little wooden bench, with a brass plaque on it, half-covered in fallen red and russet leaves.

Arabella picked her way through the long grass towards the bench.

'What does it mean, *In Memoriam Morgana?* That is not Valerian,' she said, reading out the inscription on the plaque.

'It means, don't forget her,' I said.

'Well, and I don't,' said the child, '*Jamais*. I don't forget anyone. My head is full of people.'

'Mine too,' I said.

Martha handed me the tripod and I set up the camera. When I peered through the lens, I thought, here, outside, framed by the arch and the fallen leaves, the child was almost pretty. Then too, there was a greater sense of animation about her, though I knew it was for the garden rather than the camera.

'What shall we do *maintenant*?' she said as soon as the pictures had been taken.

'Let's see if we can take out some of the weeds,' I said, and so we looked round until I found a sharp piece of wood. She took it from me and knelt down and dug out the weeds from the grass. After a moment's hesitation, because of my ankle, I knelt down too, took off my gloves, and began to scrabble around in the soil with my bare hands.

The child grew warm with her exertions, then struggled out of her coat and threw off her hat. I didn't think it was my place to prevent her, though Martha sighed and tutted. Since Arabella paid her no attention, the nurse retrieved the garments, and I thought then that Lord Darvell was right, that Arabella should not be further spoiled. In her defence, however, the exercise *was* warming; Arabella grew quite pink with it as we cleared some places in the ground.

Pink cheeks, bright eyes, and as I watched her dig, I felt a sudden pang that I had not felt since the early days of my marriage to Oleg. For I knew that I would never have a child of my own. Vampires are created, not born. And when Daedalus turned me into a creature like him, he robbed me of my chance to bring life into the world. I thought now, and not for the first time, that there had been something unutterably selfish in his actions. He had told me that he wanted us to save our fellow servants by taking their places, but he had not explained to me what the consequences of his actions would be – nor even, perhaps, thought them through himself. He had secured for himself an immortal vampire companion, but then he had died.

I was not as selfish as he, for though I was at times as lonely and forlorn as he had been, I would not now take the soul of this child to secure some solace and companionship for myself.

'We have cleared some nice little *espaces*,' the girl said then. '*C'est très joli*. The plants will be able to *respire*, no, how do you say it in Valerian?'

'Breathe,' I said.

'*Oui, c'est ça*, breathe,' she said.

'Very good, Arabella,' I said. 'And when I next come back with the photographs, I will bring you a fork and trowel.'

'And will you help me *encore*, Mademoiselle?' she asked, glancing round again at the overgrown garden. 'For there is plenty to do.'

'We'll see,' I said, and she smiled at that, because she seemed to know, as children do, that this meant *yes*.

'Well and were you successful?' demanded Lord Darvell some half an hour later, opening the front door of the mansion to us himself.

'I will know when I have developed the pictures,' I said.

'And she's going to bring me a trowel *and* a fork,' said Arabella, just before Martha took her away to change for lunch.

'That's very kind of you,' said Lord Darvell. 'I have something for you, too,' he added, and he held up what may have been a neckcloth but was now a bandage. 'Sit,' he said, gesturing to the chair in the hallway.

I raised an eyebrow.

'I mean, would you like to sit down, and I will bandage your ankle,' he said.

I sat down and stuck my throbbing foot out. To my surprise, Lord Darvell knelt down in front of me and took hold of my ankle with a grip that was both tender and assured. He then proceeded to wrap the bandage around the ball of my foot, keeping it somewhat taut, with a light pull. Just once, I gasped, but then I bit down hard on my lower lip so that I would make no further sound. After that, he began to circle his way round the arch of my foot.

'You've done this before,' I said.

He nodded and pulled the bandage diagonally from the bottom of my toes and across my foot's top. Then, with something of a final flourish, he circled the bandage once more round my ankle.

'There, see how that feels,' he said.

Gingerly, I removed my bandaged foot from his lap, placed it on the ground, and stood up.

'Better,' I said. I took a few cautious steps. 'Much better, in fact. Thank you. I wish you'd been there after the dog bit me.'

'What do you mean?' he asked.

'That's how I originally hurt my ankle. I was looking through a window and a mastiff hound attacked me. The friend I was with got sent away, and I never saw him again after that. I heard that he died.'

'That's a sad story,' he said. 'It's been a morning for them. But maybe it's time to put the sad things away. Would you like to stay for lunch?'

I shook my head. 'Thank you, but no. I need to be minding the shop and the studio this afternoon.'

A flash of blue fire flared in Lord Darvell's eyes.

'I shall have a word with Hawkins about relieving you of some of your duties. We shall want you here for gardening and the like,' he said, peremptorily.

'I wish you wouldn't,' I retorted. 'My job, the hours I work, are my business.' But then I remembered the tender way he had cradled my foot, and I relented.

'I shall come to lunch next week when the pictures are ready, if I may,' I said.

'If that's the soonest we can hope for, then there's nothing left for me to do but to order the carriage for you,' said Lord Darvell.

'Thank you,' I said and smiled. Glancing down at the bandage, I realised that his initials, *E.F.D.*, were carefully embroidered onto the fine linen cloth. So, I was right: he had sacrificed one of his neckties to me.

My intention was to keep everything that Lord Darvell had told me a secret. However, when I swept up outside the Hawkins's studio on Preston Street in a magnificent carriage drawn by a black horse with crimson plumes, Ramona Hawkins's curiosity was not unnaturally provoked. She decided that she and I must take a walk together to the stationers on Greek Street to choose some envelopes for sending out business pamphlets.

I did not think that I could refuse. She was not only my employer, she was also my only friend and confidante in this vast, strange city.

I wondered if people watching us thought we made an odd pair walking up the street together, Ramona, small-boned, with her heart-shaped face, me, both lithe and ungainly, wreathed in a purple, crushed velvet dress. Over the course of the ensuing walk, her artful friendliness and deliberate questioning drew most of what had transpired from me.

After we had selected some cream vellum envelopes from the stationers, we made our way to a pastry shop on the outskirts of Leicester Square. There was a momentary awkwardness when we realised that neither of us actually wanted a cream cake, and then we each felt compelled to buy one to please the other. After Ramona had finished hers and was licking the icing sugar from her pink lips, she gripped my arm with great enthusiasm.

'What Lord Darvell needs,' she announced, 'is a séance. That will soon find the underlying cause of this ghostly business. And I have the perfect medium for him, Madame Zozostra. Unlike *you*, she still attends our At-Homes every Tuesday.'

I recalled an energetic little woman in a turquoise and crocus-coloured turban and too many beads, as well as her enthusiastic recital of a poem of her own composition - and the ensuing chaos. Why, the canary's erratic antics had quite scared away one of my erstwhile admirers!

'Are you sure?' I said, uncertainly.

'Yes, yes,' Ramona replied. 'You should write to him today, arrange it all as soon as possible.'

'Well, if you think so,' I said, lamely. I could not understand why I was so self-effacing in conversation with her, considering all that I had been previously. For I knew that I still had something within me that was greater than any of them, that I was both ordinary and extraordinary at the same time.

All the same, when I wrote to Lord Darvell, I was as careful as I could be in how I worded the suggestion. I said that I would be delighted to accept his invitation to lunch next week, and that an acquaintance, Madame Zozostra, would be willing to hold a séance at Crowcroft Grange later that same day if he wished. I added that mediumship was a source of comfort and solace to many and might bring a measure of healing to his household.

His reply, by return post, was short and elliptical. *'If it makes you happy,'* he wrote. Still, this was enough to allow me to make the arrangements with Madame Zozostra and the séance was arranged for eight o' clock the following Wednesday evening.

In the meantime, there were still the new photographs of Arabella to develop. She materialised before me in the trays of photographic solution: her pale hair and dress forming a pleasing contrast with the darker bench and fallen Autumn leaves. I was pleased too that in this album of pictures, her expression appeared more carefree and spontaneous. If only this ghost nonsense could be laid to rest, she had every chance of becoming a happy little child. Still, I tried to imagine what having a ghost as a companion might mean to her. Perhaps it allowed her to be something or someone other than a child, or her ordinary, daily self. Perhaps it made her feel as if she were full of strength, ideas, and imagination.

I felt something like that about keeping a journal. The past, my past, leapt back at me in flashes, impossible sometimes to hold onto, and yet I wanted to give myself a history, ground myself in paper.

The day of the luncheon and the séance was grey and raining, and all the better for it. There is too much hope in blue skies, too much flurry and promise, that I can never quite live up to. Unfortunately, however, there could be no possibility of gardening today, though I wrapped Arabella's promised gift of a trowel and fork carefully in newspaper and placed them at the bottom of my bag.

My ankle being now completely recovered, I took the train to Crowcroft Grange as I had once before with Arthur. Believing that punctuality is the hallmark of respect, I arrived promptly in time for lunch, which was served not in the grand dining-room, but in the parlour. Here, there was a three sconce-candelabrum and some white porcelain plates patterned with scattered rosebuds laid out on a small, round table with a white cloth. Initially, I was served with slices of salmon and watercress, which I did not touch, along with some dry toast, which I nibbled. It had been many years since I had enjoyed the kinds of food that humans favoured, though I could still be persuaded to partake of poultry or game. But when I was offered either duck or wild hare, to be served with damson plum sauce, roast potatoes, and red cabbage, I did not know which to choose. So, I ended up with a little of both on my plate.

Two or three times, I was also offered a choice of claret, sherry, or Madeira. In the end, I chose a dry sherry, whilst I showed Lord Darvell the new pictures of Arabella, of which he wholeheartedly approved. 'Much better outdoors. Capital idea, capital,' he said. Then he told me a little about *Middlemarch,* which he had begun reading at the Hawkins's studio, and the astonishment he had felt on learning that George Eliot was a woman.

'Such a masculine-seeming intellect,' he said.

'But the Bell brothers, Currer, Ellis and Acton, they're all women too,' I said. 'The Bronte sisters of Haworth.'

'Surely not,' said Lord Darvell. Then he added, 'Though Morgana always said she didn't believe any man would write like that about love.'

Nor vampire either, I thought to myself, though there was an unintentional resemblance between Daedalus and the young Heathcliff. But I did not wish to labour the point, and instead I sipped my dry sherry. After luncheon, we took a turn about the leafless shrubbery for an hour or so, but then the chill autumn wind brought with it clouds so sombre and a rain so merciless that further outdoor exercise was now out of the question.

So, in the afternoon, we all clustered together in the parlour. Arthur sat at the bureau, poring over his schoolbooks, and sometimes, an old map; however, today there was no homework for Arabella since Miss Dulcetta was visiting her mother. So instead, Arabella took down from the parlour shelf, a jigsaw puzzle of an old abbey in Avalon, Mont-Saint-Michel. She insisted that I sit at the table with her and find all the corners, edges, and pieces of sky.

Meanwhile, Lord Darvell occupied himself with reading *Middlemarch* in a chair in the chimney gable, but his eyes wandered over to what we were doing rather more often than they perused the pages, so that I do not believe he progressed much beyond chapter three.

Later in the afternoon, Martha brought in tea and fruit cake. Then Arabella announced that she was tired, *très très fatiguée*, and well she might be in this house where no-one ever slept. So, she departed to her room for a nap. The ebon grandfather clock in the hallway was just striking the half hour for seven when Lord Darvell asked me to fetch her from her room for the séance - the medium would soon be here.

But when I peered round Arabella's bedroom door, she was fast asleep.

Her room was very pretty — no wonder she liked to spend so much time there. The wallpaper was patterned with forget-me-nots on a white background, and the carpet was the colour of the sky, embroidered with pink rosebuds. The bed where she lay was hung with white muslin curtains spotted with pale blue, looped back with blue silk cords, and her pillows were edged with lace. My eyes travelled over the blue and gold porcelain ornaments on the marble mantelpiece, the twin silver candlesticks in the shape of twisting bluebells, the oval miniatures framed in crinkly gilt, the fluted vase of pink glass holding a bunch of blush-coloured roses with deep serrated leaves, and the little bookcase crammed with picture books and fairy-tales, including, of course, *Sleeping Beauty*.

'Time to wake up,' I called out to Arabella then, and I was right, for at that very moment, there was a knock on the front door downstairs, and judging by the discordant yet musical voice in the hallway, I knew Madame Zozostra had arrived.

After the preliminary greetings were over, Lord Darvell ushered us all into the parlour: the medium, me, Arthur, and Arabella. Then Madame Zozostra locked the door and handed the keys ceremoniously to Lord Darvell. She declined to use a Ouija board on the grounds that it was vulgar. Instead, she took a glass and some pieces of cardboard from her capacious bag and asked Arabella to write the letters of the alphabet onto them. Arabella complied; for once, an obedient child.

A chill descended on us all as Arabella laid out the pieces of card in an as exact a circle round the upended glass as she could manage. Then Madame Zozostra drew the curtains, and the lanterns were extinguished, except for the three-sconce silver candelabrum on the table round which we all sat. Apart from the candlelight, the room was in near darkness.

Each person sat holding the hands of his or her neighbour on either side of him. Lord Darvell sat on my left, his fingers, warm and reassuring, and Arabella on my right: her grip was like my own, icy cold. Arthur held her right hand, and Madame Zozostra, his right, whilst the medium's other hand clasped that of Lord Darvell, and thus we formed a circle of five.

Suddenly, the glass jerked.

Madame Zozostra grabbed hold of the glass which began to skip and dance beneath her fingertips. She coughed, cleared her throat, then said, in a deep voice:

'Which spirit is this? Please, will you tell us your name?'

She put the glass back down and it began to knock backwards and forwards between the shiny pieces of cardboard, the thick, black, childish letters:

RO RE RO RE RO RE

Madame Zozostra turned to us all and said, 'Sometimes spirits are as playful as little children,' and she glared at Arabella, as if was *her* fault that the recalcitrant ghost was misbehaving. Then, 'Who are you?' Madame Zozostra said again.

The glass slowed its crazy dance back and forth, darted to the same letters as before, hesitated, then completed new words.

R O S E   R E D

Beside me, Lord Darvell gave a sudden, sharp, intake of breath. But Arabella was beaming.
'Welcome, Rose Red,' said Madame Zozostra.

H A L L O   A R A B E L L A the glass spelled out.

Madame Zozostra massaged her wrist for a moment, then sighed. Suddenly, there came a loud knock at the front door. The glass jumped up from the centre of the table, flew to the edge, teetered there, toppled off, then shattered on the floor.
'Who was Rose Red?' I whispered to Lord Darvell.
'Morgana's daughter from a previous marriage, who died,' he replied.
And then the door to the parlour flew open and a tall man with bushy eyebrows and dark sideburns stepped into the shadows. He was carrying a large, black bag.
'Many apologies for being late,' he said. 'I was detained at the sanatorium.'
'Not to worry, you're here now,' said Lord Darvell, who added, for the benefit of the rest of us, 'My good friend, Dr Charles Helton, wished to observe the proceedings. He has a theory that the physiology of persons endowed with mediumistic gifts may not be too dissimilar to those afflicted with hysterical illnesses.'
I glanced at Lord Darvell then, his long fingers clenched and jammed into his pockets, his long back tilted against his chair, his legs nonchalantly crossed, and I thought, yes, but you're missing the point. He must have read some of my disappointment on my face, for he added then, defensively, 'His work, not only in obstetrics, but also with Dr Charcot at

the Salpêtrière Hospital for patients suffering from nervous diseases has long commanded my respect and admiration.'

'That's all very well,' said Madame Zozostra tartly, 'but the contact with the spirit world has been broken. We shall have to begin again and try something else.'

So, the séance began again in earnest, with a hymn in which we all joined, and a heartfelt prayer uttered by Madame Zozostra, for divine guidance and protection. After the prayer, we sat, meditating in silence, each person once again clasping the hands of his or her neighbour - only now, with the inclusion of Dr Helton, we were a circle of six. We sat thus for a good thirty minutes, so that I began to grow sleepy, and my arms and wrists to ache. Then I started to pray to the Christian God, in case the vampire goddess Selene did not look too kindly on our activities.

All of a sudden, I felt a chilling current of air sweep through the parlour, which turned the back of my neck to ice. This was followed by the strangest thing, a luminous glow that appeared in the corner of the room. There, within that luminous glow, was the woman I had seen before in my visions: there was the tangle of red-gold hair like molten lava, and the pale ivory skin. She was dressed in a robe that seemed to shimmer, sometimes white, sometimes gold. Madame Zozostra murmured, and I heard something that sounded like a sob from Arabella, by which I judged that they could see Morgana too.

Yet when I glanced round at my male companions, Lord Darvell, Arthur and Dr Helton, there seemed to be no corresponding light of recognition on their faces. However, Lord Darvell's hand newly gripped mine, and I pressed his fingers in return.

Then the hairs stood up on the back of my neck as Arabella began to speak in a voice that was not her own. It was a voice that was broken up by the sound of weeping, a voice that seemed older than Arabella's, though with a similar Avalon accent.

'Maman, c'est moi.'

Now Arabella began to shudder with cold, holding out her arms, rigid and stiff. I watched her struggling then, at the point where opposite impulses sparked and met, where life exploded into death, heat into cold, past into future. She jerked forwards now.

'*They buried me, maman. They buried me somewhere cold and dark.*'

Life and death were speaking through Arabella, life and death were emerging from her parched, white lips, her fixed limbs.

'*They placed a great stone slab upon me. And now I do not know how to come to you.*'

At this, the visionary woman with the red-gold hair reached her arms out towards Arabella, but Arabella took no step towards her. The gap between them was too great and could not be bridged. And for all that she was so fierce and brave, the spirit of Morgana also began to shudder and cry, so heartrendingly, that even if my male companions could not *see* her, certainly they could *hear* her great distress.

It was at this moment that Madame Zozostra came into her own, winning my faith and respect for her and her abilities. For she sprang towards the vision of Morgana and began to intone another prayer, to Valeria:

'*I love the Goddess with all my heart and soul and might,
I call upon the Power of the Light.*'

In the moment after the medium had spoken, Arabella was engulfed in a powerful ray of golden light. Then a radiance rose from the child, which became a beautiful, transparent being, floating up and up: I could see the curtains and the glass tulips of the chandelier through her fair form. The radiance continued to rise, higher and higher, and increasingly ethereal, until she was no longer there.

But she had not returned to the spirit world, oh no, for Arabella fell back against her chair, smiling with what she knew had happened. And when she spoke again, it was with her own voice.

'Rose Red is with her mother now. Her spirit is with her mother in Avalon.'

'Yes, Morgana has her daughter back now,' said Madame Zozostra, and I heard something in her voice which was so rare, it surprised me. *Kindness.* Then, as we turned to the visionary Morgana, we women could see that the expression on the spirit's face had changed. All the sharp angularity of her beauty had softened, and now her face seemed simple and pretty and young. Her reddened lips moved, and I thought perhaps she was trying to thank us.

'Wait,' said Madame Zozostra. 'She's trying to say something. She wants something else.'

'That's like her,' said Lord Darvell.

'It's hard to understand what she's saying. Something like, *In Memoriam Morgana.* And something else. *Rex quondam, Rexque futurus.*'

'The once and future king,' translated Lord Darvell. 'But what does she mean?'

For a brief moment, another ray of luminous light appeared, not to rise, but to fall, this time on Arthur, so that he temporarily appeared radiant, uplifted. However, the luminous glow only lasted for a moment before it dimmed.

The vision of Morgana faded from our sight and now, despite all her prayers and incantations, Madame Zozostra couldn't persuade her to return. Arabella also closed her eyes, calling out to Morgana, seeming, by the sheer force of her will, determined to bring her back. She prayed so hard that her fair, curly hair became damp with sweat, and she fell into a slump against me. She was a thin child. I wondered why, in such a wealthy household, she was so thin.

Lord Darvell restored the lights and Madame Zozostra gripped hold of Arabella's wrists whilst I passed my smelling-salts beneath her nose. Eventually, she emerged from her swoon-like trance, and looked at me, sadly.

In the restored light of the parlour, it became obvious that Arthur was sobbing.

'Why are you crying?' asked Dr Helton.

'She told you,' Arthur said. 'She told you; she told you, she told you and none of you understood.'

'What do you mean?' asked Dr Helton.

'Don't you see? The once and future king?' said Arthur. 'She meant me. But it's no good. None of this is any good. No matter what I do, without Merlin to help me, I can't make any of it happen. The kingdom will perish in fire and blood, and it will all be my fault – but then none of you will have lifted a finger to help me, either.'

'I see what you mean,' said Dr Helton, but to Lord Darvell. Then he said to the boy, 'Lord Darvell tells me you sleep badly, Arthur. Supposing I prepare you a sleeping draught and we have a little chat.' Speaking across Arthur's head to Lord Darvell, he added, 'The treatment at Saint Cosmas & Damian's Convalescing Home would be as we discussed.'

'I won't go there,' said Arthur fiercely. 'You can't make me.'

'Go where?' asked Arabella, her eyes, wide and petrified.

'This isn't a conversation to be had in front of children,' I said. 'Arthur, Arabella, why don't you find me a story you would like me to read you and then the grown-ups can finish what they have to say.' I nodded politely to Madame Zozostra, who had impressed me with her warmth and wisdom. However, I barely inclined my head to the men before I departed with the children.

In Arabella's room, I reached into my bag and found the fork and trowel, wrapped, at the bottom. I gave them to her; she unwrapped them and placed them beneath the lamp on her nightstand, so that the silver prongs and spade shone in its apricot glow.

'I'm sorry it was raining too hard to garden today,' I said.

'The garden will still be there *demain encore*,' said Arabella.

Then the three of us sat next to each other on Arabella's bed. I was in the middle, with Arthur on my left and Arabella on my right, leaning her head against my arm.

'What did they mean about the Convalescing Home?' asked Arthur.

'It isn't something to be frightened of,' I said. 'I suppose it's just a place people go to for rest when they haven't been very well. And Lord Darvell is worried about you. You don't sleep, you hardly eat, and he doesn't know how to help you.'

'Merlin would know how to help me,' said Arthur.

'There was a Merlin once,' I said. 'He was a very wise man; some say a wizard or a magician. But he lived hundreds of years ago. You can't mean he was your foster-father?'

'Yes, I do,' said Arthur, earnestly. 'I don't exactly understand it, but it seems to me that Merlin and Morgana and I all lived once before, hundreds of years ago. But when I try to think about it too much, it all fades away, like a dream.'

'And was I there too?' I asked him. 'And Arabella?'

'You, maybe,' he said, 'but not Arabella. She's just a little girl.' He paused and looked puzzled. 'Though there was another little girl, in a stained-glass window. And a woman, holding her, passing fair.'

'I'm not just a little girl,' retorted Arabella. 'Morgana and Rose Red appeared to *me*. They wouldn't have done that if I was just *une vraie petite fille. Bah!*'

Arthur flushed, and I knew he was upset that his sister Morgana had not appeared to him, had said very little that was intelligible about him, apart from the Latin phrase, *Rex quondam, Rexque futurus*, the once-and-future king.

'But how can that be, Arthur?' I said now. 'How can you and Morgana and Merlin have lived hundreds of years ago, and then again now?'

'I don't know,' said the boy, stubbornly. 'I just know it's true. Like I know that Merlin didn't abandon me on purpose. The neighbours where we were said that he was an old man, and that perhaps he was sick and had gone away to die. But he wouldn't have done that, not without telling me, not when he was in the middle of teaching me so many things. After all, he didn't know Morgana would find me and bring me to Crowcroft Grange.'

'Well, what do you think happened to him, then?' I asked.

'I think it must have been a Magical Disappearing,' said Arthur solemnly.

'A Magical Disappearing?' I said, 'and tell me, Arthur, what was it that Merlin was teaching you?'

'He called it the Rudimentary Art of Shape Shifting. But there was so much more to learn – and so much that I have already forgotten.'

'No wonder you don't sleep,' I said to Arthur. 'That's a lot of ideas running around inside your head.'

'Sometimes I sleep,' he said. 'Sometimes I dream about how it all used to be. Or I dream that I'm floating towards a beautiful island with my sister. But when I wake up, I don't know how to get there, or how to make it all happen and then I'm so sad. And, sometimes, I wake up a long way away from where I went to sleep, and then everyone gets frightened. Even me.'

'That doesn't frighten me,' I said. 'I once went to sleep in Kief and when I woke up, I was in Lostwithiel, and it was ever such a long time later. And I had a dream once, about a king being rowed towards an island to be healed, though I don't know if he ever got there. I thought I was dreaming about my husband, Oleg, but perhaps I was dreaming about you.'

'You're the only one who believes me, then,' said Arthur.

'I believe you,' said Arabella, stoutly, *'mais m'explique encore.* Explain to me again.'

'Tomorrow, he can,' I said. 'I promised I would read you something and then you should both try to sleep.'

But the book that Arabella pushed into my hand wasn't the volume of fairy tales that I was anticipating. Instead, it was an illustrated copy of the *Hail Mary and the Angelus for Children*, written and printed in Valerian. I wondered why she had chosen that, but when I looked at the inside cover there was a picture of two children praying. The girl in the picture was fair-haired, with a look of Arabella, and the boy was dark-haired, with a look of Arthur. I thought then that though she may not be his kin, still, she is his sister, and she loves him.

'That's a very nice picture,' I said.

'You're never cross, like Miss Dulcetta,' said Arabella, cuddling into me.

'Well, Miss Dulcetta has to teach you things,' I said, 'whereas I don't have to teach anyone. I'm still learning things myself.'

'What sort of things?' asked Arabella.

'Photography, mainly,' I said. 'And people. But suppose we each take it in turns to read a page of this book, and then it really will be time to go to sleep.'

And so that was what we did, and as we each read out the words of the ancient and lovely prayers, I tried so hard to send up holy thoughts to whichever deity was still listening to me, on whichever hopeful planet or star.

After Arabella had fallen asleep and Arthur had retreated to his room, Lord Darvell asked me to spend the rest of the evening with him in the parlour. I still did not quite know what to make of him, and I felt too a curious sense of capricious shyness. I surmised that he took pride in his fine voice, so as twilight began to settle like gauze across the sky, and the evening star shone then her face, I rose, opened the piano, and entreated him to give me a song. He said he would rather sing another time, but I insisted that there was no time like the present.

So, after some protesting, he took his place on the piano-stool, and proceeded to accompany himself, for he could play as well as sing. I retreated to a window-seat, and while I sat there and looked out on the still trees and dim lawn, he began to sing, in mellow tones, the following song:

'I dreamed it would be nameless bliss,
   As I loved, loved to be;
And to this object did I press
   As blind as eagerly.

On sped my rainbow, fast as light:

I flew as in a dream;
For glorious rose upon my sight
That child of Shower and Gleam.

My love has sworn with sealing kiss,
With me to live – to die;
I have at last my nameless bliss
As I love – loved am I.'

There were other verses too, but those were the ones that I chiefly recalled. And when he had finished singing, he rose and came towards me, and his face was all kindled, and once again his eyes flashed blue fire. I quailed momentarily, then I rallied. Soft scene, daring demonstration, I would not have, and so the weapon of choice must now be prepared: a confession of vampirism.

When he sat down next to me on the window-seat, I edged a little further away.

He said that I had 'a cold little heart' and he added, rather immodestly, I thought, 'that any other woman would have been melted to the marrow at such singing, such playing.'

I assured him that I was naturally hard, very flinty, and that he would often find me so, then I added, 'for you know, of course, that I am a vampire.'

He paused for a moment, then said, 'Really?' as if he did not quite believe me. He added, 'Well, I suppose there have been rare cases of vampirism in Valerian. A notable one being Sir Pinel Le Savage – I was reading about him the other day. Although, of course, he was also cursed with many other afflictions, too mysterious and horrible to mention.'

'I have heard of him,' I replied. 'His handbook of *One Hundred and One Deadliest Poisons* remains the definitive text. But, you know, I am not actually from Valerian. I'm from what you would nowadays call Russia.'

'I did wonder at your accent. But *nowadays*? How old are you?'

'I believe, nine hundred and ninety-nine, though it is difficult to be exact.'

'That sounded exact. So – you *really* are a vampire, then?'

'Yes. I wouldn't say it otherwise. I believe the Hawkins family are too, but from a different, more modern bloodline.'

'That would explain quite a lot,' he replied. 'I was never fully convinced by their forays into hedonistic yet industrialised bohemianism.' He paused again, for a lengthy moment, then added, 'Do you think vampirism is the problem with Arthur?'

'No, I think it's something else with him. We can't all be vampires. Well, we can, but it would require a great deal of effort and besides, Creator vampires tend to be quite choosy.'

'So, you have no desire to turn me into a vampire?' inquired Lord Darvell, sounding crestfallen.

'None at all,' I said. 'But what *I* wish is to relinquish vampirism and become human.'

'It would certainly make things easier,' he replied. 'But how do you propose this should happen?'

'There is one method popular in Upper Moravia - but I always thought it wouldn't work for me, since I believed my Creator, Daedalus, to be my soulmate. Unfortunately, he was both a vampire and murdered.'

'The boy you told me about?' he asked.

I nodded.

Lord Darvell stood up abruptly and walked quite to the other side of room. When he had collected himself, he asked, 'And what is that method?'

'A vampire who finds his or her human soulmate and is truly in love can gradually return to human status again,' I said, rushing over what was tantamount to a declaration as quickly as I could. 'It is quite a simple process though I have given it a complex name from an untranslatable word. I call it *The Titrations*. It requires the vampire to make a solemn vow never to take another human life. Then he or she must drink his or her soulmate's blood, incrementally lowering the quantity each day, until he or she no longer has the desire to drink any more. On that day, the vampire becomes human.'

From the other side of the room, Lord Darvell said, in a state of contemplative dudgeon, 'I have always supposed that the blood in my veins serves a thoroughly useful purpose.'

'Yet it might serve an even better purpose in mine,' I said, as deferentially as I could, for my task was not an easy one. In my heart of hearts, I knew that a lamb-like submission and turtle-dove sensibility, whilst fostering his despotism more, would have pleased his judgement, satisfied his common-sense, and even suited his taste, less.

When there was no answer from him, I said, 'Perhaps you would call for the carriage to take me home?'

'Oh stay, stay, by all means stay,' he said. 'You can ask Martha to prepare you a room for the night. It will give me a chance to think over your extraordinary request before I see you again tomorrow.'

'Thank you,' I said, and I was about to depart, when he added, almost to himself, 'Since Morgana died, I have sought my ideal of a woman amongst Valerian ladies, Avalon countesses, Italian signoras, and German grafinnnen. I could not find her. Sometimes, for a fleeting moment, I thought I caught a glance, heard a tone, beheld a form, which announced the realisation of my dream, but I was always undeceived. How then can I know that you are what you claim yourself to be, my soulmate?'

I was surprised by his words, because I had thought that this was by far the simplest, most obvious part of the Titrations.

'Don't you just feel it?' I said.

'Well, I suppose I knew,' he said, 'that you would do me good in some way or another, at some time. I saw it in your eyes when I first beheld you, in your expression and your smile. But now everything you tell me seems different from what I believed.'

'I'm still me,' I said.

'But you're a vampire,' he said.

'And I'm honest about it,' I said.

'Well yes, you are that,' he said, and he looked as if he recalled other people and other times that would make him value honesty as a rare attribute. The strange, angry fire in his look vanished and his face softened. He stepped back towards me, still sitting on the window-seat, and held out his hand; I gave him mine: he took it first in one, then in both his own.

'I think I hear Martha in the corridor,' I said after a few moments. But still he retained my hand, and I could not free it.

'What! You *will* go?' he said.

'You said to ask her to prepare me a bed.'

'Bed. Yes. Go then, Violetta, go.' He relaxed his fingers and I was gone.

With Martha's help, I found a room for the night, but I could not sleep. I felt as if I were being pummelled by billows of trouble under surges of joy. I thought I saw at times a far distant island with white sands and a turquoise sea, and then my spirit longed to rise up triumphantly towards it. And yet I could not reach it, even in fancy, since a counteracting breeze drove me continuously back. Too feverish then to rest, I rose as soon as the day dawned.

It was a long time since I had last fed, and I thought I might yet find me some quail or peahen lurking in the mansion's grounds. Outside, in the garden, my bare feet trod the grass, soft with dewdrops, as quail's blood trickled down my throat. Then, as the early morning mist began to disperse, the river below glittered silver, like a blade.

I had expected to see Lord Darvell at the breakfast-table, but he did not appear. Since the day was fine and clear, Arabella pressed me to help her in the garden in the afternoon. In the morning, she must attend her lessons with Miss Dulcetta. Whilst she was thus occupied, I went and sat on a blue sofa in a little bookroom outside the study. Here, I proceeded to update my journal. Promptly after twelve, Arabella came bounding out of the schoolroom with her governess. Miss Dulcetta shot a curious glance in the direction of my journal, but after a moment or two, she nodded at me without any discernible malice. I thought that perhaps the visit to her mother had done her good and I wondered how more of them could be arranged.

Lord Darvell finally appeared at luncheon, looking heavy-eyed and bleary. He complained too of a pounding headache, so that I wondered if he had finished off the contents of the brandy decanter after I had departed. Perhaps the news of my vampirism had disturbed him rather more than he had admitted, or perhaps this was his customary behaviour. At any rate, with Arabella present, there was little that I could say to him on the subject. He did, however, issue an invitation for me to remain another few days.

When I protested about work, he said that he would write to the Hawkins family, telling them I deserved a short holiday. When I protested about a lack of clothes, he said that Martha had the matter in hand, that she was in the process of refurbishing some dresses from the attic for her winter wardrobe and would be happy to find me something to wear. Then, when I had nothing left to protest about, he laughed to see me so confounded, and invited me to spend the evening with him. From this, I inferred his tacit consent to my proposition. Of course, it would be embarrassing if I were mistaken.

Shortly after lunch then, I asked Martha to direct me to the nearest apothecaries in the village. I told her that I needed a little laudanum for Lord Darvell's headache, as well as some lavender water and other such items that comprise an essential part of a lady's toilette. Though she was a stout and hearty soul, I did not feel I could tell Martha the rest of my purpose, which was to purchase some syringes and a plentiful supply of bandages. For, since my adaptation of the Titrations was to be based on science rather than bloodlust, I had decided that though I myself would puncture the requisite arteries, still I would require syringes for the crimson harvest.

After I had returned with the essential items and stored them away in a drawer in my room, Arabella and I spent the afternoon in the lost garden. For all that it was bleak and bare at this time of year, still, in her fancy, the plumtree would soon bloom snow-white with blossoms and musical with bees. She said it would be like a fairy-queen's canopy. Then, too, there would be flowering cherry-trees and apple-trees resplendent with pink and white buds. That she could envisage all this when all I could see were barren twigs and shrubs, the feather of a raven newly dropped on the grass and the empty shell of some bird early hatched, was remarkable.

We went into the house and had dinner; then, that evening, the Titrations began.

My late husband, Oleg the Vangarian, was not entirely the savage barbarian that my earlier descriptions may have implied. Above all, he had wanted me to be happy. This meant that whenever foreign visitors came to our castle, I was encouraged to talk to them, in their own language, if I could. And if ever I had a desire to learn something, Oleg would be sure to engage a tutor for me. Books were very rare at that time, but whatever we could lay our hands upon, I had read, and enriched my storehouse of knowledge with their contents. Then, too, I was an ardent correspondent. Having paid for their secrecy with as many roubles as they desired, I had long been writing letters to a band of scholars from Upper Moravia about the customs, treatment, and cure of vampirism. It was from them that I had first learned of the cure which I named the Titrations.

Arithmetic has never been my natural forte, so I took some time to work through the calculations in their letters. I believed that I should begin with a transfusion of four gills of blood from the subject, injected into my own veins. This quantity should then be reduced by a half gill of blood on seven subsequent occasions, which process, if followed correctly, would allow me to transform from vampire to human. The scholars from Upper Moravia had stated that men were preferable to women as blood donors since they bleed more and are less liable to faint. Nevertheless, they acknowledged that there might be considerable difficulty in obtaining arterial blood from the human body for the purposes of transfusion: however, a true and beloved soulmate *might* consent first to the act of lovemaking and then to the opening of a vein or artery.

I rated my charms and powers of persuasion as high, but were they high enough? I felt that there would be more chance of success if I appeared to let Lord Darvell have his own way entirely, at least for this first evening, and that this would make the process more pleasant, pleasurable even, for both of us. I asked Martha for some fruit, biscuits, and a pitcher of water to be placed in the parlour, though, in fact, throughout the evening, Lord Darvell helped himself fairly liberally from the brandy decanter. I wished he would not but judged it not to be the evening for quarrels.

Later, I allowed him to play some sad song on the piano, *Rose elle a vecu,* about a beautiful flower that had a sad destiny. As he played, it occurred to me that his heart was wounded and that he sought to mend it in music. Then, as he turned the pages of his music-book, I laid my syringes on the table. I am not sure if he saw them, but a few moments later, he stopped playing, smiled, and said, 'Are you the gentle soul that will lure me to my ruin?'

I shook my head and asked him to continue playing.

As the song drew to a close, I went and lay upon the sofa and loosened my skirts. Then, after a moment or two, and with a questioning look, he joined me. There is more that could be written of this first lovemaking, but modesty impedes my penmanship. This journal, too, is an account of the finer philosophical and scientific musings of the female vampiric mind, intended for my own eyes only. Should I require literary titillation, I would read *The Memoirs of Fanny Hill.* And yet, in the sublimity of that moment, I felt something that I thought was love. I was not sure, because my heart had been so bruised and scarred by everything that had gone before. All I could be certain of was that I did not want that feeling ever to go. But, in that self-same moment, I feared it would forsake me, just as Daedalus once had.

But in that one moment how fine and lovely we were, how fair, and how exquisite it was to be alive in the world, whether vampire or human, but just to be there, together, on the sofa beside the piano, all bright and glistening in the moonlight.

Afterwards, I stepped back into my dress and approached a glass-fronted cabinet near the piano. From there, I removed a fine, golden goblet.

'Can you put that back, please?' he said, not as entirely lulled as I should have liked.

'But nothing could be too fine for my purpose,' I said.

'The goblet is a sacred vessel. It belonged to Morgana, who had received it from a relative of hers, Elaine of Astalot. It is reputed to have once held the blood of Christ.'

'Then it would be entirely fitting,' I muttered, but the stern look on his face made me comply, and instead I selected a glass with a fine, amber stem.

I approached him, sat down beside him, and licked the skin of his neck with slow concentric circles until, by the slowing of his heartbeat, I judged he was more relaxed. Then I bit into his neck's external jugular vein and began a slow, sucking process to make the blood flow to the surface more freely. If his heartbeat were to slow too much, that would, of course, be a warning to stop, so I was as careful as I could be. Then I held the glass to the scarlet fountain. Once the glass was filled, I applied the bandages to the vein.

When I recalled his tender bandaging of my ankle, I was concerned that my manner might seem brusque, but it was imperative to staunch the flow of blood as quickly as possible.

Then I sipped a little blood from the glass but transferred the rest to the syringe. The taste of it started to send me into a state of intoxication - I had to steady my shaking hands in order to inject the rest into my own veins. I had taken four gills of blood, that is, sixteen ounces, which would require around six hours to circulate my own bloodstream - although the amount of blood and time required would decrease with each subsequent Titration.

'Next time, no brandy,' I said as his blood began to soar round my system. 'It thins the blood too much and it's making me dizzy.'

'I found it necessary,' he said, a shade wanly.

'It will be easier next time,' I said. 'I won't need so much blood.' As his blood drip-dripped slowly into my bloodstream, I gave him glistening segments of tangerines, some grapes and oat biscuits from the basket on the table, all to restore his strength. Then I went and lay against him on the sofa for the next few hours, and so we rested like that, fitfully, until dawn, when the process was complete.

There were another two Titrations on two subsequent nights, but Lord Darvell and I both found the process quite fatiguing, and it was perhaps this that led to the minor quarrel that blew up in the coming days. Lord Darvell remained concerned for Arthur's health, which had in no way improved, and encouraged by Miss Dulcetta, he continued to suggest that the boy might be better in Dr Helton's sanatorium.

However, I thought since Arthur was only a child, it was unlikely that one so young would recover surrounded by sickly neurasthenics so much older than himself. I remember saying to Lord Darvell, 'Surely it would be better to send him and Arabella on holiday together, somewhere by the sea.'

'But Dr Helton is very much respected in the medical community,' Lord Darvell protested. 'He devotes endless hours shut up inside locked wards, contemplating those poor unfortunate souls smitten by all sorts of enfeebling and incurable disorders.'

'And much good that does them – and him!' I replied.

Somehow, in the course of the ensuing conversation, I declared that Miss Dulcetta's recommendation was motivated by her strong antipathy towards Arthur, an antipathy which puzzled me, since she was not required to teach him. I wondered if it was because he was a link with Morgana, and that there was some jealousy afoot – or, as I had told Arthur, his perceived unhappiness reminded her of her own. At any rate, I stated that I was by now heartily sick of her petty rivalries and vengeful plots.

    I think Lord Darvell could discern that I had Arthur's welfare very much at heart, but all the same, a slight coolness arose between us which was not conducive to the continuation of the Titrations.

I thought it would be better if I returned to the Hawkins's studio to give everyone at Crowcroft Grange the gift of missing me, as I flattered myself that they soon would. Besides, in all this new excitement, I had entirely neglected the Hawkins family, and my work with them.

    Unfortunately, I packed to depart so hastily that I forgot my journal, which I had tucked beneath the mattress of my bed. As I clambered off the train, I could only hope that no-one would find it between now and my next visit, although I reassured myself that the first and most controversial half, at least, was unreadable to anyone except myself.

    Ophelia, in particular, was pleased to see me, especially as it had been decided that she would now help me in the studio, so that Clive Hawkins found himself with two photographic pupils. Sometimes he spoke, airily, of founding a School of Photographic Arts for Young Ladies. Then the Brighton School of Photography became a fond and favourite dream, and he went as far as to have a prospectus printed, offering photographic lessons and a sliding scale of fees.

    A week or so later, a note arrived from Arabella. In her best Valerian handwriting, she invited me to tea and promised that the carriage would be available to take me to and from the station. As the horses pulled into Crowcroft Grange's courtyard, there was Lord Darvell, standing in the mansion doorway, with his hands in his pockets. His smile and subsequent gesture of welcome revealed that he harboured no ill feelings.

Over the course of tea in the parlour, he asked Arabella, 'What would you like for your birthday?'

'A ball,' announced the little girl, who was to be ten.

At first, he seemed reluctant to gratify her whim, but when, over the course of the conversation, it emerged that my birthday was just three days before Arabella's, he became more reconciled to the idea. However, Miss Dulcetta, sipping her tea in a way that was distinctly grating, thought differently.

'A ball for so young a child with her particular Avalon propensities will only encourage her Vanity,' she said, coolly. She rattled her teaspoon in her cup.

I began to wonder if, and when, I fed on her, I could stomach the mawkish blood that flowed through her veins. Damn the Titrations, which prohibited such actions!

Thankfully, Miss Dulcetta's objections were overruled.

'I fear my own propensity towards Vanity is even more pronounced,' said Lord Darvell, at which she simpered. Then he poured the governess another cup of tea, and so a measure of harmony was restored to the party.

Another Titration took place that evening, and before I left in the morning, I remembered to retrieve my journal from beneath the mattress in my old room. The next few weeks were busy, and I travelled backwards and forwards between the studio and Crowcroft Grange on several occasions.

The next three Titrations took place in this time, and we also compiled the guest list for the ball. It was to be kept short, just ourselves, Ophelia Hawkins, and Lord Darvell's friends, Dr Helton, and Lord and Lady Bloodhart. The food was ordered; and it was arranged that on the night of the ball, the ballroom would be festooned with flowers, candles, and the crystal dinner service.

Then it was the 8th of November and my birthday, a peaceful one since Miss Dulcetta was again visiting her mother. I decided to discount the nine hundred years and more that I had been asleep and number my years instead at twenty-six.

I had stayed at Crowcroft Grange the night before, and there were gifts in the morning: a pair of opera gloves and eyeglasses, a mother-of-pearl hairbrush and hairclip, an ivory-handled mirror and a cloisonne purse to put them in. From Arthur and Arabella, there was a string of ebony beads, and each seemed pleased to learn that they had the day to spend as they wished. For, later, the coachman drove Lord Darvell and I back to the studio on Preston Street. We sat opposite each other in the carriage, sometimes smiling, sometimes looking away.

Ophelia Hawkins greeted us once we arrived. She seemed to have shot up in the last few weeks, so that I was reminded of Tenniel's illustration of a long, tall Alice in Arabella's copy of *Alice's Adventures In Wonderland*. All the same, I was glad to see Ophelia no longer affecting the air of a languid, Pre-Raphaelite maiden. Instead, she bustled busily about the studio, then showed me into a small room with a wash basin and two full-length mirrors.

It is a myth that vampires do not care for looking glasses, for how else are we meant to gratify our own narcissistic self-obsession? Now I pulled my hair back and bound it so severely that it accentuated my fine bone-structure. Then I threw some cold water onto my face and applied a little rouge to my habitual pallor. I blotted my lipstick and adjusted the white cameo at my throat. The new ebony beads suited my dark dress with its pale stripes and brocade buttons. I looked what I felt myself to be, *distinctive*.

I left the little cloakroom with its bristling clothes-hooks and hat-pegs and stepped out into the studio. There I was pleased to discover a new backdrop, set up, so I fancied, in honour of my birthday. It consisted of a beautiful round oriel window with a pale green, rustic bench built into it. The window looked out onto a painting of a wild garden, with a profusion of dark pink roses and clusters of purple hyacinths. There were little ornamental trees in the foreground that gave way to a grand sweep of majestic chestnuts and oaks.

I sat down on the bench and arranged my skirts carefully.

I was pleased to discover that Ophelia would be taking the photograph. At nearly sixteen, she had a fine eye and an excellent sense of composition, and it was good that she now had something more exciting than watercolour painting as her artistic outlet.

'Keep your eyes open without blinking,' Ophelia said importantly from beneath the camera hood. 'And remember to smile,' she added. Lord Darvell came and stood beside her then, to get a better idea of the shot.

'Ideal, ideal,' he said.

I smiled and Ophelia got the picture that he wanted.

It was on my birthday, too, that Lord Darvell began to speak again, and seemingly more in earnest, about my leaving the Hawkins's studio for good.

'And do what?' I asked.

'Keep me company?' he said. 'Possibly some light gardening with Arabella?'

I couldn't tell if he was teasing or not, so I flared up anyway. For women suffer from too rigid a restraint, too absolute a stagnation, precisely as men would do, and it is wrong to laugh at them if they seek to learn more and do more than custom has decreed for their gender.

'I need exercise for my faculties and a field for my endeavours,' I said. 'It is narrow-minded to say that I ought to confine myself to making puddings and knitting stockings, to playing on the piano and embroidering bags.'

'Can you actually do any of those things?'

'I can knit a bit. I'm not bad at making pies but I don't eat them.'

'Well, I believe that all people, men, and women, should be encouraged to do what they are good at - and enjoy. I have never asked you to knit, and it is not likely that I ever shall. Besides, why eat pies when you can order steak, or oysters and champagne?'

'Isn't that a good recipe for gout?' I said. He smiled, but did not answer, a ruse he sometimes employed to make me speak further. So, I continued, 'Well, supposing that I agree, what *shall* I do?'

'Whatever you like. I'm sure you could carry on with your photography lessons if you wished, just you would be living here, not there.'

So, the following day, I handed in my notice to Clive and Ramona Hawkins. I offered to stay out the month of November, but they assured me that there was no need, since Ophelia had proved so adept in the studio that there was increasingly little for me to do. The prospect of taking me on as a fee-paying pupil instead was deemed satisfactory and we parted on good terms. So again, I packed up my few possessions and set off once more for Crowcroft Grange.

I told myself that this was just a trial co-habitation, for if I had convinced myself it was to be permanent, I would not have been able to do it. And Lord Darvell, too, was careful to treat this as just a longer visit, knowing that too much pressure was liable to send me back to the photographer's studio or to some unknown destination, before he could even order the carriage from the coach-house for me.

The second evening after my birthday had been set aside for the Last Titration. It was also the night before the ball, and the hope was that if the Titrations proved successful, I would attend the ball as a human being. As I took the last half gill of blood into my veins, I had such high hopes.

At some time around midnight, after the syringe had discharged the last of its crimson contents, I was dozing on the sofa with Lord Darvell, as was, by now, our custom. As I lapsed in and out of sleep, I remember longing that I would wake the following morning a human being. Alas, it was not to be. When I woke at dawn, the points of my fangs were still biting down into my lower lip. I was still nosferatu. And though the sensation of his ambrosial blood circling in my veins was exhilarating, somehow, it had not been enough to transform me.

Bitter indeed was my disappointment. I stood up and gazed down at Lord Darvell as he lay there. In that moment, his face was indeed the face of Daedalus, a Greek warrior far from his homeland. And perhaps he sensed I was watching him, for his eyes flew open – eyes like the sea when the storms are nigh – and he smiled. His smile, I thought, was welcoming enough that he would forgive my past murderous indiscretions.

Somehow, it made my heartache even harder to bear. I could have gone and nestled against him, but instead I slipped from the room. I wanted to be outside. I wanted to see if anything at all was growing in the Lost Garden.

There was dew on the grass. Again, I could feel it beneath my bare feet as I walked towards the Lost Garden. I held back the ivy and then pushed open the gate. Once I was inside, I could see the patches of earth where Arabella and I had cleared some space. She was trying to cultivate a garden that had grown wild, and I wondered if she would manage it.

There was a great palm tree growing at the heart of the garden which looked as if it could withstand any storm, and plants with red leaves that were nestling into its trunk. But otherwise, the paths were overgrown, and the smell of dead plants mixed with the fresh, living smell.

Underneath the tree ferns, tall as forest ferns, the autumn light was pellucid. Lilies flourished out of reach. There was a snaky-looking orchid, and another shaped like a seraph, but with long, brown, thin tentacles. Lord Darvell had told Arabella that it would flower twice a year, and that then there would be a wonderful bell-shaped mass of white, mauve, and deep purple flowers. But there were no flowers there now. It was hard to believe that there would ever be any flowers, ever again.

I crunched my way across dead leaves to sit on a bench towards the back of the garden. It was beside an old wall covered with green moss, soft and velvety.

The Titrations had failed. But why? I had followed the conditions very carefully, and in all my time at Crowcroft

Grange, I had not taken a single human life – instead, limiting myself to birds and mice. I tried now to recall the notes I had made from the letters of the Moravian scholars.

Finally, sitting there in the old garden, I realised my mistake. The Titrations did not only prohibit the taking of human life, but even the *desire* to murder. For murder in thoughts was the first step towards murder in action. And, in all my time here, I had not been able to set aside my animosity towards Miss Dulcetta. The act of hatred, I recalled now, creates toxic bitterness within the blood which prevents the formulation of human corpuscles. The vampire must remain pure in heart, thought and intention in order to achieve her goal.

I stood up now and walked along the pathway, then entered a paved, glass-roofed terrace which sloped upwards towards another clump of palm trees. Perhaps I could try the Titrations again. Perhaps I could ask for Miss Dulcetta to be sent away. Or perhaps I could learn to exercise greater self-control over my own unruly impulses and emotions.

Perhaps.

I headed back towards the house, where I tried to bury my disappointment in preparations for the ball. In the evening, Martha knocked on my door and came in with a gown that she had been altering for me over several weeks.

It was of heavy Indian silk, the colour of a foxglove, worked with fine, pale, lace, and there were seed pearls at the neck and edges of the full oversleeves. Beneath the oversleeves were tight sleeves of ivory cloth, and the underskirt was of ivory too, with mauve ribbon twisted in a border at the bottom. It had belonged to Morgana, Martha told me, but she had never worn it, thinking that the colour didn't suit her. It had been folded away in clean linen in one of the attics until Martha espied it and brought it out for me.

Once I had readied myself, I swept into the ballroom. It was glorious; the old, dark oak panels were now decorated with flowers, candles, and turquoise silk to make up a hall of shimmering light. Garlands of white flowers were tied up with turquoise ribbons.

Although he had made much of his lack of society manners, Lord Darvell unaccountably proved himself the most agreeable person in the room. He conversed with everyone present and introduced me to his friends, Lord and Lady Bloodhart, whom he had known since boyhood, and who lived in an estate, Neverfield, not five miles from his own. He announced that he wanted them to be godparents to Arthur and Arabella. And then he was so lively and unreserved, even promising to dance every dance, that Harriet Bloodhart whispered to me, 'It's good to see him so happy.'

I danced two dances with Dr Helton, to try and understand why he was such a particular crony of Lord Darvell's, from which I gathered that he had been in attendance on Morgana in her final days. The conversation, and indeed, the man himself, made these two dances awkward and solemn. I danced next with Lord Bloodhart, who was an agreeable, gentlemanly man, and then I returned to greet Ophelia Hawkins, who was wearing a long, red dress with a black sash and black evening gloves. She confessed to having missed me greatly since my departure, two days ago.

The double doors of the ballroom opened again, and Arabella burst in, looking very pleased with herself.

'Look how pretty I am,' she said, and she tried to pirouette.

She looked as light as thistledown and, as she said, very pretty. She wore a short, white muslin gown with a skirt that stuck out from her waist, like petals from a rose. The dress was embroidered all over with green stalks and leaves and white daisies tipped pink. Though she barely came up to Arthur's chest, for he was tall for his age, and she was short for hers, still she made him dance the next dance with her. And it was a fine sight to see the small, determined girl lead the great bear-like boy round the dancefloor, each trying not to step on the other's toes.

Lord Darvell then approached me and asked for the next dance. I took his hand, and he led me out onto the floor. I said that I was delighted to see him so sociable.

'And I also, you,' he replied.

'Yet previously,' I said, 'I have noticed a great similarity in the turn of our minds. We are both of an unsociable, taciturn disposition, reluctant to speak, never mind dance.'

'And yet here we are, enkindled to something like liveliness,' he said. 'How should we account for it? Is it because we each now have the same blood flowing in our veins?'

'Of course,' I said, 'we are both now blessed with that sparkling elixir.'

'Yes,' he said, 'though you have yet to give me any of your own blood in return.' He added, 'For I started to think, if you cannot become a human being, perhaps I should become a vampire.' When I remained silent, he added, hurriedly, 'Unless, of course, you are referring to the champagne?'

'Certainly,' I said, 'after the dance, let's have another glass.'

Miss Dulcetta chose that very moment to make her grand entrance into the ballroom. Her choice of gown surprised us all entirely because it was so different from her usual insipid whites and fawns, or sombre greys. This dress had a skirt of midnight black tulle that became midnight blue at the bodice, which was worked over with blue and purple sequins. Blue and purple gauzy ribbons were attached to the sleeve straps, and a sweep of shimmering blue kohl on each eyelid added to the dramatic effect. Once or twice, Lord Darvell glanced over towards her from the champagne stand, as if he could not believe the transformation.

Only because she was a governess, or more likely, because she was disagreeable, no-one wanted to dance with her. The musicians on their rostrum sent the most beautiful melodies soaring into the ballroom, to sparkle among the chandeliers, but Miss Dulcetta stayed seated on her chair by the wall. Occasionally, her slippers tapped in time to the music.

Finally, Lord Darvell took pity on her, and returning me to talk to Lord and Lady Bloodhart, he went and asked her for a dance. They swept past our alcove during a waltz, so that I heard Miss Dulcetta say, quite distinctly, that she had a birthday gift for me hidden away in the bookroom, and could he please come with her to fetch it.

However, after they had left the ballroom, they were gone for so long that I grew anxious, and quitting Lord and Lady Bloodhart and their talk of paying us a longer visit at a later date, I departed in search of them.

I found Lord Darvell and Miss Dulcetta seated side-by-side on the little blue sofa in the bookroom, poring over some handwritten manuscript pages.

'Are you reading my birthday present?' I said, as lightly as I could.

Lord Darvell looked up then and I was shocked to see how suddenly haggard he appeared. He was paler than he had ever been in the aftermath of the Titrations – in fact, it was as if all the blood had drained from his face. In the sallow light of the candelabrum, he was a spectral version of himself.

'We are reading a translation of your journal,' he said, coldly.

Briefly, I wondered how Miss Dulcetta had obtained my journal to have it translated, and then I cursed myself for the moment's forgetfulness which had caused me to leave it behind on that previous visit. But Miss Dulcetta was an intelligent, educated woman and it would not have been too difficult for her to find some scholar, translator, or librarian, perhaps from the Valerian Library, of which she was a member, to translate it. That, at any rate, seemed to be what she had done.

'And isn't that a terrible violation of my privacy?' I replied, equally cool.

'Sybilla here was worried about me, about this family. She thought we should know who you really are.'

'Oh, so it's Sybilla now, is it? I doubt whether the tormented musings of a troubled young girl from over nine hundred years ago bear much resemblance to the person I am today.'

'But you killed all those people,' said Lord Darvell, 'and you drained a grave-robber of his blood.' Was it my imagination, or was there a tinge of jealousy to those final words?

'Yes,' I said, wearily. 'I'm a vampire and I was hungry. But all the rest of it is historical. Those events have little or no relevance to the present day beyond the fact that they were necessary. Otherwise, I wouldn't be standing in front of you now, having this conversation.'

'But you're a murderess,' said Miss Dulcetta, in as dramatic a tone as she could muster. 'All those innocent lives.'

'They weren't particularly innocent,' I said. 'They planted an adder beneath a horse's bones to murder Oleg, for instance.'

Miss Dulcetta made as if to protest, but I held up an admonishing hand. 'Look like the innocent flower but be the serpent under it. You'll recognise that quotation, Miss Dulcetta, from *Macbeth*. But could you please leave us now?'

She gave me a baleful look but since Lord Darvell made no movement to stop her, she had no choice but to depart.

'And thank you so much for your gift,' I said to her retreating back. 'You alone will know what your true intentions were in giving it.'

'What do you think her true intentions were?' asked Lord Darvell, after she had gone.

'Oh, well, let me see. Could it possibly be to sow misery and discord? To make everyone here as unhappy as she is herself?'

'But why would she do that?' he inquired, so that I reflected that the best of men can rarely discern the true malice of a woman, since it is anathema to them.

'Perhaps to discredit me and force my departure, so she could take my place,' I said. 'At any rate, her motives were hardly noble or pure. The first time I was here, I told you she should go, but you wouldn't listen.'

'I'm not in the habit of taking advice from photographer's assistants with sprained ankles.'

'Well, perhaps it's time you started. Anyway, as I recall, you *asked* for my advice, then didn't take it. I was Regent of all of Kief and I crushed little adders like her daily beneath my feet.'

'Your imagery is a little extreme,' said Lord Darvell, mildly. 'You can be vehement without resorting to hyperbole.'

By now, I was barely able to take in the import of his words. 'You didn't listen,' I said, 'and now everything is ruined. The pair of you have only yourselves to blame.'

After a moment's pause, he said, 'Does everything have to be ruined?'

'I can't say that the evening has turned out entirely as I'd hoped,' I retorted.

'You didn't answer the question.'

'And no more will I,' I said. 'Carry on reading my journal. I hope you find it sufficiently titillating company. And when you have finished analysing my every word, perhaps you can think about what the impact of your own actions has been.'

'No, but Violetta…'

'But me no buts. No wonder the Titrations haven't worked. Reading my journal behind my back is the action of a coward. I don't believe there's enough courage in your blood for my purposes.'

'And a little too much megalomania in yours.'

'Now that you have insulted me in every conceivable way, I shall leave you to your evening's reading,' I said, and so departed. I did not return to the ballroom. Lord Darvell had ruined the entire celebration, and everything else besides, so he could be the one to say farewell to his guests.

I tossed and turned throughout the night, and the following morning, I was the first to rise. On the hallway table, I found a note from Ramona Hawkins. Since I valued her common sense, I decided to walk towards the station and then take the train to the Hawkins's studio.

Around eleven o' clock, I walked down Conduit Street, then turned into Preston Street and soon I was standing on the pavement in front of their house. I hadn't noticed it before, but there were a few slate tiles missing from their roof. I pushed open the glass doors and made my way up the stairs to the first-floor studio. Ramona was sitting there at a walnut-coloured desk, poring over a ledger book. She looked up when I entered and smiled, but her glance was cool and appraising.

'We were sorry not to join you at the ball last night,' she said. 'A prior engagement with Clive's uncle prevented us from attending. However, Ophelia seems to have had a good time, though she regretted not saying goodbye to you at the end.'

'That's my fault,' I said. 'Something alarming happened - and all my manners disappeared.'

Ramona paused and put her pen down. She smelled clean and practical, of cotton and citrus, starched and ironed. She was neat and tidy as a new pin, and I thought she would always know what to do in any given situation. She gestured towards the ottoman opposite her desk, and I sat down.

After a few moments, I said, 'The governess has a grudge against me and has revealed some terrible things about my past to Lord Darvell.'

'And?' said Ramona. 'Simply deny everything.'

'Unfortunately,' I replied, 'they are all true. And already things are changing between us. He slept in his dressing-room last night. What shall I do? He told me before that his good opinion, once lost, was lost forever.'

Ramona took a cigarette from a gold, embossed cigarette case in her drawer, lit it, began to smoke with every evidence of enjoyment - and did not answer.

'Answer me,' I said as she puffed out a cloud of smoke into some artificial narcissi, white with orange flame-like trumpets, placed in a vase on the desk in front of her.

218

'You're asking me something difficult,' she said, after a few moments. 'I'm going to tell you something difficult. You should pack up your things and go.'

'Go, go where? To some strange place where I shall never see him?'

'Well, you could always come back here,' said Ramona. 'You would have your old room and your old work, again.'

'I appreciate the offer,' I said, though I was not sure I did. 'It's very kind of you. But it's not what I want. I only left three days ago.'

'Well, what *do* you want?'

'Just to be happy,' I said. 'And to be loved. Only,' I confessed, in a small voice, 'I'm a vampire.'

'Yes,' said Ramona, 'we thought you might be. Clive has an unerring knack for identifying those of our kind. And there are more of us about than you might realise. Is that all the trouble between you and Lord Darvell? Because vampirism really isn't the social handicap it used to be.'

'Not just that,' I said. 'I was experimenting with a process I called the Titrations in order to become human. But it didn't work.'

Ramona blinked and said rapidly, 'The Moravian Method? But that's considered very dangerous - as well as a betrayal of our kind.'

'I believe I am of an older bloodline than you,' I said then. 'For I have been a vampire for over nine hundred years and Lord knows that's long enough. I'm tired of it.'

'And so, you call on their Christian God, and not on Selene, for help,' Ramona said, pettishly. Then she paused and looked at me more closely. 'Nine hundred years? Who *are* you?'

'I am Violetta Valhallah of the House of Vladimir of the Sabre,' I said, proudly. 'I was the wife of Oleg the Vangarian, and after his death, I took over the Regency of Kief.'

Now there was a glimmer of respect in Ramona's eyes, green with flecks of grey near the pinprick pupils.

'And that is what Lord Darvell has discovered about you?' she demanded. 'The man's a fool if he lets it matter.'

'I don't think he's a fool,' I said. 'But I stand condemned by my own hand. The governess gave him a translation of my journal, and I think, from comments he made about gravediggers, some of the later parts, too.'

'There are always problems with governesses,' sighed Ramona. 'I can't abide them. Snivelling, wretched creatures. Though it's not exactly their fault. Status incongruence is becoming a real social problem. Well, and so the man read a few things he didn't like. But a woman's past is her secret garden. If he goes snooping, then he has only himself to blame.'

'That's what I told him,' I said. 'But I think he objects to the mass murders.'

'Another time, another place,' said Ramona airily, flicking ash. A moment later, and she lit herself another cigarette. 'You can go and remind him that the conditions of the Moravian Method prevent you from taking another human life. You can promise him that, in any case, you will never do so again. And if that isn't enough, there's no pleasing him. You can still come back here.'

'But I don't want to,' I said.

'Come now, my dear,' said Ramona, 'you're being foolish, yourself. If a man doesn't treat you properly, you pack up your things and go. If he wants you, he soon comes after you.' She flicked away more ash, which had fallen onto her ledger. 'I, myself, hardly ever drink human blood these days,' she added. 'Clive thinks it's bad for business.'

She reached into her desk's pigeonhole and drew out a manila envelope from which she removed a black-and-white portrait of me. There I was, my dark hair bound back severely, my pale face, my dark eyes. Then too, the details of the white cameo at my throat were clear and precise, and contrasted well with the black lacy material of my dress, and my dark velvet shrug.

'Ophelia's picture of you turned out well,' Ramona said. 'Take it back with you and give Lord Darvell something to be pleased about. Speak nicely to him and make him understand. You are letting little things spoil your happiness.'

I sighed then at the word *happiness* and shut my eyes. For a moment, I could see a tall man slouching in a chair, pretending to read a book, his eyes shifting like clouds and sunshine. I could see a little girl hitting a croquet ball through a hoop on the lawn, smiling at her success, as her brother walked through the grounds with a spaniel at his heels. I could see it all, fixed forever like the colours in a stained-glass window. Then I opened my eyes. Ramona was pushing the manila envelope with the photograph inside it into my hands.

I took the train back to Crowcroft Village with its constellation of lights marking out the houses. Then I walked across the fields towards the manor. I passed the church with its low, broad stone tower against the sky, and its bell, tolling the hour. Three in the afternoon, but the ground was hard, the air was still, the road was lonely, and it was so cold and dark that it felt much later.

From my vantage point on the hill, I could look down on Crowcroft Grange; the grey and battlemented hall was melancholy yet imposing, its woods and dark rookery casting shadows all around. Some blue smoke rose from its few chimneys; it was only a mile distant.

Despite the cold, I lingered there awhile until the sun began to sink beneath the trees, turning crimson and clear behind them. There was the crescent now of an approaching moon, pale and cloud-like. How long it was since I had last prayed to the moon goddess, Selene. Perhaps she had quite forgotten me, and if I were to pray to her now, she would turn a deaf ear to my prayers. And yet, beneath the moonlight, everything was clear and still, and the streams ran beside me. Amongst the ripplings and whisperings, I began to take the final steps home.

The way seemed easier now, and presently, I pushed open the gates and passed through into the courtyard. There was the long, low front of the house, with candlelight emanating from the bow-windows. I entered the door, and crossed the hallway, then passed through another square hall with high doors all around. The double illumination of fire and candlelight dazzled me, contrasting as it did with the darkness outside. Next, I climbed the three flights of staircases to my old room, then sat on the bed, to look out through the window.

I was on a level now with the crow colony and could see the eggs within their nests. I surveyed the grounds beneath me, laid out like a chessboard, the bright, green lawn, then the parkland, then the vast sweep of valleys and fields dotted with ancient timber, the church, the woods, the roads, all beneath that same dim skyline.

But I longed to see beyond everything that was currently presented to me, the whole busy world, towns, regions, all full of life that I had heard of, but never seen. This restlessness had always been part of my nature: this desire for life, fire and feeling agitated me to pain sometimes, and yet it co-existed with a paradoxical desire to crawl back into bed and pull the blankets over my head.

And that was what I did now. I climbed into bed and turned my face to the wall. I had no desire for supper, company, or conversation, and instead lapsed in-and-out of sleep. But I woke suddenly to the sound of the grandfather clock striking nine, downstairs in the hallway. A few moments later, and Lord Darvell entered the room.

'What is the matter?' he said. 'Why haven't you come downstairs this evening?'

'I'm cold. And tired. And dead. A fact which you never seem to recall.'

'If vampiric immortality consists of you complaining for all eternity, I'm not sure the prospect is so very appealing.'

I sat up in bed. 'I'm not sure I ever gave you that option,' I replied.

'When you went off this morning, where did you go?'

'I went to see Ramona,' I said.

'Why did you go to see her?' he continued.

'She sent me a note. My birthday portrait was ready.' I gestured towards the manila envelope on the bedside cabinet, but he seemed not to notice.

'You wanted to ask her advice, was that it?'

I did not answer. Already, I was tired of being interrogated. He sat down on the side of the bed.

'What did she say?' he asked, in a gentler tone.

'She said that I ought to make you a promise never to take another human life and if that wasn't enough, then I should go away – leave you.'

'Oh, did she?' he said, sounding surprised.

'Yes, that was her advice.'

'I want to do the best for both of us,' he said then. 'So much of what you wrote in that journal is strange, different from what I was led to believe. Don't you feel that perhaps Ramona is right? That if you made me that promise and then went away from this place for a time, or I went away – exactly as you wish, of course – it might be the wisest thing we could do?' Then he said, more sharply, 'Violetta, are you falling asleep? Why don't you answer me?' He leaned over and took my cold hands in his. 'You've been up here by yourself for a long time.'

'You go,' I said. 'I want to go to sleep here in the dark… where I belong.'

'Oh, nonsense,' he said. He put his arms round me to draw me to him. Then he tried to kiss me, but I pulled back.

'Your mouth is colder than my hands,' I said. He tried to laugh, then stood up from the bed to draw the shutters.

'Sleep, then,' he said. After he left, I realised he had forgotten to take the photograph with him. It still lay in its manila envelope on the bedside cabinet.

I am not sure how well I slept that night, or whether I slept much at all, and all the sorrowful days that followed blurred one into another. One evening, Lord Darvell came to me, and told me that he too had trouble sleeping, that he was afflicted by the most appalling dreams.

He said that in his dreams, he saw me dressed in ivory lace, approaching him from one of the Grange's crumbling stone doorways. He stumbled towards me in relief, his arms outstretched. But then he perceived that I carried a bloodstained knife.

How was I supposed to answer that? For everything that Miss Dulcetta had shown him in my diary was true. The translator she had found in the Valerian Library had done his job only too well. And, as time went by, Lord Darvell's nightmares grew no better. If I hadn't disliked Dr Helton so much, I might have suggested that his lordship talk to his friend.

One morning, it was all a bit too much. And though it was not entirely what I wished to say, I found myself recommending that Lord Darvell travel to Russia, and find some historian who could give him an accurate account of the so-called atrocities that Violetta, Regent of all Kief, had committed against the Drevlians. This historian might be able to explain the barbarism and savagery of those ancient times in ways that I could not, might give him some insight into how a woman alone was driven to commit crimes which she would later bitterly regret. At the very least, it would give him a change of air and scene.

Besides, I thought if I had to spend one more day looking at his mournful face, strange things might occur.

His passage on board a ship bound for the Port of St. Petersburg was arranged and booked. Before he left, we discussed whether Miss Dulcetta should be dismissed, but he thought I might need assistance with Arthur and Arabella, and that the girl's lessons should not be interrupted. Then we said our sad farewells.

'I wonder if we will ever see each other again,' I said. 'The lotus flower hath no toil, but still, it ripens, fades and falls.'

'Nonsense,' he said, and some other words that sounded like expletives, but I had already stopped listening. 'Violetta,' he said then, more sharply, 'do you intend that I should go one way in the world, and you another?'

'I do,' I said. 'At least until you have stopped judging me.'

'We could go to Russia together?' he said.

'Prejudice doesn't make a good travelling companion,' I replied. But my voice trembled as I spoke, and I reached out to smooth his hair with my hand.

'God bless you then,' he said.

'And God keep you from harm,' I replied.

Then the blood rushed up to his face, and the fire flashed in his eyes. He held his arms out, but I evaded the embrace.

'Farewell,' I said, as I slipped from the room. And the cry of my heart added, 'Farewell, forever.'

After Lord Darvell had gone, I was sadly proven correct in the matter of Miss Dulcetta. Her final act of cruelty was to hurt and undermine me by hurting the boy. For, in his lordship's absence, she took it upon herself to write to Dr Helton, telling him that Arthur's sleepwalking was no better and that he needed the care of the Convalescing Home. And, with his legal guardian in Russia, I lacked the authority to prevent Arthur's enforced departure when they came for him. Nevertheless, I applied to Lord and Lady Bloodhart for their advice. They were kindness itself, and agreed that under the circumstances, I could do little except dismiss Miss Dulcetta, and then visit Arthur at Saint Cosmas & Damian's Convalescing Home and ensure that he had everything he needed.

Two days after the sanatorium doctors had assessed Arthur and taken him away, I entered the schoolroom. Arabella's morning lessons were over, and she had gone to visit her garden, so I came and stood in front of the desk where Miss Dulcetta was still seated. Such was her foolish insolence that she would not even raise her eyes to me.

'Miss Dulcetta,' I said, whilst she continued to keep her eyes fixed steadfastly on the globes in front of her. 'This family are grateful for your services, but they are no longer required.'

She looked up then, quick enough!

'What do you mean?' she said. 'You have no authority…'

'On the contrary,' I said, 'I am caring for Arabella in Lord Darvell's absence, and I don't wish her to be exposed to unwholesome influences. Her godparents, Lord and Lady Bloodhart, are of the same opinion.'

'This has nothing to do with Arabella, and everything to do with revenge,' Miss Dulcetta replied.

'In the matter of Arthur, whom Arabella loves, you far exceeded your professional responsibilities,' I said. 'Such a clever woman as you are, could you not foresee how this would distress us all?'

'We're not all visionaries,' she said. 'Or vampires.'

'That is by-the-by,' I said. 'You are being dismissed, effective immediately, with a month's pay in lieu. You should go and pack your things now and the coachman will drive you to the station.'

Miss Dulcetta looked me full in the face now, and her expression was bewildered and bitter.

'Where do you expect me to go?' she asked.

'Back to your mother?' I said. 'I will supply you with the necessary references so that you can find another situation.'

'I quarrelled with my mother the last time I visited,' muttered Miss Dulcetta, and her face began to swell up in front of me as if she were going to cry.

Her face a balloon that I wanted to burst. Bang! Her face in red shreds.

'Better a mother than a murderer,' I said softly, and all my hatred of the last couple of months crystallised into one, venomous look. I do not think she will forget that look quickly, nor the sudden gleam of my fangs. At any rate, it made her quit her chair and the schoolroom to begin packing for her departure.

Yet, after she had left, I wondered how I could become human when I was assailed by such vengeful emotions. I thought I had grown so wise in Valerian, and I had tried so hard to act with self-control. But despite what I had told Lord Darvell, perhaps my innermost being was still no more than the half-savage vampire of Daedalus's creation. Or perhaps I was just not ready to be human, since I did not know how to remove hatred from my heart. Instead, I let it flourish there, a flame I could not extinguish.

As the weeks passed and still there was no word from Lord Darvell, I grew despondent, then began to lose hope entirely. I felt as if I were sickening from sorrow and inanition; often I had no desire to feed, but only to grieve. At night, I cried, stormy, scalding, heart-wrung tears, but somehow, as dawn rose each day, despite feeling that my head was dizzy, my sight, dim, my limbs, feeble, I was still able to rise and care for Arabella.

For a vampire does not give in to her emotions. A vampire masters them.

Aurélie found herself skipping over the next few pages of the journal now, for, despite Violetta's protestations, there was much that was simply too painful to read. She paused briefly on a couple of sentences: 'There is a sword that divides us from each other, from our past and our future selves. Why is the sky now broken into pieces?' But she flicked through the pages again, and suddenly there came a day when the handwriting was more purposeful, and the sentiments too, for Violetta had written:

Much good all this does me! Nor Arabella either. For with Lord Darvell gone to Russia, Arthur to the sanatorium, and Miss Dulcetta to her mother, there is no-one here for her except Martha and me.

She was crying last night, crying on my lap, her head pressed against me, her arms clutching me. There was snot crusted beneath her nose, and her tears ran onto my hands. It seemed to me that I was no longer shut in and absorbed wholly in my own pain, for now I could feel hers. I wanted to comfort her, to draw the pain out like a splinter with a needle, to make it all better. But all I could do was hold her to me, hope that she felt safer crying into my lap then by herself in the dark. As her gasping tears slackened, so she relaxed against me, tired out. She said her prayers then, and went to sleep, meek as a lamb.

However, the very next morning, one of those elliptical letters from Lord Darvell arrived, which, judging by the date at the top, had been written many weeks previously. It must have been delayed, but I could not suppress a curious leap of the heart as I read, *'I was wrong to leave as I did. Bring Arthur and Arabella to me and let us see what we can do with our lives.'* And so, that same morning, I asked Martha to care for Arabella, then took the train to the sanatorium in Shoreditch. I intended to show Dr Helton the letter from Lord Darvell, and request Arthur's release into my care so that we could all travel to Russia together.

Emerging from the station, and crisscrossing a lattice of streets, I presently located the sanatorium building, converted stables, which loomed out in front of me. Above the arched doorway, the name was enamelled in red. Large, red, letters with a bright, red shine. *Saint Cosmas & Damian.* I pushed open the door and stepped inside, my head held high. My long taffeta skirt swished on the floor behind me. The entrance hall and corridor were tiled and smelt of soap and beeswax.

Soon, I was knocking on Dr Helton's office door. After a moment's pause, he called out, 'Come in,' and I entered. His office was large and full of bookcases and tables covered with books. I perched on one end of his leather sofa, awkward and nervous. My hands felt sweaty inside my gloves.

After the preliminary greetings, occasional words from Dr Helton's discourse detached themselves from his sentences and floated towards me, bumping against the leather furniture, the dark, mahogany shelves. *Hysteria. Delusion.* Whilst he was speaking, I studied the pictures on the wall behind his head.

They were all pictures of the same young girl in a rough white robe, resting inside a cot with bars. In the first picture, she was sitting up, her arms raised in supplication, her hands clasped in prayer. In the second, her arms were raised more in astonishment, and her face was upturned in rapture towards a light. In the third, her eyes were closed, and her mouth was twisted into a strange smile. When I saw that smile, I stiffened, then took a deep breath and sighed. More than ever, I was convinced that this was not the right place for Arthur.

Dr Helton had fallen silent. He was looking at me looking at the pictures of the young girl in the white night-dress. I took out Lord Darvell's letter and showed it to him. He noted down his friend's address in St. Petersburg and said that he would send him reports on Arthur's progress.

'But as for releasing him at such an early stage of his treatment, it is out of the question,' he said firmly.

'Is Arthur making progress?' I asked, equally firmly.

'All aspects of his medical treatment will be dealt with in the reports to Lord Darvell,' said Dr Helton.

'Well, can I see him while I am here?'

'We can only permit supervised visits with authorised family members from the third month of treatment,' said Dr Helton.

'But Arabella and I are intending to travel to St. Petersburg, to join Lord Darvell, and so it may be some months before Arthur next has visitors. Surely, under these circumstances, you can make an exception?'

'The treatment process must be respected if it is to be successful,' said Dr Helton.

'And if Lord Darvell writes to you himself, requesting the release of the boy?'

'I shall, of course, be happy to follow my good friend's wishes. However, my dear, I feel sure that he will approve of our work here.' Dr Helton smiled then, a genuine smile that reached the shadows of his brown eyes. 'Surely, Miss Violetta, you wish to have Arthur restored to you in the fullness of his health, content and purposeful? Besides, you can write to him while you are away, although I will be required to read the letters to make sure that there is nothing distressing in them.'

Blood-craving? Mass-murder? Perhaps I would leave the letter-writing to Arabella.

'Then I don't think there's much more for me to say,' I said. I stood up from the sofa. 'Good day, Dr Helton.'

'Good day, Miss Violetta,' he said, bowing slightly to me from behind his desk as I opened the office door.

Once I had stepped out into the corridor, Morgana seemed to be just ahead of me, a green wisp of smoke drawing me onwards, a green rope leading me out. She didn't want me to spend a moment longer here than was necessary. She would find a way to free her brother where I could not. And so, she delivered me out into the sunshine, into the colours and noise of the busy street, before she vanished.

I took the train back to Crowcroft Grange to help Martha and Arabella pack for the long voyage from London to St. Petersburg. I gave Martha the keys to the house and asked her to care for it in our absence. I was not sure whether to dismiss the rest of the servants but decided that this was a decision for Lord Darvell. Then, whilst we were in the midst of our preparations, I removed the sacred chalice from the cabinet in his study. I am not quite sure what my intentions were. When I tucked it inside my dress, I felt as if I were stealing a little piece of happiness, something shiny, which was not, after all, meant for me. But I told myself that I would give it back to him when I next saw him.

I also pasted the translated pages into my journal. Arabella asked me to keep some draft papers of hers safe too, some fairy tales and a letter she had written to her old landlady, so that the leather covers of this book creaked and strained with all the additional parchment. Then I fixed my birthday portrait to the inside cover. It had a sentimental value for me and besides, I did not know when I would return to these shores again.

A day or so later, and we were driven to the Port of London. Soon, the bosun was piping us on board our ship, *The Hummingbird.* The Captain himself greeted us once we had reached the top of the wooden ladder. His hands were leathery, firm and capable as they gripped mine. Then he showed us to our cabin in the poop, an upper and lower bunk with little legroom.

'I shouldn't complain if I were you,' I said to Arabella's remonstrations. 'Down in the hold, the passengers only have a hammock or a pallet.'

'I want a hammock,' said Arabella. 'It would be very fine to swing backwards and forwards and then fall asleep.'

'There isn't the space,' I said. But -

'I think we can arrange that for the young lady,' said the Captain, before he departed to set sail. Later, we heard him shout, 'Heave away.' And then the great chain clanked, and the anchor rose out of the water. The sailors chanted; the bosun whistled, and to a response of, 'Aye, aye sir,' there came the swish of unfurling sails. Soon the wind was loud, and the sails were high, and *The Hummingbird* began to lurch and roll away from Valerian's shores.

One evening, some days later, Arabella began to clutch her belly and complain of feeling sick. I wanted to go into the hold to locate some herbs for her from our travelling chest: ginger and arrowroot. The Captain gave his ready consent and provided me with a sailor, Seth Pettigrew, as a guide. I followed Seth down the stairs to the main deck. Here, children were shouting out and playing *Hot Cockles*. From somewhere came the sound of a penny whistle.

As we passed the group of children, the ship gave a sudden lurch and I stumbled against the sailor.

'Forgive me,' I said, 'I thought I had better sea-legs.'

'Don't fret,' Seth replied, 'it's a fine game with so fair a player.'

But his attempt at gallantry was wasted on me because all I could think of was my great hunger. I stared at the bulbous veins on his neck, protruding beneath a spiky tattoo of a rose

231

and anchor, and I thought, do not trifle with me. I could devour you, had I not promised faithfully never to take another human life.

Whatever else I may be, I am a creature that keeps her promises.

We were about to descend into the hold when another voice called out from the deck,

'I think I've caught something.'

'Did the Captain tell you that you could fish here?' asked Seth.

'No more than he told you,' said the other sailor, shining a lantern in our faces, then looking me up and down. In the light, I began to pick my way between the fishing lines and the shoals of slippery fish. Then this sailor shone his lantern back over the rail, jerked his rod up, and a fish landed with a watery smack at our feet.

'You've brought me luck, I think,' he said to me.

I nodded, and followed Seth down into the hold, which reeked of salt beef, dried peas and smoke. There were goats and pigs quartered there, and even a brood mare, her whinny mingling with the creak of beams and the slap of waves. Then we made our way further down into the compartment near the fo'castle, and the sailor waited whilst I rummaged around inside the travel chest.

Its contents smelt wonderful: oatmeal, sugar, figs, pepper, suet, tallow, and even the tang of wine vinegar. Right at the bottom were little muslin bags full of herbs and seeds: camomile, vervain, ginger, arrowroot, rosemary and feverfew. I pulled out several of the bags, but in doing so, my hand brushed against a small, dead mouse. Finally, food, I thought. So, I tucked the bags and the mouse's little body into my reticule and then I followed Seth back up on deck.

When I had gotten rid of Seth, whose flirtatious advances were both tedious and problematic, I bit into the neck of the mouse. As its viscous blood squirted into my throat, I felt some measure of relief. But still the ship tipped and heaved, the sky turned yellow, and the sea looked like glass. A storm was approaching which would keep us bound to our cabins for the rest of the night. Fortunately, with infusions of ginger and arrowroot, Arabella soon recovered from her seasickness.

To obtain further rats and mice, I decided to befriend the ship's cat. Whilst seeming to feed or pet him, I intended to rob him of the corpses of his victims, and then feast on them myself. I resolved to creep out at night, once Arabella had fallen asleep. But after the first night that I stole the cat's mouse, he would have nothing more to do with me, nor can I blame him.

A few nights later, I found Arabella in her hammock, crushing a couple of garlic cloves beneath her fingernails.

'Why are you doing that?' I asked.

'Seth the sailor gave them to me,' she said. 'He said it would protect me against shipwrecks and drowning, monsters, evil spirits and storms.'

'But we've already had a storm,' I said. 'So, it doesn't work.'

'Well, but I didn't have any garlic then,' said Arabella.

'It smells horrible though,' I said. 'Don't you know they call garlic the stinking rose? Besides, you might be repelling powerful spirits too. What about Morgana – and Rose Red?' And me?

'*Bah!* I didn't think of that. What should I do with it then?'

'Throw it over the railings, say a prayer and tell Seth not to be so superstitious.' Though, of course, if Seth hadn't planted his garlic on Saint Dumitru's day, he would die anyway. The garlic-bulb is a head and demands a human head.

Arabella frowned, as if something didn't quite make sense, but she did as I asked.

The voyage proved to be a miserable, desultory time, lightened only by fantasies of murdering sailors or by actually stargazing on deck. One night, however, I was furious – furious with all men, and particularly with Lord Darvell. And so, I squeezed rat's blood into the sacred chalice and was about to drink from it, then throw it over the ship's railings, out into the sea. But something, some vestiges of goodness or conscience, stopped me. I poured the blood into another glass and drank from that instead.

As I did so, I remembered our conversation from the evening before the ball, before it had all gone so terribly wrong. He had said that, above all, it was Arabella and Arthur who most needed care and compassion.

'And seeing you both with them, it is hard to believe that you are a vampire.'

'What do you mean?' I asked.

'The way you are all at ease in each other's company. Your instinctive tenderness.'

'I have many instincts. Not all of them are tender.'

'And yet,' he said, 'I cannot help but feel that what they need, especially at this stage in their lives, is a mother's ways, a mother's…'

'That is not something to ask of me, Lord Darvell,' I replied. 'That is something to ask of yourself.' I thought about adding that I had a fear of being made use of, but I was concerned about possible hypocrisy given that I had often fed on human-beings.

In any case, despite his professed fears, Lord Darvell had left me in charge of the children whilst he went off to Russia. If he genuinely believed I was so terrible, he would not have granted me such a great responsibility.

Ah, it wasn't fair. I was still a vampire. The Titrations hadn't worked. Yet it seemed that in this way, he would try to make me human, tender and flawed. Almost I might have suspected him of some stratagem, if only his fear had not been so real. But what was I to do now?

I reminded myself then that I had never lacked courage, no matter how savage and hungry the world, nor myself within it. Perhaps courage, after all, was the strong and necessary backbone to love.

Now I drained the glass and threw it into the sea, where it scattered beneath me, glinting on the blue and green waves and on the white foam that rose and parted, so carrying its shards far away.

Another night, almost three weeks to the day since we had first left the Port of London, Arabella and I were again out on deck. It was now too late and dark for us to continue our game of shuttlecock and battledore, so we had laid aside our rackets and over the crashing waves, we were searching for the evening star.

Instead, we glimpsed – land.

'The Port of St. Petersburg.' I said, pointing ahead.

'*Que c'est belle,* the lights,' Arabella said.

For my homeland, stretched out before me now, seemed entirely different from the vast, phantasmagorical landscapes where once I walked. Now there were elegant, Baroque buildings and shapely domes next to the Peter-Paul fortress and the Summer Pavilion, all dotted with fairy lights that glimmered out across the harbour.

Although the shore was fast approaching, still I had not decided what I should do. I was taking his daughter to him, but I was not human. I was not prepared to watch them all grow old and die, just as I had watched Oleg, whilst I remained exactly as I was. That did not seem fair to anybody. Oh, he might say again that I could turn him into a vampire – and certainly, he seemed to have the right instincts and disposition, so much so, in fact, that sometimes I wondered who the real vampire was, him or I. Still, that would not be the right thing to do. There was some cruelty in it, and just as I had resolved never to take another human life, so too had I resolved to make no more vampires.

The prow of our ship began to clear a new path for us towards the shore.

The return ticket to Lostwithiel was still in my cloisonne purse. Perhaps I would leave Arabella with Lord Darvell, then travel back to the churchyard, the tomb, the coffin. There, in its hallowed, tranquil space, I would sleep again, and in those quiet slumbers, be restored to the alpha and omega of my being. And, as I yielded to the darkness of my coffin once more, and the light dimmed all around me, Proserpine returned to the Underworld, perhaps my inner light would burn more brightly.

Only - my homeland lay there in front of me, gleaming with its rich patina of mystery and promise.

Soon, Arabella and I would be rowed to shore, and there, on the quayside, find the carriage that was waiting for us. Then, eventually, we would arrive at the hotel in St. Petersburg where he was staying, and the parlour, where they will have heated up the stove for us. And there, in the corner, toying with a glass of vodka or brandy, his hair tinged with grey, he will be waiting.

Lions Are Better-Looking

By all their best calculations, it was the middle of December sometime in the late Ninety-Eighties, though they were not quite sure, since they had been forced to rely on their own brains for the calculations. Now the intrepid Travellers of Space and Time, that is, the dwarves, the erstwhile companions of Snow White and Rose Red, were busy playing cards in their circus-trailer on the outskirts of a small village, Astalot.

On the plastic table in front of him, Pippin, son of Guinan, laid down a seven, eight, and nine of clubs, and then a seven of hearts, a seven of diamonds, a seven of clubs and a seven of spades.

'Rummy,' he called through a mouthful of Wotsits.

Voldip, another of the younger dwarves, threw down his hand in disgust. 'I was so close,' he said. 'Can I have the clockwork mouse as a prize anyway?'

Kilkenny, one of the undertaker dwarves, sighed. 'It's not just *your* mouse, Voldip. It is a rare prize for which we must all strive and achieve. Don't be such a sore loser.'

Guinan, their sometimes elected, sometimes self-appointed leader, sighed too. 'Lads, lads,' he said. 'Anyone would think our Noble Mission for Queen Morgana was to win mice at cards. We have far, far more important things to consider.'

'It's hard to consider anything important when it's so cold,' said Voldip, and Dagonet nodded and sneezed.

'I say one of us pops down to the corner shop and gets some tinnies in,' Dagonet said. 'I'll go, if someone gives me the cash.'

'No, stay here,' said Kilkenny. 'It's just started snowing. And I think there's still some under your bed.' He glanced out of the trailer window at the other circus trailers dotted around the park, with their scatterings of starlight and snowflakes. He had a fond liking for the mermaid in her trailer across the way, and for a moment, he hoped she was warm enough on this chill, winter evening.

By day, the mermaid swam round-and-round a great glass tank of salt water, pale, mysterious and gleaming, with spotlights artfully illuminating her light blonde hair, white skin and freckles, the sheen on her curvaceous silver tail. She looked a bit like Kylie, Kilkenny thought. Maybe she bleached her hair with lemon-juice, like *Smash Hits* said Jason did. But when she was out of her tank, the mermaid had legs enough to walk on dry land, a thing that no-one could really understand, though Kilkenny thought he would like to try.

Then too, behind the bars of their cages, beneath the glitter of the moon, Kilkenny could tell that the circus animals sensed snow. The elephants were squatting on their haunches and turning their great heads away from the moon's nervy light. And despite pelts of charcoal and flame, the tigers shivered and paced the blood-strewn straw, their tails twitching, ceaselessly.

Next door to the dwarves' trailer was the lion-tamer's, Alain, he called himself. And there, inside his trailer, a young lion lay asleep beneath the plastic table. Now Alain approached him with an outstretched hand, but the lion remained tawny and oblivious as unlit fire.

'Mielle, food,' whispered the lion-tamer. The lion's ears twitched. One eyelid flickered.

'Let sleeping lions lie,' called out the girl, Aurélie, his companion for the evening. She was rocking backwards and forwards in a chair jammed beneath a shelf weighed down with books: a few peeling paperbacks, some detective novels, a couple of hardbacks, Volume One of a leather-bound *Complete Works of Shakespeare*, and a notebook with the front cover ripped off.

Now Alain crouched down on the peeling linoleum and buried his hand in the lion's harsh, velvet mane. He soon found the ecstatic place beneath the chin. There rose up a full-throated purr, like the satisfied buzz of a hidden hive of bees.

'Why don't you come and join us?' Alain said, turning to the girl.

'It's cold where you are,' she said, 'I've just got warm over here.' She pulled her purple and pink striped cardigan more tightly round herself and patted the embroidered blanket on her lap, as if, Alain thought, she was ninety.

'I'll switch the heater on,' he wheedled, and he untangled the heater's cable and plugged it into the socket.

When the hot air began blasting out, she raised a shapely eyebrow and made a *mou* with her pretty mouth. Still, she plucked the embroidered blanket from her lap, and drifted over towards them. Then she crouched down next to Alain on the floor. Soon their hands were lost in the great cat's fur.

'A rather odd Nativity,' Alain said. He glanced at their reflections in the trailer's window. He was all pale face, forehead and gleaming glasses, whilst her blonde-gold hair fell in a thick curtain to her waist.

The lion shifted his head from Alain towards Aurélie, then closed his inscrutable eyes.

'That means he's smiling at you,' said Alain, wanting Aurélie to smile. He suddenly wondered if the Strong Man's woman was here to see him, or the lion. That was the danger of using an animal to do his courting.

'Oh well, at least he likes me,' said Aurélie. Her lips twisted upwards. Despite her lipstick, he noticed that the skin of her mouth was very dry, flaking at the edges, like powder from butterfly wings. It was an awkward, pinned butterfly of a smile.

Alain wondered why it was that all women smiled like that at him. That was how Odette, his last girlfriend, a ballerina with pink frosted toenails and impeccably arched insteps, had smiled when she told him that she was leaving the circus. Oh, she had cried a bit too, had thrown her arms round the lion, and soaked his mane with her tears. She even said maybe she could take him with her until Alain told her it was out of the question – a lion-tamer without lions cuts a sorry sight in the circus-world. But then, she'd been the one to help rear him from a cub, had even given him his name, Mielle.

Their parting had been sad and sweet, like pain dipped in honey.

Now the lion shook his head away from Aurélie's caressing hand. His chin trembled and a clicking sound emerged from the back of his throat. His front paw reached out to swat a fly. When he missed, Alain caught the fly for him with two fingers and offered it to the lion.

'Hors d'oeuvre, Mielle,' he said, glancing at Aurélie. For a moment, he longed to bury his face in her golden hair.

But Aurélie looked away first. She bent down and her lips moved slowly against the lion's ear. She smiled an enigmatic smile, then turned back towards Alain.

'I never had a pet,' she said, moving to sit cross-legged on the floor.

He was about to ask why, when there came a terrible noise from the dwarves' trailer next door, a most rumbustious banging, thundering, crash and commotion.

'What on earth are they doing?' he asked.

'The dwarves?' said Aurélie, 'I don't know, but they're a funny bunch. That Guinan with the eyes was trying to tell me something about time-travel the other day. How easy it was with the right tools, nudge, nudge, wink, wink. I had no idea what he was going on about. Then he kept saying if he gave me some spell-books, would I read them.'

'That's the trouble when you're irresistible. Strange pickup lines wherever you go.'

'I don't think it was that,' said Aurélie. 'He said he needed some help. That he needed someone to produce a master version from the two spell-books to generate an entire beautiful, magical, cosmic enchilada.'

'Yeah, you want to watch him. He probably says that to all the girls. A pinch of mysticism and stardust. A bit of New Age, Old Age, new-fangled, old-fashioned spirituality to get them hooked.'

'I don't know. If I could understand what he meant, I might help him.'

Just then there came another almighty crash.

'Shall we go and see what they're up to?' asked Alain.

'Oh, I don't know, maybe later. They can be a bit much and I've only just got here,' she said, pouting in what she hoped was an irresistible way.

'As you wish,' he said. 'You were saying something about pets before?'

'Oh yes, just that there were no animals allowed in our apartment,' she said.

'Where you lived with Emil?' His heart speeded up its count in his chest. But since he wasn't used to jealousy, he diagnosed it as the effect of a long night spent teaching Mielle to waltz. The lion's excuse-me. The great waltz from *Onegin*. One, two, three, one, two, three…

Her eyes flew to his face. Normally they never mentioned the Strong Man's name. Then her expression softened. 'Catch Emil living in an apartment,' she said. 'No, this was before, with my mother. Just outside our village.'

Alain waited for her to continue. When she didn't, he said, 'Was it so terrible there, that you had to run away and join the circus?'

'Not terrible,' said Aurélie, opening her eyes very wide. Now he noticed, as if for the first time, their exact shade of translucent green, their long, dark lashes, at variance with the pearly lustre of her skin. 'And I had already run away to art college first. Only mum was a teacher, you see,' Aurélie added.

'I used to be a teacher too,' said Alain, softly, nodding towards the shelf of books above the rocking-chair. 'Drama workshops for local kids. We're not such a bad bunch.'

Aurélie bit her lip. 'Mum isn't so bad either. I mean, she's not like Emil. Didn't hit me or anything. Just, you know, she'd left home when she was young, after some big falling-out with *her* mother, my grandmother, Arabella. It sounded like Granny was a bit of an adventuress. She was carted off to Russia by a vampire when she was just a kid. I mean, not quite like that, and it all worked out. I found the vampire's diary and some papers a few years ago, and it was all okay.'

'What do you mean, you found a diary?' asked Alain.

'Oh, there was some art student installation thing on a train, and I found an antique journal there. Some of it seemed familiar, and when I finally started speaking to my mother again, she was able to verify some of the things from the diary as our family's history. I hadn't really realised when I was reading it. But it's funny that I found it there, just like that, like it had been put there, just for me.'

'What did your mother tell you?' asked Alain.

'Oh, that after the trip to Russia, Granny never really lost her taste for travel and adventure and – and spiritualism. The polar opposite to my mum. And then, you know, King Arthur II provided funding for Granny to travel back in time and help Queen Morgana found a school in Avalon. He had a ward from that era, Nessa, whom he wanted to receive the right kind of education. And Granny intended for the school to be really progressive and exciting, magick and spells and séances on the curriculum, that kind of thing.'

'That does sound exciting,' said Alain. 'Did she start the school?'

'Yes, she did,' said Aurélie. 'Brunwych's. It got to be quite famous in Avalon. Just my mother didn't want to go there. She insisted on staying on the Grand-Ile to go to the local college and study maths, which must have been very disappointing for Granny. But, like I said, they never really got on.'

'So, you never met your grandmother?'

'No, Granny was always too busy overseeing her school in Avalon, and anyway, the rift was too great. Besides, having been so disapproving of *her* mother and *her* lovers, *my* mother didn't feel she could own up to her one silly fling – and me. I mean, she was embarrassed about it. She was already in her forties by the time I was born.'

'That's a bit sad. Surely with a baby on the way, they could have reconciled?'

'You would have thought so, but mum has her stubborn streak, too. And her pride. Anyway, by the time I was growing up, it was just homework homework homework all the time, for both of us. No television after eight o' clock for me, and migraines for mother. She used to sit there in dark glasses at the table, with piles of marking to do. Sometimes she didn't even have time to eat. She used to tell me to make myself an omelette if I was hungry.'

'And did you?' asked Alain, wondering whether there was anything left in his own fridge. Normally Aurélie never stayed long enough for conversation, let alone something to eat.

'Yes,' said Aurélie, 'I'd take my plate and lie down on the white fur rug with it, and sometimes I'd fall asleep.'

Mielle turned his lazy golden eyes back towards the girl and repeated his full-throated purr.

'Oh,' Aurélie said, sounding pleased.

Alain leaned forwards and crouched down. 'Dust of gold that gleams, vague starpoints in the mystic iris of his eyes,' he breathed against her neck.

'What's that?' Aurélie said, jerking her head back, revealing a little blue mark above her breastbone. Not a bruise, Alain realised, but a tattoo. A phoenix.

'Charlie B.,' he replied.

Beneath lowered lids, Aurélie continued to regard him, blankly.

'You know, Baudelaire,' he said. 'One of Avalon's finest poets. A dog is prose, a cat is a poem.'

'I've never heard of him before,' said Aurélie.

'Oh,' said Alain, straightening up and reaching beneath his glasses to rub his eyes. This was proving more difficult than he'd thought. 'I'm sorry you haven't heard of Baudelaire. That's what you get for hanging around with Emil. A distinct lack of culture.'

'Don't we all make our own culture? You may find you're not aware of all *my* frames of reference.'

Alain looked nonplussed, then smiled and reached over the rocking-chair to the bookshelf. From between two books, he took down a slim volume covered in brown paper.

'Let me see,' she said.

So he showed her the front cover, *Les Fleurs Du Mal*, written in his own long-ago, schoolboy hand. Then he sat down on the chair, settled his glasses on the bridge of his nose, and opened the book somewhere in the middle. He began to read, '*Mère des souvenirs, maîtresse des maîtresses...*' He liked the sound of his own voice, emerging from the concave of his chest, a full, rich, mellifluous actor's baritone. 'Like Orpheus's lyre,' Odette used to say when she first knew him. He paused for a moment, to give Aurélie the chance to pay him a similar compliment. But she didn't say anything, just peered at him from beneath her dark lashes. He watched as her pupils narrowed to pinpricks but he didn't see that the compliment was in her rapt, luminous eyes.

'I'll carry on reading,' he said, nettled.

As she listened, Aurélie started to pick at a bit of skin that had come loose from the bed of her thumbnail. Then she stopped, not wanting to spoil the sophistication of her first-ever manicure. 'I wish he hadn't mentioned Emil,' she thought. Flowers of Evil, that was Emil, certainly. After all, there was the car he'd stolen from his cousin, the huge sums of money he'd 'borrowed' from his poker-playing friends, not to mention the original Strong Man he'd beaten up to take over his job at the circus.

'Are you alright?' asked Alain, breaking off his recitation.

'No,' she said, 'but please keep reading.' Alain wasn't handsome, like Emil, but she liked to look at him. Especially now, when he was reading, and his eyes blazed behind his glasses and his voice varied somewhere between lion's fur and sandpaper rasp.

'*Mère des souvenirs, maîtresse des maîtresses.../Nous avons dit souvent d'impérissables choses*,' he declaimed.

Suddenly, she remembered the moment when she took her violin out of its case, after her first music lesson, to show it to the stranger who was chatting her up in the local cafe.

'She's beautiful,' Emil had said. He reached across the checked tablecloth to take the violin in his arms. 'Shaped just like a woman,' he added, and winked at her.

'Le Violon d'Ingrés,' she said, feeling proud of herself and her scholarship education at Valerian College. 'You know, Man Ray,' she added, twisting her hair through her fingers. Surely he'd heard of him? Apparently not. 'Well, we all make our own culture,' she said, smiling at him. 'Probably there's things you know that I haven't heard of.' Then, with a tact beyond her years, she changed the subject. 'You know, they say the Devil created the violin because he was lonely, and envious of God's creation of woman.'

'I'm lonely,' Emil replied, winking at her again. 'And I always wanted a violin.'

'My Granny got a queen's violin mended,' said Aurélie. 'But the queen didn't want it anymore, and Granny couldn't play it, so she passed it down to me.'

'You've a canny Granny,' he said. 'Has she given you anything else?'

That evening was the first time she went back to his trailer. After that, she only returned to the flat she shared with her flatmates for her stuff. Though apart from her sketchbooks and graphite pencils, Emil took pretty much everything she owned anyway, all her portable property. The opal necklace that her best friend Harmony had given her a couple of years ago, for her twenty-first birthday. A silver bangle that had belonged to her mother. And of course, the violin.

'After all, it's wasted on you,' Emil said. "You can't play it and I can.'

'But I was just starting to have lessons,' Aurélie mumbled.

'Give it up,' he said. 'You only like the colours of it. Whereas I – can actually do something with it.'

Alain stopped reading suddenly, snapped shut the book.

'You're a million miles away,' he said.

'I'm sorry,' said Aurélie. 'That was lovely. It's just I started thinking about Emil.'

'Emil? Why?'

Aurélie adjusted her thoughts. 'If he ever found out I'd been seeing you…'

'You're not obliged to,' said Alain.

His voice had changed, thought Aurélie. It wasn't beautiful anymore. And perhaps Mielle had noticed it too, the distinct froideur, because he stood up, stretched and padded over to the far corner of the trailer. Now that he was equidistant from them both, he began to wash himself.

'Triangles,' said Alain.

'What?' said Aurélie, watching as the lion bestowed his attention on one particular paw.

'Lions. If there are two people in a room, lions like to form a triangle shape with both. It's a way of giving them equal attention.'

'I never knew that,' said Aurélie.

'Well, you don't know much, do you, Aurélie?' said Alain.

There was a moment's silence. Then, 'Are you worrying about Emil because you're still in love with him?' he asked, more gently.

'No,' she said. 'I'm just scared of what he would do if he ever found out I'd been here.' She said the words before she thought them through, then realised, they were sort of true, and sort of not. But she turned towards Alain, her eyes flashing fire and tears. 'Because,' she said, 'I know you're not going to stop seeing him. He'll still come to your trailer for poker games, parties…' There, she'd said it now, revealed the elephant in the trailer, one of the bones of contention between them.

'It would look more suspicious if I did stop inviting him,' said Alain. 'Besides, you're not going to stop seeing him either.'

For a moment, Aurélie thought she heard the sound of a violin, sonorous, liquid, heart-breaking and beautiful. Alain was right, she wasn't quite ready to give up Emil yet. Emil's potential to be better than he was, the rare, gentle look in his blue eyes. But then, it wasn't a violin she could hear, after all, just Mielle yowling and pawing at the door to be let out.

'Stupid animal,' said Alain. 'He knows how to push open the door.' But he held it open for the lion anyway. With the door ajar, they could both hear, all too clearly, yells and thumps from the next trailer, and something that sounded like the table falling over.

'They haven't stopped fighting yet,' he said, looking out. 'Last week, they sent a frying pan flying right through their open window. Come on, we'd better tell them to stop or else there'll be a racket all evening.'

Aurélie stood up from the floor and straightened her skirt. She pulled on her fur-lined boots, arranged her cardigan, reached for her jacket and grabbed her bag, ready to follow Alain next door.

The dwarves apparently couldn't hear them knocking above the noise they were making, so Alain pushed open the unlocked door.

'Trailers are meant to be locked after 9pm,' he muttered.

Aurélie followed behind him, clapping her hands together to warm them up, murmuring, 'Says who, the trailer park police?'

The dwarves' trailer was slightly larger than Alain's, with a couple of sofas in the sitting-room area that looked as if they could become pull-out beds. There were also a couple of bedroom extensions. Then too, the dwarves seemed to have one large portable heater between them to keep the place warm, though currently it had tipped over with the falling table. There were some ebony pipes on the floor too, as well as what looked like fishing nets, and some scattered cards, with diamonds and hearts showing uppermost.

There was also a small clockwork mouse, though the silver key had fallen out of it. The mouse lay, half-buried, beneath wrappers of Wimpy burgers and empty packets of Wotsits and Frazzles. Amongst the beer, cider and Fanta cans, there was even a bowl of ice-cream with chocolate Magic hardening on top of it, that had somehow survived the upended table.

Alain sighed, bent down, and picked the table up.

'Did we ask you to do that?' asked Guinan, belligerently. 'We might have been conducting a religious ritual on our very own upended table.'

'Were you?' asked Alain.

'No,' said Guinan, 'just Dagonet found a few tins of cider under his bed, and it got a bit rowdy.'

'Well, can you keep it down, lads?' asked Alain. 'I'm trying to entertain a lady.' He gestured towards Aurélie, who stepped out in front of him.

To Guinan, she seemed a celestine vision with snowflakes like crystals melting on her hair and the shoulders of her jacket. Her blonde hair was full of luminous snow-light, and her face looked as if had been carved from a white rose petal.

'Hey, we know you,' he said.

'Yes,' piped up Pippin, 'from a long, long time ago.'

'No, I don't think so,' said Aurélie, 'I only met you the other day, with Guinan.'

'I think we'll have to agree to disagree,' said Pippin, 'though all the time travel does get a bit befuddling.'

'What are you doing with this joker?' Guinan added, in a lower voice, though he didn't really care if Alain heard him or not. One of the advantages of being a dwarf was that you could pretty much say whatever you liked: you were unlikely to get thumped. 'I thought you were with the other one.'

'I like lions,' the girl said and smiled.

'Well, it's in your blood, my dear,' said Guinan. 'You know your ancestress Rose Red married Lowenhardt, the Lion Baron of Astalot?'

'Er, no, I didn't,' said Aurélie. 'What are you talking about, please?'

'My mistake,' said Guinan. 'And there was I, thinking your mother must have told you all your family history.'

'Only some of it,' said Aurélie. 'I mean, have you heard of all of *your* ancestors?'

'Both heard of them, and *met* them,' said Guinan proudly. 'I made it my business to seek them out since the Celestine and the Time Travelling Spell came into our possession.'

'See, that's the kind of stuff they keep going on about,' Aurélie complained, turning to Alain.

'Do you want to leave?' asked Alain, putting a protective arm round her shoulder.

'Let's stay a bit longer,' said Aurélie. 'You told me about the time travel last time, Guinan. But what do you mean about the Celestine?'

Guinan gestured towards another dwarf. 'Allow my compadre, and fellow Space-Time Traveller, Voldip, to enlighten you.'

Aurélie raised a curious eyebrow.

'The Celestine,' sighed Voldip, taking a small, blue stone out of his stonewashed blue jeans pocket. 'Don't you five-footers know *anything*?'

He approached her and gestured for her to bend down. Then he held the Celestine very close to her, not to her eyes, but to her forehead, and muttered something about the third eye. In the midst of darkness, there appeared a flicker of blue, like a gas flame. Except it reminded her of other things too. Bluebells, butterflies, something beautiful but also the silver-blue of a sharp blade. Then, as the blue flame dispersed, she saw a whole world in miniature, which shone with an amber glow. Dragonflies were skimming the grass and long avenues of apple-trees were blossoming.

'Oh, it's lovely,' said Aurélie, straightening up.

'Yes, it is,' said Voldip. 'It's the Fruitful Isles,' he added. It seemed to her that his shrewd eyes were watching her closely. 'Where all our old heroes and heroines go to rest until we can persuade them to join us again.'

'But I would think they'd never want to leave, it looks so beautiful,' said Aurélie.

'Ah, and that's the problem,' said Guinan. 'Which is why we need your help.'

'*Me*? Why?'

'Partly because of your bloodline. As I was trying to explain, you are the granddaughter of Arabella De Lys, who was herself the daughter of Delphine De Lys, who is an ancestress of Elaine of Astalot's brother, Torre. Elaine herself is the daughter of Rose Red and Lowenhardt the Lion Baron and the granddaughter of Queen Morgana of the Fruitful Isles. Before she became a priestess, Elaine found the Holy Grail, but it was later stolen by,' he sighed for a moment, then continued, 'Various people… and then, the vampire.'

'I don't understand. You don't mean Violetta, do you?'

'Yes,' said Guinan. 'I do. Let me explain. Due to Merlin's curse, Queen Morgana was already greatly weakened by the time Queen Victoria came to the throne – that is to say, she died in Valerian, and became a ghost. If it hadn't been for the vampire and the medium helping to return her and her daughter to the Fruitful Isles, things would be even worse than they are now.'

'I read about the séance in Violetta's diary a few years ago,' said Aurélie. 'But I didn't know how much to believe.'

'Violetta's diary?' said Guinan. 'That's a valuable artefact, that is. Queen Morgana acquired it from Violetta's carriage in St. Petersburg and asked me to plant it on the centenary train for you to find.'

'It's currently in a shoebox in my cupboard,' said Aurélie. 'I can show it to you, if you like.'

'Thanking you kindly for the offer, but it's best in your possession, at least for the time being,' said Guinan. 'Anyway, from the diary, you'll have some idea that Morgana did what she could to get Arthur back onto the throne, but as a ghost, things were quite difficult for her. And then, Arthur was meant to reign after Victoria for many, many years.'

Aurélie tried to remember her history lessons from school. Surely King Arthur's and Queen Sophia's Victorian reign had been brief and unremarkable? So many magnificent plans that never really came to fruition.

'Without the companions of his old days, Arthur lost heart, came to doubt himself,' added Guinan. 'He and his queen abdicated - and then the dark days were truly upon us. But he promised he would come back if he could have the support of his knights. Which is why we need *you*,' said Guinan, pointedly.

'What do you want *me* to do?' she said, more ungraciously than she intended.

'The spells from those two books I was telling you about, the *Cardoeil Spell Book*, and the *Camelot Spell Book*, are notoriously difficult to read,' said Guinan, and he reached beneath one of the sofa-beds and pulled them out. The *Camelot Spell Book* had a dark red cover that was blackened with age; the other had no cover at all and was tightly bound with string to stop it falling apart even more. 'I'm the seventh dwarf of a seventh dwarf, and even I can only read some of them.'

'Yes, you told me that already,' said Aurélie, glancing curiously at the runes on what she presumed was the title page.

'But,' said Guinan, and his face glowed ruddy with cider and enthusiasm, '*but*, my dear, if you can find a way to read them, and somehow unite the spells of Morgana and Merlin, of Avalon and Valerian, you would bring about great healing to this land. You would create a realm of such beauty and power that all the old heroes and heroines, the kings and queens, the wise, the good and the powerful, would want to leave their safe havens in the Fruitful Isles and return to Valerian.'

'And then King Arthur will want to come back, too?' she asked.

'Exactly,' said Guinan. 'You've hit the nail precisely on the head.' He thought for a moment, and added, 'well, we can but hope. And if it doesn't work, a shot of rum in the Holy Grail and a good kick up the backside might do the trick.'

'But you don't have the Holy Grail,' said Aurélie. 'You just said, Violetta has it.'

'Yes, I know,' said Guinan. 'And Queen Morgana is currently consulting with her priestesses and astrologers to learn whether it would be the right course of action to travel back in time to the Valerian Victorian era and take it from her.

The trouble is, there are now so many different timelines opening up, it's all getting a bit complicated.'

'And who's fault is that?' asked Aurélie.

'We do our best,' said Guinan, with as much dignity as he could muster. 'The Time Travel spell is a tricky one. I've spent many years refining it, but it's still a bit trial-and-error.'

'I've had about as much of this as I can take,' said Alain. 'It's all nonsense. Have you ever thought of going into pantomime, lads? Or else, you've been smoking the wacky backy again.'

Guinan grinned but didn't reply.

Alain folded his arms, and said, 'I'm going back to my trailer. Aurélie, are you coming with me?'

Aurélie shrugged and he started to leave without her. But while his back was turning, she quickly took the spell books from Guinan, and stowed them in her handbag.

'Wait for me,' she said.

'Remember to lock your door,' Alain called to the dwarves from outside. 'This is a circus. You don't want to let the tigers in.' He stood still for a moment, whistling for Mielle, then turned and said to Aurélie, 'I'm sorry you had to listen to all that.' He, too, made no real attempt to lower his voice as he added, 'Honestly, I go past their trailer sometimes and the air reeks of marijuana. Didn't you see the Turkish pipe on the shelf and the pipes on the floor?'

'No,' said Aurélie. 'I just liked listening to their stories.' But she resolved to say nothing more of the dwarves for a bit since it seemed to annoy Alain.

Alain whistled once more for the lion, who came padding back through the snow towards them. He unlocked his own trailer door, opened it, and then the lion edged his way inside ahead of them.

Once they were all back inside, Aurélie stamped the snow off her boots, then switched the heater back on. She huddled beside it for a few minutes, while the lion very deliberately picked his way across the peeling linoleum towards her. Then he paused in front of Aurélie and started to knead the ground with his paws. Once she was warmer, she took her jacket off and sat down in the chair, watching him.

'Making pastry,' said Aurélie.

'I thought you said you never had a pet?'

'I didn't. Even if the landlady had agreed, mother would never have got me one. She wanted it quiet, just the two of us.'

'She didn't have any boyfriends or anything, after your father?' asked Alain.

'No,' said Aurélie. No more men. Just the certainty of mathematical equations she could always make right.

'What do you think she'd think of you now?' asked Alain. 'Breaking hearts in circus trailers?'

'She'd disapprove,' said Aurélie, with a small, unhappy smile, recalling her mother's number eleven frown. 'Too many lovers. Too much sleeping around. Too, you know, arty. She didn't even like it when I got the art scholarship to Valerian because it meant I was going away from her. And she doesn't much like animals, never mind the circus.'

Alain leaned over, took her hand, and squeezed her fingers.

She returned their pressure, but his hands were cold. She shivered and instead bent to fondle the lion. How soft his fur was. So much softer than the white acrylic rug where she used to fall asleep at home, in a parlour with walls, drapes, candles and porcelain, all white as falling snow. How strange, though, just for a moment, she thought she glimpsed her mother's face in the glitter of the lion's eyes. Her mother Catherine, her first great love, after all, beautiful and fierce, soft, and flushed and golden.

'I'll make us some dinner,' said Alain then, in a gentler tone.

'Omelette,' she called out to his retreating back.

Outside the trailer window, the snow began to fall for the second time that evening. Snowflakes, like white feathers, like forgetting, but like remembering, too. White lines sketched in the gates, the fence, the metalwork of the trailers opposite.

The world disappeared beneath a blanket of ice and snow. Just the tops of hedges showed white, the tips of reeds, silver. The moon lit up the acrobats practising their highwire walk, the jugglers blowing on their cold hands, whilst huddled away in their own trailers, the clowns were painting on their smiles.

Through the trailer window, the rays of the moon turned Mielle the colour of *crème brulée* and orange blossom honey. Now, he pressed his lithe young body against the girl's hand and purred again. The sound mingled with the rapid swish of the tamer sharpening his knives in the kitchen. Then Mielle arched his spine and placed a front paw on her lap. His claws caught her skin through her skirt, making her shiver. She moved to disentangle him from the new fibre mix.

Mielle let out a growl of protest, but the sound soon settled into his habitual, full-throated rumble.

Then the tamer came back, with a plate of fried eggs for Aurélie, and some chicken for Mielle. The lion pushed the carcass forwards with his nose, covering his mane with grease and blood. But as he worried the meat, out of the corner of his eye, he noticed that his companions were no longer eating.

They were kissing.

Then, suddenly, they weren't there at all. Where did they go? The lion looked round for a moment, then returned his attention to the chicken carcass.

'It's freezing out here,' the girl said a while later as she reappeared from the bedroom. She sat down in the chair to pull up her stockings. 'You know,' she added 'it wasn't quite like I said it was.'

'It never is,' said the man, following her out, tightening his belt buckle.

'No, it's just that, every morning I always woke up in my own bed.'

'What are you talking about?' asked the man.

'Well, then I knew that my mother had carried me there without waking me. Then I knew that she loved me.'

Mielle shifted his great head towards the man, interested to hear his response. But the man just dropped his eyes again, refusing to meet the girl's gaze. He picked up the dirty plates from the floor and returned to the kitchen section at the back of the trailer to do the washing-up. So, the lion came and rubbed his head against the girl's legs. Almost at once, he felt her sigh.

Then Aurélie stood up and checked the hem of her skirt. She took a little cracked mirror out of her handbag. The butterfly of her lipstick had flown away. She reapplied it, in thick, greedy smudges.

She crouched down again.

What was she up to? The lion blinked as she held the compact mirror to his face.

'Handsome Mielle,' she said.

The lion's sudden nod jerked the mirror out of her hand. She bent down to pick it up.

'So, you do understand me, then,' she said. 'At least, when you want to.'

She sat back down in the chair, took the two spell-books out of her bag and began to flick through them. She found that every page had a wide margin which enclosed a scribbling, scrawling rectangle of text, written in an ancient language, underneath which were miniscule annotations. And yet, she found that rather than trying to read the text, if she placed the image of it within her mind's eye, she could get at the sense of it. By using this method, she could understand the spells quite easily, though there seemed to be strange energies pulsating from the words.

She began to wonder whether what Guinan had said was true, that Morgana of Avalon, and Elaine of Astalot, and all the rest of them, were her ancestors - and that because of her powerful bloodline, she was the one chosen to unite their fractured lands. It might take months and months of careful study, but if she could combine the powerful spells within these two books, their lands might again be healed. And then Morgana, Arthur, Lancelot, Merlin, all of them, could return to the Kingdom of Valerian.

Aurélie turned over the pages of the spell book and glanced down at a spell in front of her. Now she found herself repeating the words, *Tirra Lirra*, an old water magick spell from Avalon.

Suddenly, the compact mirror fell from her lap and shattered on the linoleum-floor.

Seven years' bad luck. Aurélie leaned down to pick up the pieces. Was it her imagination or was there smoke rising from the mirror-shards? Smoke that took on the shape and likeness of an elderly, wizardly gentleman. She shook her head, and the gentleman started to fade away, until nothing but the glimmer of the moons and stars on his cloak remained. Still, the pieces lay there, a glassy mist of blonde, jagged fragments.

Mielle watched as she tried to pick up a bit of broken glass. Then she gasped. 'It burns,' she said, and let it drop. She turned back to the spell-books and flicked through the parchment pages again.

Another spell caught her attention. In crabbed, Gothic lettering, someone had written: *Reversal of Vampirism*. Beneath it, someone else, the wizard perhaps, had added in a different script, *(without the need for Titrations.)* There was another note beneath that: *Mention to Sir Pinel?* Aurélie glanced down at the list of ingredients, and saw that the spell required the chalice, the sacred chalice, the Chalice that had once belonged to Joseph of Arimathea, the receptacle of the most holy and precious blood of Christ. The Holy Grail.

'Just the chalice?' thought Aurélie, 'or do they want Christ's blood too?' She tried to recall what Guinan had told her, and what she already knew, about the Holy Grail. She remembered that when the Fool gave the chalice to the Fisher King, and he drank from it, the king was restored to health and life, and that the great lands laid waste around him bloomed again. But was Arthur the Fisher King? Or was that someone else? And who was the Fool? Because she could already think of several different candidates.

At any rate, the Holy Grail seemed to possess its own powers of healing. The author of the spell claimed that with some water or wine in it, and a priest's blessing said over it, a draught from the sacred chalice could reverse the *Cruel Curse and Terrible Affliction of Vampirism.* Aurélie remembered then that Guinan had told her that Violetta had stolen or taken the Holy Grail with her. Oh, that was when she left Crowcroft Grange, thought Aurélie, remembering what she had read in Violetta's journal. Though the journal itself had concluded abruptly: the last entry of the volume Aurélie possessed was written on board the deck of the vampire's ship just as it was nearing St. Petersburg.

Aurélie remembered that Violetta had suggested she might return to her coffin in the tomb of St Swithin's churchyard, and so sleep through to better times. If that were so, might it be possible for Aurélie to travel to Lostwithiel now, and find her, to reveal the contents of this spell? Then Violetta would have the option of becoming human, again. As long as she still had the Holy Grail, of course.

Though, hadn't Guinan said something about a Time Travelling spell before? If Aurélie could find it in one of the books, then perhaps it wouldn't be too difficult to locate Violetta, wherever she was, and even the Grail, if necessary.

Perhaps. Though, first of all, she would get her violin back from Emil, then pack up her things. Because, really, there wasn't anything keeping her here. It was time for her to run away from the circus and go travelling again. Except – well – she would miss the animals, especially the lions, especially this one.

Now, in front of her, the lion's eyes were wise as living amber and he pushed his head against her hands, so that she was forced to lay down the book. She felt the bristles of his muzzle and the sensation of his rough lapping tongue against her burnt fingers. Finally, he raised his head, swallowed hard, bared his teeth. A sound forced itself from his throat, something like a growl, but more than that, something harsher, more guttural, that tore apart his very soul.

In Valerian, they are the three most difficult words in the language. But, thought Aurélie, stroking the lion's golden head and remembering, in Avalon, they trip off the tongue, sweet and light as honey.

'You said something?' Alain called out from the kitchen sink, above the clatter of crockery and the sound of the dripping tap.

Printed and bound by CPI Group (UK) Ltd, Croydon, CR0 4YY
16/12/2023
03627604-0001